QUARTERBACK TRAP

ALSO BY DALLAS GORHAM

The Carlos McCrary PI Mystery Thriller Series

Six Murders Too Many

Double Fake, Double Murder

Quarterback Trap

Dangerous Friends

Day of the Tiger

McCrary's Justice

Yesterday's Trouble

Four Years Gone

Debt of Honor

Sometimes You Lose

QUARTERBACK TRAP

CARLOS MCCRARY PI, BOOK 3

DALLAS GORHAM

ePublishingWorks!

Book and cover design by eBook Prep
www.ebookprep.com

December 2021
ISBN: 978-1-64457-249-8

ePublishing Works!
644 Shrewsbury Commons Ave
Ste 249
Shrewsbury PA 17361
United States of America

www.epublishingworks.com
Phone: 866-846-5123

ONE

The woman stumbled from the elevator into the lobby, catching her spike heel in the crack between the elevator and the tile floor. *Dammit, why did I wear these shoes?* She glanced at her watch: 3:30 a.m. *Too late to go back and change; he might wake up.* She bumped open the lobby door into the parking garage with her hip. She thumbed the key fob of her rental car, listening for *beep* of the horn.

She jerked to a halt as a dirty white van, tires squealing, pulled sideways in front of her, blocking her way. The side door of the van opened like the mouth of a secret cave. Rough hands seized her from behind and half-carried, half-dragged her toward the dark hole.

"What the hell...?" Her red Prada purse dropped to the pavement, its contents scattering everywhere. Her cellphone skittered across the pavement and disappeared beneath the van.

Two men in black shoved her into the van and onto the second-row bench seat where a third sat. He grabbed her arm and yanked her over beside him. One man climbed in after her and turned back to the one remaining at the open door. "Grab her purse and find that cellphone."

The man outside slammed the sliding door closed, scooped up the purse, and dropped to his knees to stuff the contents back in the purse. Closing the purse, he retrieved the phone. He trotted around to the driver's side, jumped in, tossing the items onto the front passenger seat, and cranked the engine. As the van roared away, a tire rolled over the rental car key fob, crushing it.

Carlos McCrary

Bob Martinez eased through the crowded coffee shop toward my table, fist bumping and high-fiving breakfast customers as he went.

I stood and waved. Bob was a half hour late. That wasn't like him.

"Hey, Eighty-Eight, great to see you," he said in Spanish.

I had to smile. "It's been twelve years since I wore number eighty-eight, Bob."

"You'll always be Eighty-Eight to me."

We shook hands and Bob pulled out a chair. The starting quarterback for the New York Jets lifted the stainless-steel covers from the two plates. "This my breakfast? Pass the salsa, please."

Bob was speaking Spanish, the language he spoke when something was bothering him. I went along with him and switched to Spanish as I slid the dish across the table. "Two orders of *huevos rancheros* with brown rice and *refritos* on the side, like your text said."

"Thanks, buddy. Sorry I'm late. It's always a madhouse when I'm in public." He eyeballed his phone before he smothered his food with salsa. "I never know how long it'll take to get anywhere."

"You're starting in the Super Bowl. It's natural that everyone wants a piece of you. It must be like being on stage all the time. Is it tough to handle so much attention?"

Bob shrugged. "You do what you gotta do. I'm used to it by now." He checked his phone again and frowned, then dug into his *huevos rancheros*. "These folks are football fans. It wouldn't be right to ignore them."

"Your text didn't say what to order for Graciela. Where is your gorgeous fiancée?"

A frown flashed across his face. He stuffed a forkful of *huevos* in his mouth. "Gracie doesn't eat breakfast," he mumbled as he rolled a tortilla in his fingers.

A small boy approached the table and waited for my famous friend to notice him.

Bob set down the tortilla and wiped his hands on a napkin. "Hey, sport. How's it going?" He asked in English.

The boy blushed and blurted out, "How come everybody calls you the Mexican Muscle?"

Bob grinned at the nervous youth. "What's your name, son?"

"Travis McKinnon, sir."

Bob shook hands. "Bob Martinez. Pleased to meet you, Travis."

Over the boy's shoulder, Bob noticed a middle-aged man in a Jets T-shirt watching from a nearby table. The man smiled and shrugged. "Is that guy in the Jets shirt your dad?"

Travis glanced back at him. "Yes, sir. I asked him why they call you the Mexican Muscle. He didn't know."

"Lots of people ask me that. A sportswriter for a Cleveland newspaper came up with the nickname when the Browns drafted me six years ago. I'm Mexican-American like my friend Eighty-Eight here, and I'm kinda big. The nickname stuck, even after the Browns traded me to the Jets."

The boy pivoted to me. "Why does he call you Eighty-Eight? Do you play for the Jets too?"

"No. I wore number eighty-eight when Bob and I played together at Theodore Roosevelt High School in Adams Creek, Texas. I was a tight end and Bob played quarterback. We've been friends ever since."

"Oh." Travis leaned back toward Bob. "Can I take your picture?"

"Sure thing." Bob waved the boy's father over. "Why don't you take a picture of Travis and me together?"

The boy's father took out his cellphone.

Bob grinned at the boy. "Did you know that where I was born, Travis is a famous name?"

Travis's eyes grew wider. "Where's that, sir?"

"Texas. William Barrett Travis was a hero of battle of the Alamo. Lots of people in Texas are named after him."

"I'm from New York."

"Well, I am too—now. I live in New York City." He wrapped his arm around the boy's shoulder, and they both faced the camera. "Say 'Go Jets.'"

After giving Travis's father a fist bump, Bob picked up the tortilla and used it to scoop eggs onto his fork. "Kids like Travis make it worth all the hassle." Bob was speaking Spanish again.

My friend should have been on top of the world with the Super Bowl a week away, but instead he seemed troubled. "Something's bothering you. What's on your mind, *amigo*? Does it have anything to do with you checking your phone every five seconds?"

Bob had switched back to English. "I'm sure it's nothing, really, Eighty-Eight." He scooped up a mouthful of rice.

"When a guy says 'it's nothing, really,' it means there's something there. What is it?"

Bob's mouth drew into a thin line. "Gracie wasn't there when I woke up this morning."

"Wasn't where?"

"In our hotel suite. In our bed, for God's sake. The players have a curfew before a big game, and there's no game bigger than the Super Bowl. I left the party at 10:30 last night. Gracie was having a good time and said she wasn't ready to leave. She said she'd be along later and not to wake her in the morning. She wanted to sleep in."

He downed some orange juice. "The alarm woke me at six. Her side of the bed hadn't been slept in. I've been calling and texting every five minutes since then. Her phone goes straight to voicemail. Frankly, I'm freaking out a little." He finished his first order of *huevos rancheros* and attacked the *refritos*.

"Have you looked for her?"

Bob ate mechanically. "That's why I was late to meet you, buddy. I asked at the front desk. Then I went to the concierge in case she left a message, a note, anything. Nobody's seen her this morning."

"Has Gracie ever done anything like this before?"

"What do you mean 'like this'?"

"Disappeared without telling you."

Bob glanced over his shoulder to make sure no one was nearby. He lowered his voice. "Once or twice... when she was using."

I lowered my voice too. "Using? You mean drugs? That's bad news."

"Don't I know it." Bob chugged the rest of his juice and signaled the server to bring more. "I'm scared as hell that Gracie scored some drugs last night after I left. She could be off god-knows-where doing god-knows-what with god-knows-who." He ate without enjoyment, refueling an empty tank. He scooped the last morsel of rice from the first plate, set it aside, and tackled the second plate.

I sipped my coffee. "When the three of us had dinner in New York two weeks ago, Gracie seemed fine."

"She doesn't talk about her, ah, former problem."

"I never heard any rumors that Gracie was an addict."

Bob shrugged. "So far, we've managed to keep it under wraps. I sent her to rehab last summer under another name while I was at training camp. She stayed there through the pre-season and came to our season opener against the Steelers. She's been clean ever since." He frowned and poked at his food. "At least that's what she tells me."

I figured Bob needed my help. "What do you intend to do?"

"I don't know, Eighty-Eight. My schedule is jammed all day. I gotta go to the airport in an hour to ride into town on one of the team buses. That's a big photo op for the local media. We have a team meeting after that. I can't search for her any more until late this afternoon."

"I don't want you to worry all day. I'll find her for you."

"Hey, that's right. You're a private detective." Bob's mood brightened. "Can I hire you to find Gracie for me?"

"No, you can't hire me. What are friends for if you can't use and abuse them occasionally? You would do the same for me."

"Chuck, the Jets pay me over fifty million dollars a year. If Gracie has gone and done something stupid, finding her will take more time than you think. I'll pay you the going rate, whatever it is."

"Are you sure about this, Bob? I don't make fifty million a year, but I'm not cheap either."

"Don't forget the endorsement deals, Eighty-Eight. They're good for another forty million. Yes, I'll pay. Where do you want to start?"

I pushed the plate aside and slid a notepad from my pocket. "Where was the party?"

I dodged dozens of people wearing New York green and white or Dallas blue and silver as I pressed my way through the crowded hotel lobby.

The concierge desk took up a chunk of one wall. Banners for both teams hung on the wall behind the desk, the Super Bowl logo between them. Two men and a woman in hotel uniforms stood behind the marble desk.

Bob said he had talked to a man named Ronald earlier. I read the nametag of the nearest concierge. "David, I'm looking for Ronald."

"That's him." He waved at the other man. "Hey, Ron, this guy wants to talk to you."

Ronald walked over. "How may I help you, sir?"

"I'm trying to locate Graciela Perez, Bob Martinez's fiancée. Have you heard anything from her since Bob was here earlier?"

"Are you a guest in the hotel?"

"Why do you ask?"

"I know Mr. Martinez and Ms. Perez by sight, but I don't know you. I'm sure you understand."

"I'm Chuck McCrary." I showed him my private investigator's license. "Bob's a friend. I'm doing this as a favor—not professionally. You keep guest confidences, right?"

"Of course, sir."

"Graciela was a no-show at breakfast. Bob is concerned about her. I offered to confirm that she's all right. They may have gotten their signals crossed. Can you help me out?"

"I saw Ms. Perez and Mr. Martinez yesterday to hand them their dinner reservations, but I haven't heard from Ms. Perez since. Sorry. Did you try their suite?"

I knocked and waited a minute. Graciela hadn't answered the call I made from the concierge desk, so I didn't expect her to be in the suite. I knocked again, then opened the door with Bob's keycard.

"Gracie. Are you here? It's Chuck McCrary. Hello?"

Silence.

I hung the Do Not Disturb sign on the doorknob and closed the door. The maid had not yet serviced the room. Two soft drink cans lay half-crumpled on the coffee table. Yesterday's newspaper was scattered on the floor. A laptop on the desk was plugged into an outlet in the base of the desk lamp.

When I entered the bedroom, I noticed the bed sheets mussed on one side only. Opening the walk-in closet, I studied the clothes hung on both sides. Bob's clothes occupied three feet on the left; Gracie's took up the rest.

The shelf above the rod held a pink suitcase and an overnight bag with the initials *GP*. The pink suitcase was empty except for the normal travel stash of a packet of instant decaffeinated coffee and four wrinkled packets of coffee creamer and sugar-free sweetener. The overnight bag had a New Jersey highway map in a zipper compartment.

A variety of women's clothing in different lengths, styles, and colors was wedged into the eight-foot length of the closet. Just what I would expect from a fashion model. Four boxes sat on the shelf above the closet rod; a dozen pairs of shoes lay haphazardly on the floor. I picked two shoes at random—one was size seven, the other a seven-and-a-half. Two negligees hung inside the closet door. A faint hint of perfume filled the air.

I opened the boxes that sat on the shelf. Two contained purses with logos of designers so famous that even I, a barbarian with as much fashion sense as a tree stump, recognized them. Each purse was empty except for a small pill box with two kinds of colored pills. The third box held a larger designer purse with a similar pill box and an envelope folded into a zipped inner compartment. Inside the envelope, I found a baggie containing white powder. *This can't be good*, I thought.

After sticking my fingertip into the powder, I touched a little to my tongue. My tongue went numb. Cocaine. The fourth box was empty. I replaced then all.

Under Bob's side of the bed were two brown leather suitcases. Three more pink ones, also with designer logos, were wedged beneath the other side.

The bathroom shelf held the usual toiletries. Two prescription bottles in Graciela's name were shoved to the back of a cabinet drawer—methamphetamine and an anti-anxiety drug advertised on television. The pills were identical to the ones I'd found in the purses. *She keeps a handy-dandy supply of diet pills and downers in all her purses. Have drugs—will travel.*

I opened the first of three louvered doors—the toilet compartment. The seat was up. That figured. Bob would have been the last one to use the toilet.

Another door led to the bathtub. Salon-brand shampoo and conditioner sat on the edge of the bathtub. The used soap in the dish was damp. So was the crumpled towel in the tub. The bathmat showed small footprints pressed in the plush nap. They looked like size seven.

A third door opened to the shower room. Bob's shampoo and a plastic hair scrubber sat on the marble shelf. Bob's soap was wetter than the soap in the other soap dish. A wadded towel lay across another plush bathmat, this one with man-sized footprints in the nap.

The only object of note in the kitchen was a pink tablet computer plugged into an outlet. The name *Graciela* was painted on the back in red nail polish that matched the shade of one of the bottles I had noticed in the bathroom. I stuck the tablet in a plastic laundry back from the closet.

I waited outside the locker room at the Jets practice facility for the team meeting to adjourn. Bob strolled out the door with a group of massive football players. It's not often that I'm in a crowd where most of the people are bigger than I am. Bob waved at me.

We walked out to the field and sat on a sideline bench. "Here's your keycard back."

Bob slipped the card into a pocket. "What did you find in my room?"

"Her pink tablet computer. I took it in case we need to examine it later. That okay with you?"

"Sure. Long as you bring it back."

"Good. Does Gracie take birth control pills?"

"Yeah, sure. Why?"

"There weren't any in the bathroom cabinet or drawers. How many bags did she bring to Port City?"

"Oh, geez, let me think…She had five matching suitcases and an overnight bag."

"One of the suitcases wasn't in your room."

Bob frowned and almost said something, then stopped. "I don't know what to say."

"That's all right. One more thing…when you got up this morning, was the toilet seat up or down?"

"I didn't notice."

"It's important, Bob. Close your eyes and think back to this morning."

Bob closed his eyes, then opened them so wide that the whites showed all around. "The seat was down, and I left it up before I went to bed last night."

"Gracie returned to your room after you fell asleep. She took a bath, packed a suitcase, and left before you woke up."

"Jesus, now you're really freaking me out." Bob stopped as another player approached. "Wait a sec, Bomber. I'm talking with an old high school buddy. Be with you in a few." He lowered his voice. "How do you know she took a bath?"

"I have magical powers. Also, I found damp soap and a damp towel in the tub, and woman-sized footprints on the bathmat."

"I should have noticed that stuff."

"*Nah.* You couldn't see the tub from the shower, and raising a toilet seat is second nature to any man."

Bob shrugged. "I understand Gracie being quiet when she came back to the room, so she wouldn't wake me. She's real considerate like that. And I understand her taking a bath before bed. But why would she pack a bag and leave again in the middle of the night?"

"I didn't find her toothbrush or deodorant either. She planned to skip out on you."

"Why would she do that?"

"Why indeed?"

TWO

The time index on the computer monitor read *02:21:24*. The surveillance video showed Graciela exiting the elevator on the thirty-seventh floor. She tottered unsteadily down the corridor in a gold lamé dress with a neckline that plunged nearly to her waist. She carried a pair of gold sling-back stiletto shoes in her left hand. A gold-sequined evening purse with a long gold chain hung near her waist. She clutched the purse in her right hand like she was afraid it was planning an escape.

That same dress was hanging in the closet of Bob's hotel suite. I had noticed the matching purse in a box on the shelf above. The shoes had been dropped on the closet floor. Wherever she'd gone, she had changed clothes after the party.

Wally, the hotel security guard, glanced at the wall clock. "Is that who you're looking for?"

"Yes, thanks." I wrote down the time the video was taken. "Can we access the elevator video to determine where she got on?"

"You do know I have other duties, right?" He stared into his empty coffee cup as if he could will it to refill itself.

"Wally, that woman is a guest in your hotel. She is missing and maybe in danger. Finding her trumps your duty to refill your coffee."

The guard scowled, then punched the keyboard. The picture switched to split screen, high-angle shots from the elevator car's top corners. "I'll run this back one minute earlier."

Two men rode in the elevator. One wore a well-tailored black tuxedo and one was stuffed into an ill-fitting business suit. The second man had a shaved head and a crooked nose. He tugged at his collar and loosened his poorly knotted tie. Part of a neck tattoo peeked put above the shirt. The men stood side by side against the back wall.

"Zoom in on the tattoo. *Hmm*. Can't tell what it is, but I recognize it from somewhere. Probably a prison tat." I gestured at the screen. "Keep going."

Seconds later, the doors slid apart and Graciela boarded the elevator, walking carefully. Her purse swung from the shoulder chain. A thirtyish couple followed, arm in arm. The man wore a blue tuxedo that matched his date's long, blue cocktail dress.

"Must be Cowboys fans," I said.

Graciela lifted a champagne flute to her lips, drained it, and placed it on the elevator floor in the corner. She steadied herself with a hand on the wall and straightened up. Her face came into sharp focus on the monitor.

Wally froze the picture. "Is that who I think it is?"

"That depends on who you think she is."

"The Latin Angel...what's-her-name? The super model..." He snapped his fingers. "Graciela! That's it—she's Graciela, ain't she?"

"Right on."

"I saw on TV where she's the fiancée of that Jets quarterback, Bob Martinez—the one they call the Mexican Muscle."

"Right again."

The guard seemed more engaged in helping me now. He pointed to the lower left corner of the screen. "See this indicator? Graciela got on at the third floor, where the Palm Paradise Pavilion is. That's where ESPN threw that fine, fine party." He punched the keyboard and the video played again.

Blue Tuxedo put his arm around the woman in the blue dress and copped a feel. She moved her left hand down and stroked his crotch discreetly, if you can stroke a crotch discreetly in a crowded elevator. She winked. His jacket gapped open to reveal a silver cummerbund. Their mouths moved as they talked.

"I don't suppose you have audio, do you, Wally?"

"Too many privacy issues, man."

"Just as well—that conversation's gotta be X-rated."

"Nowadays, that's NC-17," Wally said. "It means no children under seventeen."

The woman leaned her head on Blue Tuxedo's shoulder, blew in his ear, then kissed him with her mouth open. The other two men stood in the back, oblivious to the enthusiastic display of lust. Some people have no romance in their souls.

Graciela leaned her head against the side wall, seemingly unmindful of the other people in the car. The door opened on the eighteenth floor and the two Cowboys fans wobbled off, groping each other as they went.

The door closed and Graciela came to life. She straightened up and spoke over her shoulder to Black Tuxedo.

He slid an envelope from his jacket and leaned closer to the woman. Crooked Nose watched. Black Tuxedo and Graciela exchanged words as she opened her purse and stuffed the envelope in it. She wrapped her hand around the top of the purse, covering the clasp.

Graciela flashed a plastic smile at Black Tuxedo as the elevator door opened. Crooked Nose exited first. His jacket bulged under his left arm.

"Freeze that, Wally. I want a printout of that frame."

"Yeah, yeah, anything you say." Wally tapped the keyboard. "Is that bulge a gun?"

"Yes."

"And that tattoo on his neck?"

"Fairly sure it's a prison tat."

Wally shivered. "Geez, maybe Graciela's in danger after all." He played the video again. Graciela said something to Black Tuxedo. He waved and followed Crooked Nose from the elevator car.

Wally pointed at the screen. "They're on 34."

I wrote that on my notepad. "Let's come back to that floor in a minute, and we'll learn which rooms those two men went into."

On the screen, Graciela leaned against the wall and took off her shoes. This time she grabbed the purse in a death grip. She valued whatever she had stuck in there.

"What do you think was in the envelope?"

"His Grandma's cornbread recipe."

We watched the video until Graciela exited the elevator. No one else entered or left the car. "Let's go back to 34 now," I said. "Is there a camera in the hall?"

Wally punched the keyboard again. "Okay, hall camera on 34 coming up."

Crooked Nose took one step into the hall and checked both directions. His shiny, bald head nodded an *all clear* to Black Tuxedo before he exited.

"Freeze that too, Wally. I need several blow-ups of those guys."

The two men stopped at a door. Black Tuxedo pointed back toward the elevator, said something to Crooked Nose, then entered a room on the right.

"All the units on that side are suites overlooking Seeti Bay. The rooms on the left have a city view and they're smaller."

Crooked Nose entered a door on the left.

"What suite number did that guy in the tuxedo enter?"

"I can't tell from the video; it's too far down the corridor to make out."

"Can you access the keycard files and tell me which rooms on that floor were entered at—" I glanced at the screen, "2:20 a.m.?"

"I didn't think of that. Hold on." The guard swiveled to another computer and dragged the keyboard over. "The boss is in suite 3406. The ex-con is in 3405."

"Thanks, Wally." I wrote that down. "Now let's review the elevator video again and spot where those two guys got on."

Wally ran the video back three minutes. "They're already on the elevator."

So I noticed. "Run it back another three minutes."

The elevator held another couple. They got off on 26. The empty elevator rose and stopped at 34. Black Tuxedo and Crooked Nose got on and took their positions at the rear of the car. For the next six minutes the two men stood motionless. The elevator went down to the lobby, up to 39, and back down to the lobby. Other people got on and off, but the two men never moved. Finally, Graciela and the amorous Cowboy fans got on.

"You think those two guys were waiting for Graciela to get on that elevator?"

"Do fish swim? Let's go back to the floor camera on 37 and watch for Graciela to come out of her suite."

Brian Wallenda, manager of the Super Bowl headquarters hotel, spread the stack of pictures across his desk. Even on Sunday, he wore a suit and tie. "What you're asking is highly irregular, Mr. McCrary."

"I certainly hope it's irregular and that a guest disappearing from your hotel is not a regular occurrence. This may involve a guest's safety. The guest is Graciela Perez, the fiancée of the Jets starting quarterback. That's why I asked you to meet me here on a Sunday."

"I'm well aware of who Graciela is. I don't live in a cave." Wallenda pursed his lips. "Frankly, if not for the potential danger to a guest, I wouldn't entertain your request—not without a search warrant."

"Mr. Wallenda, the man with the prison tattoo carried a gun. He and the man in the black tuxedo rode the elevator up and down twice, lying in wait until Graciela arrived. All I want you to do is help me identify the men in the elevator with her."

"That would require accessing the hotel's reservation system and our guests' personal information." He slipped a finger inside his collar and tugged. "That goes against all my hotel training."

"How about having a guest kidnapped from your hotel? Does that go against your training?"

Wallenda's face blanched. "I...I, uh, I don't know what to say. We've never had anything like this happen before." He straightened up. "You don't know she was kidnapped."

"I don't know that she wasn't, either. I do know she was with two suspicious men and now she's disappeared." I'd had enough of this guy tiptoeing around the issue. "Can we go off the record, Mr. Wallenda?"

Wallenda raised an eyebrow. "About what?"

"Times being what they are, we both know that it would not damage the reputation of the Port City Palace if Graciela were discovered to have a controlled substance in her hotel suite."

"The Palace is a big hotel." Wallenda shrugged. "No one

expects us to control what goes on in our rooms or what guests bring in with them. And everyone knows what celebrities are like."

"Right. But if Graciela obtained the controlled substance from another hotel guest in your elevator, and that guest was accompanied by an armed ex-con bodyguard, and your surveillance cameras captured the exchange…" I gestured to the photos on the desk, "and that guest later disappeared from your hotel in the middle of the night…"

I let the implication hang in the air for a second or two. "That would look bad for the Port City Palace if the news media or the cops discovered that you ignored the potential danger to a guest— especially a high-profile guest like Graciela."

"Should I call the police?"

"Not yet. The police never take a missing person report seriously for the first forty-eight hours, unless it's a child or there's evidence of foul play. Let's keep my investigation low-key for now. If we're lucky, your hotel will avoid any bad publicity." I hoped the manager liked the idea of no bad publicity.

Wallenda's brow knitted. "If I've learned anything in thirty years in the hotel business, it's that things you hope won't come out, always do. Always. More so with a celebrity. It's purely a matter of time." He pushed the stack of pictures together. "You're right. We have to do something. Okay, Mr. McCrary, we keep it off the record. Now tell me: What's going on in my hotel?"

"That's what I intend to find out. When I do, you'll be the second one to know—after Bob Martinez."

"Come in, Mr. McCrary. Whatever this big emergency is that can't wait until tomorrow, it better be a matter of life and death, or else I'm gonna be pissed." Giselle Foreman, the chief accountant for the

Port City Palace, peered at me over the top of her reading glasses. "Since I can't be mad at my own boss, you're next in line. Do I make myself clear?"

Clearly, Giselle Foreman wasn't feeling the love. It didn't take the world's greatest private investigator to know that I wasn't talking to Miss Sunshine.

"Yes, ma'am, and I appreciate your help."

"Now convince me this was worth missing a family trip to the beach on a beautiful Sunday afternoon." She sighed. "Okay, okay, I know it's not your fault. The boss may know all about managing a hotel, but he stopped using computers about the time they installed more than ten buttons on them. He said to help you any way I can, keep your visit under my hat, and not to ask questions." She gestured to a chair across from her desk. "Let's get this over with."

I slid the pictures across the desk. "I need to know who these two men are. They're in rooms 3405 and 3406."

"That's all?" Foreman glanced at the pictures. She slid a keyboard in front of her. "Why couldn't this wait until tomorrow?"

"It was Mr. Wallenda's decision to call you in. I agree with that decision, but he should be the one to tell you why it's important."

"Well, he has conveniently gone home and left me holding the bag."

"I sympathize with you. If it's any consolation, this wrecks my Sunday too."

She waved it off. "Forgive me; I'm venting…3405 and 3406, you said? Let's see…those rooms are both registered to XPVV Corporation. They checked in at the same time with a corporate American Express card." She pushed the keyboard aside. "That doesn't help, does it?"

"Did they sign a register card?"

Foreman glanced at the screen. "They arrived yesterday. Our guests sign a computer screen with a finger, but you know how bad those signatures are. Usually they sign with just a squiggle on the screen. That signature is scanned into our data base." She pulled the keyboard over again. "Here they are." She rotated the monitor so I could examine it.

The two signatures were illegible squiggles.

"Wally, this is Raymond Snopolski, my associate." I had called him in for an extra set of eyes on the case.

"Call me Snoop." They shook hands.

"Show Snoop that security video of the third floor lobby where Graciela got on the elevator. The one we looked at earlier. Okay to pull up a couple of chairs?"

"Sure thing, Chuck." The hotel security guard glanced at my friend and occasional employee. "Snoop, was it?"

"Yeah, I used to be a police detective. I did a lot of snooping."

Wally nodded and punched the keyboard. "Here's the Latin Angel getting on elevator number four."

"Go back three minutes. I want Snoop to see her arrive at the elevator lobby."

Wally punched the keys. "Mr. Wallenda said I should do anything you want and not tell anybody about it." He typed in the new command. "Here's the lobby three minutes earlier."

Graciela was already there, standing near elevator four.

I pointed at the screen. "She waited next to elevator four. Everyone else is waiting near elevators one and two."

Snoop shrugged. "Human nature. The party was at the end of the floor nearest to elevator one. People leaving the party naturally stop at the first elevator they come to."

"But Graciela didn't." I turned to Wally. "Run it back three more minutes please."

"Right. Here it is."

Graciela was not in the lobby.

"Play it in real time, please, Wally."

Six hotel guests in evening dress walked into the picture and waited near elevator one. Elevator two arrived and all six got on. More guests entered the picture. They got on elevators four, three, and one.

Graciela entered the picture with another couple and two single women. The five of them smiled and chatted as they waited for an elevator. Elevator one arrived again. The man in the group waited for his date and the two single women to get on. He swayed back and forth as he waited for Graciela to board next. When she didn't, he spoke to her and bowed with an exaggerated gesture for her to go first. She shook her head and said something. He shrugged, waved to Graciela, and lurched into the elevator.

The elevator doors closed. Graciela walked carefully—like drunks walk—to elevator four and waited.

"Snoop, she waited specifically for elevator four."

"Graciela must have known the guy in the black tuxedo would be on elevator four."

"That's what I figure. Continue, please, Wally."

Three other elevators arrived and departed. Graciela sipped champagne. The couple in the blue tuxedo and blue cocktail dress entered the picture and waited near elevator one, arms wrapped around each other. The green light went on above elevator four. Blue Tuxedo took his date by the arm and steered her toward the elevator. Graciela peered into the elevator for a second, then followed them through the open doors.

"She made sure Black Tuxedo and Crooked Nose were in the car before she got in," Snoop said. "The three of them planned that meeting."

"That's right," I said, "and they went to an awful lot of trouble not to do it in a public place."

I pushed the stop button and sank to one knee. "You're too old to squat, aren't you, Snoop?"

"I can do everything you can do, bud, just not as fast. But since you volunteered, be my guest."

"Here's the mark where she caught her heel in the elevator door."

"Like in the security video." Snoop released the *stop* button and followed me into the elevator lobby.

We examined the floor all around.

"She got off the elevator, suitcase in her left hand, and walked to that metal door with her right hand inside her purse. Maybe she was reaching for the key fob." I mimicked the motion we had watched on the video. "She bumped the crash bar with her hip and twisted around to back through the door..." I bumped the door like Graciela had and backed through it into the parking garage. "...and vanished."

Snoop followed me to the parking deck. "What kind of first-class hotel doesn't have security cameras in the parking garage?"

"The Port City Palace kind. No sense complaining, Snoop. We work with what we have."

I surveyed the parking deck. "I don't know whether to hope her car is still here or whether it's gone. What's that?" I pointed at something on the concrete deck.

Snoop walked over and squatted in the driveway. "My squat's not really broken." He grinned at me and pulled on a rubber glove. "It's a squashed key fob. Probably somebody drove over it. We can fingerprint it to test if it's hers." He picked up the fob. "This has a rental car company key ring on it. If I can make out…" He moved a few feet to hold the crushed plastic under an overhead light. "I can read the license number." He showed it to me.

"Good work." I glanced around. "There, the red Mustang convertible." Walking over, I slipped a small Maglite from my pocket. When I shined it in the window, I noticed something unusual. "It's unlocked." Opening the door, I tried unsuccessfully to squeeze into the driver's seat. "This seat is positioned where a five-foot-seven woman like Graciela would have it." I moved the seat all the way back, sat down, and inhaled. "That's the same perfume I smelled in Bob's closet in their hotel suite."

I found a button on the instrument panel and popped the trunk. "Check the trunk. I'll examine the rental contract."

Seconds later Snoop returned. "Trunk's empty."

I handed Snoop a thick cardboard folder. "We won't need the fingerprints from the key fob. These rental papers were in the glove box. This is her car all right. You'll just have to get another key fob at the car rental office."

"I'll head out to the airport. Maybe we'll learn something from the GPS after I get the new fob."

"I'll pay another visit to the security office. Maybe I can find something useful from the garage cashier videos."

———

A green Mercedes eased into the picture and rolled to a stop at the garage exit. The time indicator showed *03:33:45*. The driver's window slid down, and he reached his arm out to the exit console and swiped a keycard across the reader.

"Freeze that, Wally. Now zoom in. The driver's wearing a tuxedo. Zoom in on the French cuffs. I want to examine the cufflink."

Wally expanded the picture until the cufflink showed in blurry detail. "A lion's head, maybe? You want a picture, Chuck?"

"Yeah. It looks like the cufflinks the guy in the tuxedo on the elevator was wearing. Save a jpeg copy on this." I gave Wally a stick drive, which he inserted into the computer. "Now pan over to the windshield sticker and get me a print."

Wally focused on the corner of the windshield. "That Mercedes is from Mango Island."

"Yeah. Now switch to the camera at the rear. Zoom in on the license plate. Print and save that to the stick drive also, please."

Wally clicked the keyboard. "Done...and done." The picture moved again.

The yellow-striped gate rose and the Mercedes glided forward.

"Freeze that. Let's have the front view. Zoom in on the men in the front seat. Can you enhance the picture?"

Wally moved his shoulders back and straightened in his chair. "I can make this computer do everything but brew coffee." The screen transformed into close-ups of the two men. "Those are the same guys who were on the elevator with Graciela."

"Yep. Let's print and save that one too."

"Right," Wally said. The Mercedes moved out of the frame.

"Do those consoles at the entrances and exits record parking charges from the electronic coding on the hotel room keycards?"

"Yeah, sure. That's how we charge guests for parking."

"Which hotel room was the Mercedes registered in?"

Wally moved the mouse and glanced at a second monitor. "Room 3406."

"Just like we thought."

An ancient white Ford Aerostar van entered the picture and approached the garage exit.

"Freeze it there. Advance a couple more frames. There. Switch to the rear view and zoom in on the license plate."

"Hey, those are New Jersey plates."

"Lots of Jets fans in Jersey," I said. "That's where they actually play their home games. I need another picture."

Wally did something and the image expanded. "Shazam." He ran the video again. "Those rear windows are tinted so dark I can't see inside."

"Yeah. The back could be full of people and you couldn't tell at night with the reflections of the lights."

The van stopped at the exit console and the window rolled down. An arm in a dark T-shirt swiped a keycard and the gate opened.

I tapped the screen. "There's one man in the front seat. What keycard did he use?"

Wally consulted the other monitor. "Room 3405."

"Crooked Nose and the man in the tuxedo were in the Mercedes. Obviously, they had other men working this. Let's have a close-up of the driver."

Wally leaned toward the screen. "That's useless." The driver wore a New York Jets hat that obscured his face.

"Not quite. Get me a picture of his Jets T-shirt."

"Right." Wally ran the videos for the next fifteen minutes, but no other vehicle left the garage.

"What time did the van enter the garage?"

Wally consulted his computer. "It didn't enter on that keycard. The driver must have taken a parking ticket like a non-guest." He scanned more video files. "Here it is. It entered at 1:26 a.m. and the driver took a paper ticket."

"Yeah, but it used a hotel keycard, room 3405, to exit. That means the driver met with Crooked Nose."

"Let's get a better view of the driver when he entered."

Wally leaned back in his chair. "Would you look at that? Two men in the front seat, both in black Jets T-shirts and hats."

"Neither of those two guys drove the van out. The driver who exited wore a different Jets shirt. The two guys in the front must have been in the back when the van left."

I knew now that Graciela had been in the back with them. But why?

THREE

B ob Martinez gazed up from a table for two in the back corner of the hotel steakhouse and stood. "Thanks for coming, Eighty-Eight. Have a seat."

I shook hands and slid out a chair. I nodded to the server who had shown me to the table. "I'll have what he's having." I glanced at Bob's food. "But one steak, not two."

Bob waited for the server to leave. "What have you learned so far?"

"Plenty." I handed the Jets quarterback the pictures one at a time and briefed him on each one.

Bob held one picture up. "Who are these guys in the elevator?"

"I hoped you might recognize them."

"Never saw them before. What about that XVVP corporation that rented their hotel rooms?"

"XPVV," I corrected. "Don't know yet. Snoop is tracing the corporation. It doesn't show up on the Florida Secretary of State's website, so it's out of state. Snoop will search until he finds something, but there are lots of states to research. He'll begin with

New York, New Jersey, and Delaware. Lots of corporations are chartered in Delaware, even those that do business elsewhere. We should have info tomorrow."

"Can't he research those websites tonight?"

"Snoop went to the airport to get a new key fob for Gracie's car," I said. "It's after hours on a Sunday, so it won't be easy, and he's gotta sleep sometime. Tell you what: I've got another operative—a computer geek who's the best in the business. He specializes in rush jobs and sleeps at odd hours, but he's expensive. You want me to sic him on the XPVV Corporation tonight?"

"Gracie is missing; the money doesn't matter."

"I don't want you to be surprised when this case gets real expensive, real fast. I need a retainer."

Bob pulled out his wallet. "Of course. This has morphed into a bigger project than we thought. You don't need to carry me on the cuff. Would ten thousand be enough for right now?"

I lowered my voice. "Don't tell me you carry that much money around with you."

Bob laughed. "Of course not. *Mamacita* didn't raise no stupid children. I carry a couple of blank checks for emergencies."

"Then make it for twenty thousand."

Bob filled out the check and pushed it across the table.

I stuck it in my pocket. "Thanks. I'll let you know if I need more. If I don't use it all, I'll refund the rest."

Bob swallowed a bite of steak. "*Amigo*, I would trust you with my life, so I trust you with my money. You don't need to explain. Do whatever it takes to find Gracie."

"Right. The video showed Gracie reaching for her key fob when she got to the parking garage, which means she intended to drive somewhere." I fished one picture from the stack in front of him. "She carried this suitcase."

Bob frowned at the picture. "That's one of her matching bags.

She uses that one to carry extra clothes to a photo shoot. That must be the one that wasn't in the suite."

"You have any idea where she was going?"

Bob shook his head. "Did you find anything in her car?"

"No, but without the key fob, we couldn't start it. Snoop should have the new key fob later tonight. Maybe the GPS will tell us something—if she used it."

"Gracie loves gadgets. I guarantee you she used it. I know she visited her mom and dad."

"She must know the way to her parents' house."

"Yeah, but it's over thirty miles to Little Havana. She would have used the GPS to tell her the best way to get there in case there was a traffic delay on I-95."

"You know any place else she would have gone?"

"She had an appointment with a lawyer about our prenuptial agreement, and she shops anytime we travel together." He made a weird face. "Boy, does she ever love to shop."

"She dropped the key fob and it got run over. Look at this picture." I thumbed through the stack of prints. "Something surprised her to make her drop it. She had already unlocked the car with the fob. Maybe somebody ambushed her and pushed her into that old Aerostar. The Aerostar followed the green Mercedes out of the garage. Remember, there were at least three men in that van."

"You got an ID on the van yet?"

"We're working on it, but the New Jersey DMV records can't be searched online and their office won't open until tomorrow morning. We may not have it until noon, maybe later. You know how DMVs can be."

Bob grunted.

"We might get the DMV to move faster if I asked one of my Port City cop buddies to run it."

"No cops. No FBI. No nobody other than you and your people. Keep this on the down low."

"Suit yourself."

Why was Bob so averse to using the cops? I had already found enough evidence to convince the PCPD to open a missing person case. And the fact that the Aerostar had New Jersey plates made this an interstate crime, so the FBI could easily take jurisdiction, even if it hadn't been a kidnapping.

My meal arrived. I waited until the server left. "Gracie took an envelope from one of the guys in the elevator, and her body language indicated she knew them, or at least the guy in the tuxedo. The two men left the garage in the Mercedes right before the van did. I traced the Mercedes license number. It belongs to XPVV Corporation. It has a Mango Island resident sticker on the windshield." I showed him the picture.

"That's great. Call Mango Island and ask them whose car it is."

"It's not that simple, Bob. The address on the car registration is a Port City post office box. I'm not a cop anymore. People don't talk to me unless they feel like it, and Mango Island—the entire island—is a private club. I know from experience that they won't share any information without a warrant. Liability issues and such. This is not a police missing person investigation—at your request. I can play the sympathy card, but that's the only influence I have. You won't let me tell anyone she's missing."

"Don't tell anybody yet, Eighty-Eight. You've made progress, and it's not even twenty-four hours. Keep this on the down low for now, okay? If you hit a dead-end, we'll think again about the missing person option."

I stabbed a bite of steak. "You're the client. It's your money and your fiancée, but, *amigo*, you're making me play with one arm tied behind my back."

I punched the start button and the red Mustang's instrument panel lit up.

"The rental contract says the car had 7,826 miles at the time Gracie rented it. The odometer shows 8,004 now, so she drove… 178 miles."

I tapped the GPS screen. "Here's the *recently found* list. Judging from the distances of these addresses from here, I'd guess these last five are Gracie's, maybe the sixth one too. The seventh one is Disney World. That's over two hundred miles away, and she drove only 178 miles, so that would be from the previous driver."

I scrolled up. "Write those addresses down, Snoop. I'll check the last one first—oh wait, that's this hotel. She must have entered it to find her way here from the previous address."

After I entered the previous address on my cellphone, a map popped up on the screen. "That's a rough part of town. Bob was afraid Graciela was doing drugs again. She could score some in that neighborhood."

"If she did, then what did the mook in the black tuxedo pass her in the elevator?"

"Don't know yet. Cash, maybe?"

I entered the next address and studied the map on the screen. "This is a residential neighborhood in Miami's Little Havana."

"Maybe she has family there."

"Her parents. She was born in Miami." I keyed the next address. "That's Vicky Ramirez's office building. At dinner a couple of hours ago, Bob said that Gracie had an appointment with her lawyer. Could it be Vicky?"

"Vicky's firm does family law and prenuptial agreements," Snoop said.

DALLAS GORHAM

"Of course, it's a big building. Vicky's firm isn't the only law firm in that building."

"What's the fourth destination?"

"It's in Naples." I punched the address into my phone. "It's a hotel. Naples is over 100 miles from here. Gracie drove only 178, so she didn't drive there."

"Why would she enter the address if she wasn't going there?"

"Lots of reasons. She may have wanted to know how far it was, or she was thinking of going there but changed her mind." I shrugged. "Read the address before that and you'll spot something strange."

Snoop examined the GPS screen. "175 Beachline Causeway. That doesn't make sense, there's nothing on the Beachline. It just runs across Seeti Bay from downtown to Port City Beach."

"I don't recognize the address either. We'll follow her GPS log backwards and research them all."

I slipped the Mustang into reverse and backed from the parking spot.

"You don't have the hotel keycard for this car."

"I'll use the paper ticket I took for our car when we came in. We'll get another ticket when we bring this car back."

We exited and I stopped at the curb by a fire hydrant. I selected the trip log from the GPS screen and zoomed in until the display showed individual streets.

"All those blue lines loop back to the Port City Palace. How you gonna tell which way she drove?"

"I find the last place she went on the GPS map." I swiped the map screen, following the blue line.

I cruised the block at idle speed. "Notice anything suspicious, Snoop?"

My old buddy scoffed. "I don't notice anything that *isn't* suspicious. Check out that guy in the hunting vest. He must carry his inventory in his pockets."

A young black man wearing a Port City Pilots baseball hat and three-hundred-dollar sneakers stood under a streetlight near the entrance to the alley, thumbs hooked in his yellow hunting vest. His pants hung below his buttocks, revealing dark grey underwear. His eyes widened in recognition of the red convertible we drove. A gold tooth gleamed in his smile.

I slowed to a stop and pressed the button to lower the passenger window.

Pilots Fan sidled over to the curb. He leaned down to peer through the window. "You lookin' to do some business, my man?" he said to Snoop.

I got out and regarded him over the roof of the car.

Pilots Fan backed up. "I'm clean, man. I ain't carrying nothin'. Search me if you want."

I walked around to the sidewalk. "This your territory?"

"Who wants to know?"

"Relax, dude. We're not cops."

"Why you carrying a piece?"

"I'm private. I only want information." I slipped a hundred-dollar bill from my pocket and held it where Pilots Fan could appreciate it. He licked his lips and stared at Ben Franklin's face.

I showed him Graciela's picture. "You do any business with this woman yesterday?"

Pilots Fan reached for the bill and I jerked it away. "Answers first."

He stared both ways up and down the street. "I seen the car you're in, and I seen the chick. Fine, fine stuff she was. She stop

across the street." He pointed. "But she don't buy nothin' from me."
He gripped the bill but I didn't let it go.

"Who did she buy from?"

The man glanced up the street. "Fast Eddie. He works the other side of the street."

I released the bill and he stuffed it in his pocket. I gazed across the street. "Fast Eddie over there now?"

"That'll cost you another Benjamin."

I squinted at the other man and said nothing.

"It's good information, dude. I wouldn't shit you or nothin'. That's worth a Benjamin."

I moved my hand toward my pocket. "Where is he?"

"Show me the money first."

I waved the bill in front of him.

"Fast Eddie, he works the next block up the street."

"You know his last name?" I waved the bill again.

A contact in the Port City police sent Eddie Yanez's mug shot to my phone. I glanced at it again as I pulled to the curb. My cop friend told me Yanez was a runner and would bug out at the first sign of trouble. "You'll never catch him," were his exact words. Fast Eddie.

I got out and stood by the driver's door five yards from Yanez. Let Mohammed come to the mountain.

He glanced at me. I waved. He narrowed one eye but didn't move.

I slipped a hundred-dollar bill from my pocket and held it where Yanez could practically sniff it. I stuck it back in my pocket.

He eased closer and stopped ten feet away. "I'm listening."

"I'm not a cop; I'm a private investigator. I only want information." I held up Graciela's picture.

He came closer and took the photo. His eyes rounded when he examined it in the streetlight, but he said nothing.

"Yesterday. She drove this red convertible." I held up the hundred. "What did you sell her?"

Yanez smirked. "I didn't sell nothin' to nobody."

I waved the bill. "An easy hundred, Eddie."

Yanez shrugged and reached for the bill. "Okay. I tell you."

Snoop walked around the corner of the house and handed the Maglite back. The sun had risen, but the backyard and driveway were in shadow. "I peeked through the garage window. Regular junk stored in it. No car."

"Since there's a Honda SUV in the driveway, they must own two cars. Maybe they went out for early breakfast." I rang the doorbell. A dog barked behind the house.

"There's a mutt in the backyard," Snoop explained. "Cute little guy."

I waited a minute then knocked. The barking erupted again. "They're not out of town unless they have a neighbor to feed the dog. We'll wait."

Ten minutes later, a shiny Ford Fusion parked in the driveway and a middle-aged couple got out.

I opened the driver door. "You be bad cop."

"Why am I always bad cop?"

"With my movie-star looks, no one would believe me as bad cop. You, on the other hand…"

Snoop scoffed and opened his door. "Movie-star looks… maybe Quasimodo in *The Hunchback of Notre Dame*."

We met the couple as they walked to the front door. "Mr. and

Mrs. Perez? I'm Chuck McCrary and this is my associate, Raymond Snopolski." I handed them each a business card.

The man glanced at the card. "Is that Graciela's rental car you're driving?"

"Yes, sir. She and Bob Martinez are friends of mine. Can we talk inside?"

"What can we do for you, Mr. McCrary?" Horatio Perez asked.

I set my Cuban coffee on the table. "Please, call me Chuck. We're trying to find Gracie."

"What do you mean?" Evangelina Perez asked. "Is my *Graciela* missing?"

The dog's ears perked up at the mention of Graciela's name.

I noticed that the woman had slightly stressed "Graciela." Maybe she didn't like the nickname. "Saturday night, she and Bob attended a TV network party at their hotel. Bob left at 10:30, but Graciela stayed a little longer. When I met Bob for breakfast yesterday morning, he told me she never came back to the room."

"Then where is she?" Horatio asked.

I decided not to tell Gracie's parents what we had seen on the security videos. There was no point worrying them yet. "We don't know, sir. Bob is worried, and he asked me to find her. I spent all day yesterday searching."

"Well, you certainly began early today." Horatio Perez glanced at his watch. "Evangelina and I serve breakfast to the homeless at our church every Monday before we go to work. We came home so Evangelina could take her own car to work."

"I'll try her right now." Evangelina picked up her cellphone and called. She held her husband's hand and they sat on the couch.

Snoop and I waited.

Evangelina squeezed Horatio's hand as she listened to the voicemail message. Her eyes glistened. Her hand shook as she set the phone beside her Cuban coffee. "Straight to voicemail," she said to Horatio. "That means her phone is turned off."

Horatio laid a hand on hers.

"We'd like to ask you a couple of questions that might help us find her."

Evangelina twisted her hands in the folds of her skirt. "Anything we can do. Anything."

"Was Graciela worried about anything when she came to visit?"

Horatio shook his head. "Same old Graciela. She was excited about Bob playing in the Super Bowl, of course." He glanced at Evangelina. "We all are. In fact, he got us good tickets—twenty-five-yard line."

Evangelina smiled and reached down to pet the dog. "I think Graciela came mainly to play with Gordo."

I gestured toward the dog. "That's Gordo?"

The woman smiled. "Graciela named him that because he was so fat when he was a puppy. *Gordo* means—"

"Fat. I'm Mexican-American. I speak Spanish."

Evangelina smiled.

I continued, "Gordo is Graciela's dog?"

"We bought him from a rescue shelter when Graciela was a girl. She and Gordo were inseparable. She went to modeling school in Miami instead of New York so she wouldn't be separated from Gordo." The dog cocked his ears at the woman and wagged his tail.

"Graciela's career took off, and Evangelina and I told her she had to move to New York City. That's where she could find the media connections and the rich people—for her career. She took Gordo with her so she wouldn't be lonely among all those strangers." He scratched Gordo behind the ears. "But he didn't do so well in that city atmosphere. We brought him back to live with us. Gordo's fifteen years old now."

"I see. Did Graciela mention she was in any kind of trouble?"

"No, no, of course not," Horatio said.

"Was Graciela using any drugs?"

Evangelina's lips pressed into a straight line. Her gaze cut to Horatio. "Graciela would *never* use drugs. *Never*." The woman fished a handkerchief from a pocket and twisted it in her hands.

Horatio's eyes narrowed.

I nodded at Snoop.

He plunked his coffee cup on the saucer with a clatter. "Mr. and Mrs. Perez, we all know that's not true." He leaned toward the couple. "I know you both love Graciela, but you can't protect her by lying to us. We're trying to help her. She may be in trouble. In fact, we think she's in danger. Was she using any drugs?"

Evangelina buried her face in the handkerchief and sobbed.

Horatio wrapped an arm around her.

"We're sorry to bring up such an ugly subject," I said, "but we need the truth. What can you tell us about Graciela's drug habit?"

Evangelina's eyes blazed. "It's that man Jerry Greenbaum's fault."

I opened my note pad. "Jerry Greenbaum?"

"That's her agent," Horatio said. "He told our baby girl that heroin would help control her weight."

Evangelina sobbed again. "She got addicted. She's been to rehab twice. Bob even paid for it last summer. That man is a godsend. Is she using again?"

"We think so," Snoop said, "but we thought it was cocaine."

"It could be both," I said. "Did she tell you where she planned to go after she left here?"

The woman stared into space for a moment. Tears streaked her cheeks. "She had a party to go to Saturday night to make an appearance for the media people who would be there. That must be the network party you mentioned. That was the only plan she told me about."

"What time did she leave here?"

"Right after lunch."

"What was she wearing?"

"A fawn-colored, knee-length skirt with a taupe linen shell, and matching gold earrings, and a bracelet and necklace we gave her for Christmas." She smiled at the memory. "She looked stunning."

"What about shoes?"

"Brown sling pumps with gold straps and four-inch heels. I asked where she got them. I hinted that she might give me a pair for my birthday. She's so generous."

I wrote that in my notebook. "What time did Graciela get to your house?"

"About five o'clock."

Horatio noticed the surprise on my face and smiled. "Not five a.m. It was the previous day—five p.m. Friday. She treated Evangelina and me to dinner at our favorite restaurant on *Calle Ocho*. She insisted on paying. She hadn't planned to spend the night, but we had an extra bottle of wine at dinner. We made her stay over."

"She slept in her old room," Gracie's mother said. "Gordo slept on the foot of the bed like he did when my Graciela was a little girl." Tears flowed again.

Snoop reached across the coffee table and patted her hand. No more Bad Cop. I didn't blame him; she was hurting. Horatio seemed about to cry too.

I waited for them to compose themselves. Time was important, but I didn't want to put undue pressure on Gracie's parents. They looked almost unraveled as it was. "Graciela had an appointment with a lawyer before she visited you. Do you know what that was about?"

Evangelina wiped her tears with the handkerchief. "Oh, that was about her prenuptial agreement. She met with her attorney that afternoon and came to visit us after she finished. She and Bob are getting married in a few weeks, you know. And they both have successful careers." She tried to smile.

"Doesn't your daughter have a lawyer in New York City?"

"Of course," Horatio said, "but the wedding will be here in Miami and her New York attorney said she should hire a lawyer familiar with Florida law. Her New York attorney recommended the woman Graciela met with on Friday."

"Did Graciela tell you her name?"

"It was something Latin—I think she's Cuban like us," Horatio said. "Graciela gave me her business card so I would know who it was in case she called. It's in a drawer in the kitchen." He left the room.

"Would you or Chuck like more coffee while Horatio is up?"

Snoop glanced at me. I shook my head. "We're good."

In a few minutes, the man returned with a business card. "This is her card. You can take it with you if you want."

I glanced at the card and smiled. "That won't be necessary, Horatio." I handed the card back to him. "Victoria Ramirez is my attorney too."

Vicky Ramirez greeted us in the reception area. "You said it was urgent, so I cleared a slot. You've got fifteen minutes. Hello, Snoop. Nice to see you too."

"We appreciate you squeezing us in. We'll be brief."

She led us to a nearby conference room. "You want coffee?"

I waved it off. "Thanks, but we can't stay long. We came from meeting with Evangelina and Horatio Perez, Graciela's parents. They told us you're representing her with the prenuptial agreement."

"You're wasting your time. Chuck, you know I won't confirm or deny who my clients are, let alone which matters I represent them on."

"I know, Vicky, but this is different. The reason we can't stay is that Gracie is missing and every hour is precious. We think she's in danger. Bob Martinez hired me to find her." I told her about the breakfast meeting with Bob. "I called Bob on the way over here. Gracie told him you're her attorney. It's not a secret, but I don't want to know anything about your negotiations with Bob's attorney. I only want any information that could help us find Gracie. Will you at least help me with that?"

Vicky patted my knee. "Sorry, big guy. I would if I could, but I have no idea where Graciela is."

Drumming my fingers on the convertible's steering wheel, I stared over the turquoise water at the white, steel skeletons of the container cranes on Columbus Island rose across the ship channel. Columbus Island had been dredged from Seetiweekifenokee Bay in the early twentieth century to make the port. Two rusty island freighters were moored across the choppy water. The Monday morning commuters had cleared the Beachline Causeway. Traffic was light.

"What do you think?" Snoop asked.

I had parked Gracie's rental in the terminal parking lot for the Mango Island Ferry. "I've driven past this ferry terminal a hundred times. I never knew its street address was 175 Beachline Causeway."

"Gracie must've met someone on Mango Island."

"Well, duh." I zoomed the GPS trip log to maximum. "She parked the car here. She didn't take it on the ferry."

"How can you tell?"

I pointed at the image of Mango Island on the GPS screen. "If she had started the car to drive off the ferry on the other end, the GPS log would have recorded it. No blue log line on the other side; ergo, she parked here."

"Ergo? You're giving me *ergo*?"

"Hey, I went to college too," I said. "It means 'therefore'."

Snoop sniffed. "I knew that, smart ass. Anyway, Gracie had to have met someone here, ergo, someone who lives on Mango Island."

"The Mercedes was from Mango Island."

"But who owns the Mercedes and why did she meet him? She met him in the elevator later... if he's the guy she met, which we don't know."

"Or she walked onto the ferry and went to the island as a foot passenger." I opened my door. "Let's go find the security footage."

"I want to be Good Cop this time."

"I'll throw you for it. One, two, three...Paper beats Rock. Sorry, Snoop, you're Bad Cop again."

We walked to the Mediterranean-style building at the edge of the parking lot. A brass plaque said *Security* on one of the doors. I pressed the doorbell and waited. The lock buzzed and we entered.

A large man in a neatly-pressed turquoise jacket with gold trim sat at the desk behind three computer monitors. He smiled, straight white teeth gleaming. "Can I help you, sir?" His accent was Caribbean, or maybe Bahamian.

I glanced at the guard's name tag and handed him a business

card. *Maybe I ought to add a logo of a knight slaying a dragon.* "Alphonse, I'm Carlos McCrary. This is my associate, Raymond Snopolski." I held up Graciela's picture. "Did this young woman cross to the island as a pedestrian on Saturday after 1:00 p.m.? Maybe your security video could tell us."

The guard didn't look at the picture. "May I see your card, please?" His smile faded a bit.

"I gave you my card."

"I meant your *membership* card, mon. Mango Island is a private club."

"I'm not a member; I'm a private investigator. Did this young woman cross on this ferry on Saturday afternoon?"

Alphonse stood and gestured toward the door. "Sorry, mon. Mango Island is only for members and guests. We take members' privacy seriously." He pronounced *privacy* in the British fashion. "You and your friend will have to leave."

I stared at Snoop.

Snoop leaned across the desk. "Alphonse, you may be in trouble—legal trouble, if you know what I mean."

The guard frowned. "I don't understand."

Snoop took Graciela's picture from me and thrust it at the guard. "I'm sure you recognize this woman."

Alphonse did a double take and grabbed the picture. "That's the cover girl, mon. Graciela. The one they call the Latin Angel. My teenage daughter has a Latin Angel poster on her bedroom wall."

"That's right. She's so famous she uses one name, like Beyoncé or Shakira. She's missing, Alphonse. And the last place she was seen was in *your* parking lot Saturday afternoon." Snoop jabbed a finger at the guard. "She parked that red Mustang convertible out there," he pointed through the window, "right where it's parked now. Then she *disappeared*. We don't know how that car got back to the hotel. So, if you value your members' *privacy,*" he pronounced it like Alphonse had, "the last thing you want is the FBI and the Port City Police in here searching for a famous model who's been kidnapped. They would invade your private island, guns drawn, and take it apart house by expensive house."

I lifted a hand. "Easy, Snopolski."

He sneered at the guard. "Do you want the authorities to run roughshod over your beautiful island, Alphonse? We only need a little information."

Alphonse appeared skeptical. "If Graciela was kidnapped, why hasn't it been on the news, and why aren't the FBI and the cops here already?"

I lowered my voice to a whisper. "Her fiancé is Bob Martinez." I waited for Alphonse to recognize the name.

Alphonse had no reaction.

"You know...Bob Martinez?" I repeated.

Alphonse scratched his head. "Am I supposed to know that name too, mon?"

"Super Bowl quarterback Bob Martinez of the New York Jets?"

Alphonse smiled. "Quarterback...is that American football? In Jamaica we play cricket, mon."

"There she is...Saturday." I read the time off the screen and wrote it on my notepad.

Alphonse scrolled the security video of the parking lot in reverse until we watched Graciela's rental car drive backwards into the frame. "I'll keep going backwards until we see her arrive." He ran the video backwards some more. Graciela backed butt-first out of the car and walked backwards toward the ferry. It would have been funny if it hadn't been so serious.

"There," said Snoop. He tapped the screen. "She was on the island four hours."

"Not quite, mon. It takes thirty minutes each way for the ferry to get there and back."

"Fine; she was on the island *three* hours. Let's review the video from the other end. We'll see who met her on Mango Island."

"That video is in the guard house on the island, mon. You have to go over there."

We waited for the last of the cars to bump off the ferry. Our steps rattled on the metal deck of the *Islandhopper III* as we disembarked. We walked beneath the thatched roof of the small terminal waiting area to another Mediterranean-style security building that was the twin of the one on the causeway.

It was twilight and streetlights had come on in the parking lot. I pressed the doorbell, listened for the buzz, and opened the door. "Did Alphonse call you?" I said to the guard behind the desk.

"You must be Mr. McCrary," said the guard, also with a Caribbean accent. He seemed skeptical.

"And you're Terrence?" I stuck out my hand.

Terrence considered my hand like it might be a trap before he shook it. He sniffed. "I don't like this. It's against policy."

"Alphonse said he would clear it with you."

Terrence wrinkled his nose like he smelled a dead rat. "I've queued the video when the young lady arrived as Alphonse instructed. I still don't like it. It's against policy."

"We think she's been kidnapped."

Terrence sighed. "Come 'round this side where you can see."

The frozen picture came to life. Graciela wobbled across the steel deck in her stilettos and took the same walk under the thatched terminal that Snoop and I had taken a few minutes earlier. She disappeared from view.

Terrence changed to a different view. Gracie crossed the parking lot to a turquoise golf cart with a white roof. A bald man in a pastel green guayabera shirt and khaki Bermuda shorts stood beside the cart. It was Crooked Nose from the hotel elevator.

"Freeze that," I said. "Do you recognize that man, Terrence?"

Terrence scrutinized the screen. "No, mon. There are over six hundred condos and fifty houses on the island. I don't know them all." He zoomed the picture, and the man's neck tattoo sprang into high relief. It was a spider web. Terrence frowned at the picture.

Snoop began to say something, but I placed my hand on his arm. "Could you print us a screen shot, Terrence?"

"It's against policy."

"Never mind, I'll do it myself." I photographed the screen with my phone. "Okay, play it now."

Graciela sat in the back seat without speaking to Crooked Nose, and the cart moved out of frame.

"Terrence, do the golf carts have license plates?"

He frowned. "Yes."

"Please fast forward to the cart bringing her back. We can maybe find a picture of the number."

"It's against policy, but…" Terrence punched his keyboard. The picture skipped ahead three hours. "It should show up any second… there." The video switched to slow motion.

This time Graciela sat in the front seat. She smiled and talked to the driver. He wore a Panama hat, a red guayabera, and white shorts. The bald man with the neck tattoo sat in the back seat. "Freeze that," I said. "Zoom in." The driver's face was in shadow. "Too much contrast. Can't make it out. Move a frame at a time, and let's try to get his face in the sunlight."

The cart stopped and the driver walked around to where

Graciela stood. He removed his hat and the two exchanged air kisses. It was Black Tuxedo from the Port City Palace. "There," I said, "zoom in and I'll take a screen shot."

The cart wheeled across the parking lot and the license number came into view. The guard zoomed in. "Number 1217."

I wrote that down. "Who does it belong to?"

Terrence swiveled his chair and rolled across the floor to a two-drawer file cabinet. He slid open the top drawer and flipped through a metal box of cards. "All the latest nineteenth-century technology. We use index cards for the golf carts. Here it is." He pulled a card from the box. His face hardened. He shoved the card back in the box. "We don't have that number on file. Sorry, mon." He tried to close the file drawer.

I grabbed his wrist and jerked him away from the file cabinet. Shoving his chair out of the way, I yanked the drawer open. A metal box stuffed with index cards was inside. I found the card for 1217 and read it.

"You never got nothing from me, mon. You understand me? I didn't tell you nothing. I don't want nothing to do with him."

I stuck the index card in my pocket. "Don't worry, Terrence. He'll never learn about it from us."

———

Snoop and I returned to the red Mustang and I fired it up and drove calmly from the parking lot.

"You want to tell me what's going on? You didn't say a word on the ferry all the way back from Mango Island."

"Didn't want to be overheard, Snoop. Terrence was terrified when he read the owner's name on that index card. The walls on that ferry could have ears. Wait until I park somewhere. We gotta think about this."

A half mile from the ferry terminal, I steered the car into a side street on one of the residential islands to park. The car decelerated, and I felt a tap against my left heel. I threw the gear shift into *park* and glanced at the floorboard. It was a flip-phone. I picked it up. "This slid out from under the front seat, Snoop."

"You mean you didn't search under there, bud?"

"Uh-oh. I sense another teachable moment coming on." Before he took early retirement, Snoop had been a Port City police detective longer than I had been alive. When I was his partner, he taught me most of what I know about the detective business. He was my go-to guy when I didn't know what to do. To call him a mentor would be a gross understatement of the depth of our friendship. He was more like a second father.

"No, *sensei*, I only searched the glove compartment. I found the car rental contract, and I thought *Oh goody* and stopped searching. I got distracted by the rental contract and left the search half done. Let's have the lecture."

"Okay, consider yourself lectured to." He opened the passenger door and squatted by the curb to peer under the passenger seat. "Hand me the Maglite." He flipped the back of the seat up and knelt on the narrow floorboard in front of the convertible's slender rear seat. "Help me get this seat out."

I did. We found an unopened foil-wrapped condom beneath the seat and thirteen cents. Snoop dropped the coins in his pocket without a word. He tossed me the condom. "Maybe you'll get lucky, bud."

We replaced the rear seat and took our places in the front. I tried to switch the flip-phone on. "Battery's dead. Will your charger fit this?" I handed him the phone.

Snoop pulled a cellphone charger from his jacket pocket and tried it in the flip-phone. "Yeah." He plugged the charger into the dashboard. After a few seconds, the phone came to life. He scrolled through the address book. "There's two numbers in the contacts list. An area code 212 number for a *Jerry* and a 302 area code with no name attached to it. Evangelina said Gracie's agent was named Jerry Greenbaum. You want me to reverse look up the numbers?"

"Yeah. Write down both numbers so I can examine the phone's history."

Snoop jotted down the numbers and handed me the phone.

I punched the phone's screen. "There's a text message from Jerry."

Sharky wants his money. He is becoming insistent. You cannot ignore this any longer. He has threatened me too.

I scrolled to the earlier messages.

"The 212 number is listed under the name Jerry Greenbaum," said Snoop. "The 302 number is in Wilmington, Delaware. It's listed under XPVV Corporation."

Gracie's agent had sent the texts about Sharky. In the more recent ones, he became increasingly more upset.

I searched for texts from the Wilmington number.

Confirm you are on the guest list for the ferry. See you tomorrow. Regards, Vic.

I handed the Mango Island golf cart index card to Snoop.

He glanced at it. "XPVV Corporation. The same company that rented the rooms in the Port City Palace."

"And owns the Mercedes that left the parking garage right before that Aerostar van. Terrence noticed that XPVV name, and he clammed up. He knew enough about it to be scared." I tapped my cellphone screen. "Call Flamer," I told the phone.

The phone call went through. "Flamer, I'm putting you on speaker. You got anything on XPVV Corporation yet?"

"It's a Bahamian corporation with a registered office in Newark, New Jersey. The New Jersey address is in care of Lambrusci &

Partners. Lambrusci is a law firm with ties to organized crime and a few legitimate casinos. The firm has an office three blocks from the Double Down Casino in Atlantic City." Flamer paused. "Oh, yeah, and the Double Down Casino is owned by a privately-held REIT."

"What's an REIT?" asked Snoop.

"Real estate investment trust," Flamer responded. "Some tax thing. Guess what the REIT's registered address is?"

"The same law firm?" said Snoop.

"Give that man the prize. The same REIT owns a Double Down Delaware Casino in Wilmington."

"Someone named Vic sent Graciela a text from a phone in Wilmington that's listed for XPVV Corporation."

"*Hmm.* You want me to investigate the Delaware casino?"

"Yeah," I replied. "Anything on the Aerostar van?"

"I ran the Jersey plates. It belongs to Lambrusci & Partners."

"Okay. Another link to the Double Down Casino maybe." I glanced at the index card. "Find who really owns the house at 176 Mango Drive on Mango Island. There's probably a land trust or a corporation involved. If there is, find out who's behind it."

FOUR

Bob Martinez chugged Gatorade as Snoop and I sat on the bench beside the practice field. "Okay, Eighty-Eight, what have you found so far?"

"We traced Gracie's movements using the rental car's GPS log." I filled him in on the details. "Did Gracie mention anything about going to the Beach Cabana Resort in Naples?"

"Gracie was going to Italy?"

"No. It's in Naples, Florida."

Bob shook his head. "Why do you ask?"

"She entered the address on her GPS right after she went to Mango Island."

He shrugged. "*¿Quien sabe?*" *Who knows*?

"Okay. Next, do you know anyone named Sharky?"

"Who's that?"

"Somebody Gracie's agent said wants money from her. Did she ever mention a Sharky?"

"Not that I recall."

"Could he be her drug dealer?" Snoop asked.

Bob glared at him and crushed the Gatorade bottle. "Gracie's clean—ever since I sent her to rehab."

I spoke to him in Spanish. "You're living in a dream world, friend. Didn't you hear me tell you that she bought cocaine from a lowlife named Fast Eddie Yanez in northwest Port City? It's a drive-in drug take-out market." I switched to English. "This was in the bottom drawer of your bathroom cabinet." I handed Bob a yellow prescription bottle.

Bob read the label. "It has Gracie's name on it. What's Desoxyn?"

"It's a highly addictive methamphetamine," Snoop said, "often prescribed for weight reduction. It's popular with New York fashion models. I researched the doctor who prescribed the pills. He's a Park Avenue drug pusher for the rich and richer. Sources with the NYPD say he runs a pill mill. They've tried to shut him down, but they can't touch him."

"That's not all I found." I handed Bob another bottle. "She had this Xanax, an anti-anxiety psychiatric drug—also subject to abuse—prescribed by the same doctor."

Bob eyed the two yellow plastic bottles like they might bite him.

"Look at this picture I took yesterday morning when I searched your hotel suite. I found those purses on the top shelf of your closet."

"I recognize them. They're Gracie's."

Pulling three hot-pink plastic pill bottles from my jacket pocket, I said, "One of these pill bottles was in each of those purses." I unscrewed the lid of one. "Notice those pills?"

Bob peeked inside the bottle.

"Gracie rat-holed a supply of Desoxyn and Xanax in all of the extra purses. All three stockpiles are identical. No matter what purse she grabs, she always has her drugs handy. These stashes are her version of the old American Express commercial: 'Don't leave home without it.'"

I paused for him to absorb all that. "Then there's the cocaine she bought."

Bob stared across the artificial turf, but I don't think he saw anything. Nor did he say anything.

I plucked a plastic baggie from my jacket. "This was left from the batch she bought off the drug dealer I told you about. I found it in a purse she left behind."

Bob shook his head, still studying the turf. "If she's back on the drugs, she must be sleeping off a cocaine episode. She'll come back." He raised his gaze. "She always comes back."

"It's been over twenty-four hours, *amigo*. Pull your head out of the sand—Gracie is in trouble. There's a reason she asked the doctor for an anti-anxiety drug. She's stressed and afraid. She's into something way over her head."

"But she knew those guys from the elevator. You said she met them on Mango Island the day of the party. She *knows* them, for crissakes. How could they have kidnapped her? Besides, she carried a suitcase. She intended to go somewhere where she'd need a couple of changes of clothes is all."

"I hope you're right. I didn't find her toothbrush in your suite, so she planned to be gone at least overnight. That's why she took the birth control pills with her. Just because she knows the guys in the elevator doesn't mean they're friends. Maybe they have something on her—something she's afraid of. They might have threatened her or be blackmailing her. Maybe she took the suitcase to run away from them." I slipped the baggie of cocaine back in my pocket and held up Gracie's tablet computer. "It's time to search this for clues." I stuck the tablet in my briefcase. "We think the main man is named Vic. Does that name mean anything to you?"

Bob shook his head. "No."

"This Vic guy has a connection to the Double Down Casinos in Atlantic City and Delaware. Does that name ring any bells?" *Did the hint of an expression cross Bob's face?*

"Nope. *Nada.*"

"The Atlantic City casino is connected to a Newark law firm with ties to organized crime—Lambrusci & Partners. You ever hear of them?"

Bob didn't say anything. A whistle blew in the distance. He jammed his helmet on and jumped to his feet.

I stood too. "Gracie is in danger, even though she may not know it. You should file a missing person report with the Port City police. That way the cops can help me search for her."

He shook his head. "You're making progress, Eighty-Eight. Let's hold off for now. You keep on truckin'." He ran back onto the field without so much as a backward glance.

Why didn't Bob want me to bring in the cops? He must be hiding something too. What was he afraid of?

"Holy crap. Vicente Vidali is the man in the black tuxedo." Snoop handed Flamer's report to me. "Teflon Vic, the New Jersey mob boss. He's supposed to be a ghost. I didn't know anyone ever got his picture."

I set the report on my desk. "Flamer sent me a mug shot from twenty-five years ago when Vidali was booked for running numbers, but nothing since. Maybe this is the first time anyone's managed to take his picture in the last twenty-five years. The VV in XPVV could stand for Vicente Vidali."

Snoop slurped coffee and waited.

"Okay, what do we know?" I asked. "Gracie had a generous supply of drugs, so the envelope Vidali passed her in the elevator wasn't drugs. For the grand prize: What else would you pass someone in a thick envelope?"

"Cash, of course."

"Give that man the trophy. Teflon Vic owns two casinos. He handles millions in cash."

"Remember the Mango Island mansion," Snoop said. "Flamer said it belongs to a Florida Land Trust and the trustee is Lambrusci & Partners, the casino's lawyers in Atlantic City."

"Right. Mango Island is an hour's drive or more from downtown Port City, allowing for the ferry ride. Vidali took a suite in the headquarters hotel. Maybe he wants to be close to the Super Bowl action. People bet billions of dollars on the game each year." I sat up. "Snoop, you've been to Vegas, haven't you?"

"Sure. Janet and I take in a couple of shows and drop a few bucks occasionally. We go whenever we can. Why?"

"You ever bet on football in Vegas?"

"Yeah." Snoop smiled. "I'm actually pretty good at it."

That was hard to believe. Not that Snoop gambled occasionally, but that he was good at it. "I didn't think anyone won at the casinos in the long run. Does being good at it mean that you win?"

Snoop winked at me. "Like I said: I'm pretty good at it."

"But the odds favor the casinos."

"They do on the most popular games like blackjack, craps, and slots, yeah."

"But not on sports betting?"

Snoop rocked his hand back and forth. "Not so much. The casinos don't bet their own money on the games. They mostly broker for the bettors on each side of the bet. In effect, I compete against other amateur gamblers. The casinos make their money on the vig."

"The vig," I repeated.

"That's short for *vigorish*. It's another name for the bookie's commission for handling the bets. The bookie is basically a broker between you and the guy who bets on the other team."

"So the more money the public bets on the game—on both sides—the more vig the bookie gets."

"That's right."

"What happens if more people bet on one team than the other? Won't the bookie have his own money on the line?"

"Sure," said Snoop. "That's why he changes the line up or down—to attract more bets on the other side. It's like a store lowers prices to attract more customers or increases prices when demand is high."

"How do the bookies set the point spread in the first place, before any bets have been made?"

"The big casinos set the initial betting lines. Their experts analyze each team's past performance, player injuries, home field advantage, and anything else that could affect the game. Then their bookies take bets on the lines they publish. People bet on December games as early as August. A lot happens in five months."

"You mean like when a player gets injured?"

Snoop warmed to his subject. "Or the other team wins more games, or a blizzard comes in. A lot of different things make bets move to the other team. The bookie raises or lowers the line throughout the season depending on which way the betting goes. At least that was the way they did it in the old days."

"Old days?"

"Now most sports betting is online. The odds are figured by computer algorithms that respond to the customers' bets."

"So you don't have to go to the casino to bet the games?"

"Nah. I know guys who stay at home and bet on their cellphones. Janet and I prefer to go to the Vegas casinos for the entertainment."

"How do you beat that ten-percent-vig disadvantage?" I picked up my cup.

Snoop wrote on his paper again. "I pay $110 to make a $100 bet. That includes a $10 vig. If I win, I get $210. That's a five percent disadvantage on each bet."

"Yeah," I said.

"But I'm not a bookie; I don't have to bet on every game. I choose my bets carefully. I search for games where I think one team will cover the spread with better than 55% probability."

"What do you know that the other gamblers don't?"

Snoop shrugged. "Nothing, really. Maybe I read the sports section and my internet sports news feed a little more closely than most sports bettors. Some people are suckers. For example, some people here in Port City love the Pelicans so much that they'll bet on them no matter what the odds are. They're not gambling to win, so much as to support their team. It also makes the game more interesting to watch when they have money on it. It's not a rational, economic decision to bet."

"They bet for entertainment value, and you find games where other people bet with their hearts instead of their heads."

Snoop smirked. "I usually win enough to pay for our trip to Vegas or Atlantic City or wherever."

"So why not become a professional gambler?"

"I don't have the stomach for it. I'll bet three or four hundred bucks on five or six games, and I sleep all right if I lose. But if the bet was a thousand...I couldn't take that. Besides, Janet would kill me."

We laughed. "Okay, Snoop, I want you to verify the betting line on the Super Bowl at both Double Down Casino sports books."

"What are you thinking, Chuck?"

"I've got an idea how someone like Teflon Vic could fix the Super Bowl game, and it scares the hell out of me."

61

"Flamer, I want a complete report on Graciela Perez. She's the super model they call the Latin Angel."

"How good a report you want?"

"Give me the smorgasbord. Credit report, education, hobbies, friends. You know the drill."

"I'll even get you her kindergarten teacher's name."

"I'll send you her tablet. It's password protected. Can you hack it and crack it?"

Flamer scoffed.

"Also get me everything you can find on the mansion at 176 Mango Drive."

"That on Mango Island?"

"Yeah. High-rent district."

"You want blueprints too?"

Rule Five: *You can never have too much information.* "Yeah. Could come in handy."

I scrolled through the screens and selected pages to print. "Would you believe that Flamer did get me the name of Gracie's kindergarten teacher? And I thought he was kidding."

"The man takes pride in his work," Snoop said.

"He found an article in a tabloid where Gracie happened to mention she met her best friend in kindergarten. She mentioned her teacher's name and the kindergarten. Flamer hacked the kindergarten's computer files. Wow."

"We gonna talk to the best friend?"

"I'll do that alone. I want you to research Vicente Vidali and the Double Down Casinos—both of them. Go deep diving."

"Ms. Takashi, I'm Chuck McCrary. Thanks for seeing me on short notice." I handed her a business card. *Maybe I need a logo of Sherlock Holmes's deerstalker hat.*

Miyoki Takashi glanced at the card. She stepped back and held the door open with a polite smile. "Gracie's a dear friend, so it's no trouble. Bob said it was important. Come in, come in. My studio is a mess. I'm preparing a gallery exhibition. I have to finish three more paintings this week."

"I'm sorry if this is a bad time."

She appraised me like I was a race horse at a stud auction. She peeked at my left hand and nodded her approval that I wasn't wearing a ring. Her polite smile grew into a glowing grin. "I'm about to lose the light anyway."

She pushed back a stray wisp of hair with her wrist and flashed me a grin. "On the other hand, I always make time for a good-looking bachelor. You *are* a bachelor, aren't you?"

I felt my face flush. "Yes, ma'am, so far."

"Then you're twice welcome."

She led me into a spacious room that had been designed as a combination living room/dining room. The balcony overlooked Seeti Bay. The clerestory windows provided ample natural light, now fading in the late afternoon. If she owned this penthouse on the top floor of a Port City Beach high-rise, or if she even rented it, she must be a successful painter, or come from a rich family. Maybe both.

She studied my business card again. "I know why your name is familiar. You're Bob's best man, aren't you?"

"Yes, ma'am."

"Didn't Bob tell you I'm Gracie's maid of honor?"

"We men are much too shallow to talk about weddings."

She laughed. "You and I will promenade out of the church arm in arm after they say 'I do.'"

"I guess we will. It's nice to meet you."

"We'll also sit together at the rehearsal dinner."

A Nike headband held back her hair. Paint dabs in assorted colors marked the sky-blue smock. Her well-muscled bare legs were tanned below the smock. "Let me wash my hands." She wrapped the brush in a plastic sandwich bag and put it in the freezer of a small refrigerator. "Keeps the paint from drying out," she explained, closing the door.

I followed the young artist to a sink. Blank canvases in various sizes were stacked in one corner. One wall had shelves filled with tubes and bottles of paints, chemicals, brushes, and other objects I didn't recognize. An easel stood in the center of the room, her current painting half-finished on it.

She was tall, maybe five-foot-seven, even in flat sandals. I wondered what, if anything, she wore beneath the thin blue smock that reached to her thighs. I inhaled a whiff of perfume mixed with paint smell. Despite the overlay of *odeur du painte*, she smelled *really* good.

She squirted hand cleaner into her palm and rubbed it in. "Takes the paint flecks right off. Keeps the skin soft too." She winked at me. "Here, stick out your hands." She squirted hand cleaner into my palm. "Rub your hands like this until it soaks in." She grabbed my hands in hers and stroked them.

That affected parts of my body other than my hands. I wondered if that was her intention. I hoped it was.

Her hands were warm, the skin soft and smooth.

My knees wobbled a little. I felt my face flush again, so I jerked my hands away. "Thanks." *Dumb, dumb, dumb. That was the first fun you've had all day. Why did you pull your hands away, stupid?*

She ripped a couple of paper towels off the roll and handed

them to me. She took two for herself, dried her hands, and extended a hand for me to shake. "Call me Miyo. I have a feeling we're going to be good friends."

"I'm Chuck." A spark jumped between our hands—a real, physical, electric spark. The last time that had happened was with Liz Johannes at Teddy Roosevelt High School when I was a sophomore. Liz and I had become an item for three years. Maybe lightning could strike twice in the same place. Miyo's grip felt exactly firm enough.

"Would you like coffee, Chuck? Or maybe a cocktail." She glanced at the time on the stove. "It's nearly five o'clock; we can push the cocktail hour a little. Like the song says, 'It's five o'clock somewhere.' After all, we're consenting adults." She winked.

I would like anything you have to offer, I thought. *Coffee will do for a start.* "I still have work to do, Miyo, but coffee would be great."

"How about a raincheck on the cocktail? For when you *don't* have work to do." She gestured me to a seating arrangement around a coffee table. "Have a seat; I'll make the coffee." She moved with a dancer's grace to a small coffee station and poured coffee beans into a grinder.

The white sash cinched her waist and highlighted her hips. There was a blue paint dab on the back of her left calf.

"What's this about? Bob said to cooperate with you, whatever that means." She flipped on the grinder and dropped a filter into the coffee maker.

I waited for the grinder to stop. "Gracie has been missing since Saturday night."

Miyo scoffed. "That's nothing new." She dumped the ground beans into the coffeemaker and pressed a button. She smiled and sat in a canvas sling chair across from me. The smock draped open, revealing a tan thigh before she adjusted the fabric. "She'll turn up; she always does."

It took an effort to focus on her face. "You don't seem worried."

"I'm not."

"May I ask a couple of questions?"

"First, let me ask one: How do you know Bob?"

"We've been friends since first grade. We played middle school and high school football together in Adams Creek, Texas. We've remained friends ever since. Where do you know him from?"

"We met last summer when he came to South Florida to meet Gracie's parents. She figured Bob was about to propose, so she brought him over for my seal of approval. She asked if I thought he was as good a catch as she did."

She grinned at me. She had about a hundred straight, white teeth. "Gracie looks very self-assured, but she's actually insecure. Always has been. She never makes an important decision without bouncing it off me. We don't have any secrets from each other."

That was almost true. Gracie had at least one secret she had hidden from Miyo. Unless Miyo was lying too.

The aroma of brewing coffee filled the room, overpowering the smell of paint, chemicals, and Miyo's perfume. My nose was confused. "And did you approve of Bob?"

"Oh yeah. Bob's the best thing that ever happened to Gracie. He's an anchor of stability in her life. He's smart, loyal, kind, handsome, and successful—a real Boy Scout. He ticks all the boxes. The three of us have dinner together whenever they come to town."

"The three of you?" I asked. "There's not a husband or boyfriend in the picture?"

"Why do you think I asked if you were single? Would you like to apply for the position?" She smiled. "My painting career has monopolized me for the last year or so, while I built my reputation. But with this latest gallery exhibition in a few days, that phase of my career will be complete. Then I have to plan Gracie's bachelorette party."

"That's right, the wedding is in three weeks, isn't it?"

"Yeah. But after my showing, I'll have time for a more normal social life." The smock inched its way open on her thigh and she laughed and winked.

I felt myself blush again. I hate it when that happens. I lowered my gaze, then realized I was staring at her thigh. I dragged my attention back to her face and changed the subject. "When have the three of you had dinner?"

"They came down a second time before the Jets training camp. Then the Jets played a pre-season game with the Port City Pelicans here in August. Gracie wasn't with Bob, so he and I ate alone. I remember now that Bob said he tried to call you too, but you were out of town. I had an exhibition in New York in October and I met with both of them. And the Jets played the Pelicans again three weeks ago in the playoffs." She frowned for a second. "I guess that makes…four more times."

I wrote that down. "How did you and Gracie meet?"

"We were next door neighbors when we were little. We've been BFFs—and I mean *real* best friends, not social media friends—since kindergarten. Twenty years. Much like you and Bob."

"When did you last see Gracie?"

"Last week. She came to visit when she arrived in Port City. Bob wasn't coming down until Saturday. I picked her up at the airport and she spent Thursday night here. We drank wine and talked all night like school girls."

"What about?"

"Mostly about Bob and what she wanted their wedding to be like."

"She didn't have a car?"

"No. I took her to the airport Friday to pick up a rental."

"A red Mustang?"

"Yes, how did you know?"

"I'm the world's greatest private investigator."

"And modest too." Miyo gave me a smile that would have launched a thousand ships.

I hoped I wasn't blushing again. "May I see the room where she stayed?"

"I told you she's not here."

"I don't doubt that. It's simply the way I work. I need to learn everything I can about Gracie and her movements. I'm not sure what I'll learn until I learn it. It couldn't hurt to humor me."

Miyo sighed and led me down a short hall. The view of her tush was inspirational. "The guest room is the first door on the right."

"Thanks." I flipped on the light, dropped to the tile floor, and peered under the bed.

"What are you doing?"

"Seeing if she dropped something." I stood. "Might be a clue." I grinned and moved to the guest bathroom. The shower had a bar of used soap and used bottles of shampoo and conditioner. The guest towels were fresh. Someone had washed them since Gracie's visit. Was Miyo the domestic type too? The medicine cabinet contained an Ibuprofen bottle and a half-empty bottle of nail polish called Secret Stash. I hoped the name wasn't prophetic. I lifted the toilet tank lid and perused the inside.

"Wow, you're thorough. I would never think of that."

"I was a Port City cop for three years. Started as a patrol cop and ended as a robbery-homicide detective. Don't want to leave the job half-done."

I slid open the mirrored closet door, and a light came on inside. The closet held two winter coats, two pairs of warm boots, and a dozen empty coat hangers. Two cardboard boxes labeled *Christmas decorations* sat on the shelf. I closed the door.

"Thanks for humoring me, Miyo. I'm finished."

She led me back down the hall. Again, I admired her dancer-like grace.

After we were seated, I asked, "Have you heard from Gracie since she left?"

"No, but I don't expect to. The Super Bowl is a social whirl for the rich and wanna-be-famous and a media feeding frenzy, all rolled into one." She glanced at the coffeemaker and levitated herself from the low chair. I don't know how she did it, but she made the move graceful. "She'll use every spare moment during Super Bowl Week to market herself. I think she suffers from Imposter Syndrome."

"I've heard of that. Isn't that when someone feels like a fraud?"

"Yes. Gracie's secret fear is that she doesn't belong. She's afraid she only got to be a super model through dumb luck. That's just one aspect of her insecurity."

Miyo took two cups from the cabinet. "How do you take your coffee?"

"A little creamer, no sugar."

Miyo set the carafe and coffee creamer on a tray with the cups.

"How do you mean she'll 'market herself'?"

Miyo carried the tray to the table and sat beside me on the sofa. Her thigh touched mine for a moment. I hoped it was intentional.

"Gracie is *not* a fraud; she's actually quite a talented model, even though she doesn't really believe it at a deep personal level. It's difficult for a top model to *stay* at the top, even if they have the self-confidence of an eight-hundred-pound gorilla. A girl can become 'Darling for a Day' unless she focuses on her career. You should hear Gracie complain about all the crap she puts up with." She poured my coffee, then her own. The smock draped open.

I averted my gaze, but not before I glimpsed a lacy, pink brassiere.

"Gracie has to attend the right parties and hobnob with the other beautiful people. She has to schmooze with the right money people."

She set down the carafe. "And the whole time, she's just putting on an act. Gracie must stay in the public view so they keep buying magazines with her picture on the cover. And everyone she meets— and I mean *everyone*—has a hidden agenda. It gets old." She sipped coffee.

"I didn't realize it was such hard work to be famous."

"The hard part is *staying* famous. She attends three or four parties or receptions a week, eats only a couple of appetizers for the sake of appearances, limits herself to two drinks, and then eats a business meal—and holds her weight at a hundred and ten pounds. And she has to show up at photo shoots at dawn and work until sunset." She sat back with the cup in her lap. "I know I couldn't do it. I have a hard enough time attending my gallery exhibitions every couple of months. She does that stuff month in and month out. That's gotta take a toll. That's why she disappears from time to time to decompress. She's been putting up this front for years. She's great at it. That's why I'm not worried about her."

"This time may be different."

Miyo set the cup down. "Can you keep a confidence, Chuck?" She leaned against me and laid a hand on my leg. "Like a private detective's privileged communication or something?"

Her hand felt like a heating pad, even through the fabric of my pants. It was hard to concentrate. "I'm discreet, but I represent my client's best interests. In this case, that's Bob."

"Bob's okay. Heck, in three weeks, 'the two shall become one.' Don't tell this to anyone else, or Gracie will kill me. Promise?" She removed her hand from my leg and I could breathe again though my leg still tingled where she had touched it.

"Okay."

"Any famous person has to decompress from time to time;

Gracie is no different. When she goes AWOL from the supermodel media circus, she usually stays with me. I'm one of the few people who couldn't care less that she's famous. To me, she's simply my best friend. She doesn't have to pretend with me." She held her coffee in both hands and gazed at me over the rim of the cup.

"Where do you think she is now?"

"Well, she's not here, for starters." She grinned at me.

I returned her smile. "We've established that. But aren't you surprised she didn't come to you, especially since she's in the same town?"

Miyo's face clouded. "Now that you mention it, it does seem out of character. I would expect her to hide out here since she's so close. I don't know what to make of it."

"Did Gracie mention any trouble she might be in?"

"She did seem preoccupied when she first showed up. I asked her what was going on. She said she was working on a new deal that was different from anything she'd done before. She wasn't sure if it was right for her."

"What kind of deal?" I thought of Vicente Vidali. Maybe VV wanted her to be a spokesperson for the casino.

"That's the strange thing; she wouldn't say. Just that it was way different. She usually tells me everything." She shook her head. "Then we talked about Bob, and the Super Bowl, and wedding plans. I forgot about it until you asked."

"Could her new deal have to do with promotion for a casino?"

"I don't follow Gracie's career closely. I have my own business to consider." She leaned over to pick up her coffee, and her thigh brushed mine. Her smock draped open again.

Was I perceiving something that wasn't there? Miyo was affecting me more than I had expected. "I hate to hit you with this cold, Miyo, but did you know that Gracie had a history of drug use?"

"History, that's the word for it. It's ancient history. After that stint in rehab last summer, that's behind her. When she was here a couple of days ago, she said she was drug-free."

"Bob said her rehab was a secret."

Miyo's black ponytail swung as she shook her head. "I told you: We don't have secrets between us. She called me when Bob asked her to go to rehab. I told her to do it. She called me after she got out. She promised me she'd stay clean and sober from now on."

"When Gracie spent the night here, did she do any drugs?"

Miyo's shoulders slumped. Tears welled in her eyes. "Is she doing drugs again? That's why you searched under the toilet lid, isn't it?"

"It's a favorite place for addicts to stash drugs. Sometimes they forget and leave them there."

"Is that why you think this disappearance could be different?" Tears rolled down her tan cheeks. "The pressure must have gotten to her again, or you wouldn't ask me that. No, she didn't do any drugs here. I have my own history, and I won't stand for it."

"I don't mean to pry, Miyo, but your history could have relevance to Gracie since you two are so close. What are you willing to tell me about it?"

She stared into her cup.

I waited. She would respond when she felt like it. Or not. I was content to observe her forever.

She sighed. "I nearly died from a heroin overdose two years ago. Gracie called 9-1-1 and got me to the hospital. I had stopped breathing by the time they wheeled me in. If she hadn't acted quickly…"

She shuddered. "That incident scared me half to death. After they released me from the hospital, I went cold turkey. It hasn't been easy with the artsy-fartsy crowd I hang with, but I haven't had anything stronger than a Mai Tai since. God willing, I never will. Gracie knows that."

Snoop stuck his head in the door of my home office. He had let himself in with his key. "Something weird has happened to the Super Bowl betting line."

I gestured to a chair. "Any news is more than we had. Let's hear it."

Snoop plopped down and took out his notepad. "First thing I learned was that sports betting is illegal in New Jersey. But it's legal in Delaware, so I checked out the Double Down Delaware Casino."

"Good move."

"A few days ago, right after the conference championships games were over, the Vegas bookmaker line opened with the Jets a thirteen-and-a-half-point favorite. That zigzagged back and forth a couple of days. It finally settled at sixteen-and-a-half, Jets favored. Maybe a point either way. Depends on which casino you ask. The Mexican Muscle must have looked good in practice for the line to go up three points." He glanced again at his notes. "The Delaware casinos, including the Double Down, are toeing the line with Vegas—which they always do. There's only a half-dozen casinos in Delaware." He paused. "You with me so far?"

"Yeah, Cowboys plus sixteen-and-a-half is an even bet." I motioned him to continue.

He held up a hand. "*Was* an even bet. It's not anymore. Sunday the line at the Vegas casinos changed. Jets are now favored by seven-and-a- half. And the Double Down Delaware Casino has stopped taking Super Bowl bets."

"That happened right after Gracie disappeared." That was a

head-scratcher. "Snoop, I'm not a gambler. What does that mean in the real world?"

"It means the Double Down casino has taken all the bets it wants. It means somebody in Vegas bet a truckload of money on the Cowboys two days ago."

"Can you find out how much money?"

"It's hard to say, but it would have to be a boatload of money. To move the betting line nine points in one day, it would be maybe a hundred million dollars or more."

Flamer sent Graciela's tablet back to me with a note.

Password is Ama$ingGrace. Have fun.

I searched the directory and found a file with Gracie's passwords for all her online accounts and emailed it to Snoop.

The tablet's address book did not have a listing for anybody named *Sharky*. No luck, but that was no surprise. If Sharky was a drug dealer, he wouldn't want to leave any digital footprints, and neither would Gracie. A text message was bad enough. I read her correspondence with Jerry Greenbaum for the last six months. Mostly agent/client business, but he had made oblique references to "our mutual friend" and "packages." I printed copies of the emails and set them aside for further use.

Then I had a thought so simple that I wanted to smack myself upside the head because I hadn't thought of it earlier. I had not played back the flip-phone's voicemail. I felt like a fool, until I realized Snoop hadn't thought of it either. Then I didn't feel quite so stupid. Not quite.

I called the voicemail from the flip-phone. Most people never bother to set up a password on their voicemail. The default is usually 1-2-3-4, so I tried it. That wasn't it. The next most common default is the last four digits of the phone number. I punched that and *Bingo*, the voicemails played. The first message had come in the previous Saturday from an area code in New York City:

Gracie, this is me. When you come back to New York, you better have my money. Have a good time at the Super Bowl. Remember that a lot of your good times come from me. Jerry's too. If you don't pay me Wednesday after the game, look over your shoulder. Remember what happened to Tawanda Grisham. But maybe I'll start with Jerry to show you that I mean business. That way you could still have a career."

I reverse looked up the phone number. It was a burner phone.

I Googled the area code and three-digit exchange and wrote down the name of a local pizza chain. I called the burner phone's number.

"Hello."

"We know we've called you on your cellphone, but this will take less than sixty seconds, and we'll send you a coupon for a free large pizza with unlimited toppings from your neighborhood Pizza Paradise if you'll answer two questions for us. One, have you ever used your cellphone to order a pizza from anyone?"

"Sure. All the time."

"Great. Final question: Have you ever used your cellphone to order any type of carryout food so it would be ready when you got there? If so, what type and how often?"

"*Hmm*, yeah. I order Chinese from the restaurant down the block."

"Is that the only one?" I asked.

"Yeah, I think so."

"Thank you for your time. To what address should we send the coupon for the free pizza?"

He gave me an address in Brooklyn.

"What name do we address it to?"

"Sam Torrance."

I hung up. *Bingo.* I forwarded the name and address to Flamer with a note to get me a brief report on him.

I Googled Tawanda Grisham. Three years before, Ms. Grisham had been the victim of an acid attack. An unknown assailant had thrown sulfuric acid in her face and scarred her horribly. After several plastic surgeries, her face remained badly scarred. The newspaper accounts said the police suspected a drug dealer was involved, but the victim had refused to cooperate.

My heart felt like it had dropped into my stomach. Tawanda Grisham had been an aspiring Broadway actress. Her face was her fortune, like Graciela's. No wonder Gracie was taking an anti-anxiety drug. She must be wound up tighter than a banjo string.

I called Snoop at my home office computer where he was working. "What have you got on Graciela's credit cards?"

"I researched all the way to the first of last year, Chuck, about thirteen months." He glanced at his notes. "Gracie has always been a little haphazard about paying bills, but last February, payments on her credit cards got way overdue."

"Must be when she got back on the drugs."

"She stayed spotty with the payments for the next four months, until Bob sent her to rehab. Someone paid her credit cards in full on July 22, right before the Jets training camp started. That was over $80,000 and the money didn't come from Gracie's bank account."

"I'll ask Bob, but I'm almost sure he paid them. Maybe he wanted to give her a clean slate when she finished rehab."

"Whatever," said Snoop. "There were no credit card charges for the next five weeks. That had to be while she was in rehab. The last week in August, she began to charge things again."

"That would be after she finished rehab."

"Sure. In September, she paid the minimum on each card. The October payments were late, and her card balances grew to forty grand in two months." He flipped a page. "She was late again in November and she's made no payments since then. Her card balances are now near their maximum credit lines—close to ninety thousand dollars."

I sipped my coffee. "She's in debt up to her plucked eyebrows again."

FIVE

Graciela Perez

Graciela sipped Pinot Grigio and set the glass on the teak table. She rose from the chaise longue and stretched toward the sky. Her new bikini top rode up on her breasts and pinched a little. It was the only swimsuit she had packed. She tugged the top back into place and lengthened the shoulder straps—again. *God, I hope my tits haven't begun to fall.* She stretched toward the heavens again. *I haven't seen a crew member come back here for the past two days.* She removed the top and draped it across the bench. *That's better.*

She bent over and touched her toes. She spread her feet and did thigh stretches. She wondered how much longer it would take the boat to get wherever they were going. She felt lonely and bored. Why had Vic done this to her?

This was the third day the *Double Scotch* had cruised south down the Florida coast. Vic Vidali had told her goodbye before dawn Sunday at the Portside Market dock. He said the yacht would take her to the Florida Keys, but he'd been vague about the timing and the exact destination. She didn't think it should take this long. Since the yacht had cast off, she had seen only two crew members. One was the steward who remained in the main salon and galley. He fixed her drinks and prepared her meals. The other man seemed to be a general deckhand. But there had to be somebody to pilot the yacht. Speaking of that, the boat was barely moving. A girl could only work on her tan for so long, then it became tiresome. Besides, she didn't want to age her skin prematurely.

She put on her top and climbed to the sun deck on the top of the yacht. The wake spooled out behind the vessel. She made out a few of the taller buildings on the mainland miles away on the western horizon. *We should be off the Keys by now. But the Keys don't have that many tall buildings. We must be passing Miami, or maybe Coral Gables. What's that? That's the Turkey Point nuclear power plant. We haven't even gotten to the bottom of Miami-Dade County. Vic lied to me! Why would he do that?*

The engine vibration changed. Her shadow, which had been on her right, moved toward the back of the boat. The bubbly wake curved off to the left as the yacht changed direction. Graciela's shadow traced an arc across the sun deck. *Funny, the boat is turning around.*

The buildings she had observed on the starboard side circled to the port side. *We're heading back the way we came. How strange. Vic is up to something.* A chill ran down her spine, and it wasn't from the temperature. It was 85 degrees.

The wake straightened out and the engine vibration changed again. The breeze on the sun deck had switched from left to right. Now the wind bent toward the north and freshened. *We've picked up speed,* Graciela thought. Waves splashed off the bow and spray blew back over the sides, chilling Graciela where she stood. She twirled to descend to the next deck. A rogue wave, caught by the wind, crashed over the yacht and soaked her to the skin. *Something's going on and I'm going to find out what it is.*

Graciela had not been on the bridge, but she'd been on yachts before, and she knew generally where the bridge was. She descended the carpeted steps to the bridge deck and walked forward past the owner's stateroom to the bridge door. She knocked twice, then went in.

The cabin air conditioning chilled her bare skin, bringing her nipples erect.

A man in a denim shirt and pants sat on a high stool, hands on the wheel. He pivoted toward the sound of the door opening. "Miss, you're not supposed to be in here. This area is for crew—" He gawked at her red bikini and froze. His gaze swept Graciela's body from head to foot and back. It stopped at her bikini top.

Graciela remembered she had left her beach cover up on the sun deck. She glanced down and realized belatedly that the new bikini had not been made for swimming. The wet fabric was virtually transparent. Her dark nipples showed like chocolate drops through the thin red fabric plastered to her breasts like a second skin. *Well, it's too late to go back and get it now*, she thought. Her attention swept the instrument panel and stuck on the cellphone lying there. *I may as well make the most of it.* She smiled at the sailor. "Why have we changed course?"

The helmsman stared at her breasts, speechless.

She sashayed over to the instrument panel, hips swinging like she was on a fashion show runway. *Enjoy the view, you horny jerk.* She ran her fingers across the counter from left to right and circled languidly to face the helmsman. She leaned back against the steel rail, hands behind her to display her breasts to greatest advantage. She crossed her ankles like she was at a photo shoot. *This is like modeling for the swimsuit issue, except those swimsuits aren't transparent.* She pointed her breasts at the sailor to give him a good view. "I was curious why we turned around. Perhaps you could tell me where we're going?" She smiled again.

The man came back to his senses. "Orders," he mumbled in Spanish.

She responded in the same language. "Oh? What orders would those be?" She felt behind her and palmed the cellphone.

"We're going to Mango Island." He never raised his eyes to her face.

"Well, finally. I love your boat, but it is getting a little dreary. I'd much rather spend the time on Mango Island." She smiled again, pirouetted, and left with the cellphone shoved down the front of her bikini bottom. She could have carried the cellphone in plain sight and the helmsman wouldn't have noticed it. *That'll show Vic. He can't treat me like this. I'm a partner, not a prisoner.*

She climbed back up to the sun deck and glanced around to make sure none of the crew could see her. She composed a message on the cellphone and hit *send*, then cursed under her breath. *No signal. We're too far from shore. No matter, we'll be in range eventually.* She stuffed the cellphone between two cushions, slipped into the beach cover, and resumed her spot on the chaise.

She picked up her Pinot Grigio and thought back three days to when the three men grabbed her in the parking garage...

They had thrown her into an old van that smelled of sweat and gasoline. *Has Vic learned the truth?* she wondered. *That I don't really have Bob Martinez under my spell? A tidal wave was coming in and she had to surf with it. Keep up the front.* She whirled to them with fire in her eyes. "You idiots! This is not the way this is supposed to work. I am supposed to go into hiding. Give me my purse and my cellphone." She reached between the two front seats toward her purse.

The man beside her grabbed her wrist. "There's been a change of plans."

"What change?"

"We're keeping the cellphone."

"At least let me get my purse." She grabbed her purse. "You numbskull! You scratched it when it fell on the concrete. Do you have any idea how much a Prada purse costs?"

The driver ignored her. The van rolled down the ramp and slowed as it approached the garage exit.

"Where are we going?"

The man waited until the exit gate rose. He closed the van window and drove from the garage. "Mr. V will explain."

"And where is Vic?"

"On the yacht."

"And where is the yacht?"

"At the Portside Marina."

The sun had dropped halfway to the horizon. Graciela watched Mango Island come into view. Her suspicions were confirmed. *Three days to go south and one hour to come back north. I knew this boat was just killing time.*

She wrapped the beach cover tighter and retrieved the cellphone from between the cushions. *One bar.* She hit *send* and waited until the text was transmitted, then descended three decks to her stateroom to change clothes. She didn't want to meet Vidali wearing a sexy bikini. *I don't want to appear vulnerable. This isn't working out like I planned. I need to project a more powerful image.*

She selected navy blue pants and a sleeveless white top. She wore a clunky gold necklace and a matching bracelet. White sneakers completed the outfit. They were the closest thing she had to deck shoes. She studied her image in the full-length mirror. She replaced the gold necklace with a slender silver chain and matching earrings and bracelet. *The silver highlights my tan.* She nodded approval and packed her bag.

She carried the suitcase upstairs to the yacht's salon, then she walked to the bar and reached for the Pinot Grigio. *God, I wish I had blow instead. Why, oh why, didn't I remember to stash some in my Prada?* She bypassed the Pinot Grigio and poured herself a double Scotch. *Like the boat's name,* she thought and laughed. She normally preferred Pinot Grigio but she wanted to get buzzed quicker than the wine would allow.

She had finished her first Scotch when the steward entered the salon. "We'll be docking soon, Ms. Perez. Would you like another?"

"Yes, thanks, Tomás." She wondered if the steward had been told to keep her drunk if possible.

Minutes later, mango trees laden with yellow blooms appeared through the salon windows. Graciela stood and steadied herself on the sofa arm. *I hope I haven't drunk too much.* She moved unsteadily to the window. *It must be because the boat is rocking.*

A concrete seawall rose behind the riprap. Six feet inland, a paved sidewalk and bike path circled the island. Mango and palm trees filled the grassy lawn between the seawall and the asphalt path.

The *Double Scotch* glided past the trees and through the mouth of Mango Island's private yacht basin. The yacht skimmed across the azure water toward the dock. Two sailors came on deck outside the salon windows, docking lines in hand. The engine vibrations changed when the screws reversed, then stopped. The boat drifted to the dock under its own momentum. The sailors tossed the lines to a man and woman in turquoise and gold uniforms who waited on the floating dock. The club crew moored the yacht and stood near the cleats. The two deckhands hauled out a folding aluminum gangplank.

Vicente Vidali stood on the dock in a navy-blue blazer and white pants, wearing Topsiders with no socks. His two bodyguards stood a couple of yards behind. He seldom went anywhere without them. A frisson of fear rolled down her back as she saw the bulges made by their guns. Vidali could make her disappear without a trace. She was only a fashion model, and not a particularly good one. Whatever made her think she could match wits with a mobster like Vidali?

Graciela set down the drink and picked up the small suitcase. She stepped through the sliding door and walked toward the gangway. *Get away while you can.*

The sailors secured the aluminum steps to the yacht.

Vidali climbed the steps to the gangway, followed by the bodyguards. "There you are, my dear. Let's talk in the salon." He reached for her bag. "Here, Dante will take that for you."

Ignoring the knot in her stomach, Graciela snatched the bag from Vidali's hand and stood planted in the middle of the walkway. "Let's talk in your house, Vic. I'm sick of this boat."

Vidali smiled and shrugged. "There's been a change of plans, my dear. Let's go to the salon and I'll explain." He gestured back at the open salon door.

The other crewmen and both bodyguards now stood behind Vidali, blocking the entrance to the gangway. She glanced down at the dock and her breath caught in her throat. *What am I thinking? An eight-foot drop and jumping across two feet of water. I'd probably break my ankle. And if I didn't break an ankle, where would I go if I jumped? I have no choice but to play this out.*

She stepped back into the salon, but she didn't let Vidali take her bag. That way she convinced herself that she was in control of the situation.

The steps clanged as the crew hauled them aboard. She gaped forlornly through the salon windows as the dock appeared to move away from the yacht. Within minutes they cleared the entrance to the Mango Island Marina and powered toward the ship channel. Her chin quivered. She took a deep breath and stood straighter. *Power image. I must not project weakness.* But she felt helpless nevertheless. She wished she had thought to bring her Xanax when she packed for this trip.

The mega-yacht cleared the breakwater. It turned south and accelerated to cruising speed. The ship porpoised through the swells between the Gulf Stream and the mainland.

Graciela's spirits fell and her stomach felt queasy. She set the wine glass down. After the second Scotch, she had switched to Pinot Grigio. The pale gold liquid vacillated back and forth in the glass as the table tilted. *I don't need any more alcohol right now. I have to be on my toes.* "What's this about, Vic? Where are we going?" *Power image. Never let them see you sweat.*

Vidali's smile never reached his eyes. "As I said, there's been a change of plans, my dear. We'd like you to remain aboard the *Double Scotch* for a couple of days—until the Super Bowl is over."

"That wasn't the plan, Vic. I'm supposed to go to a hotel in Naples and wait until after the game to resurface. That's what the fifteen thousand is for." She reached in her purse. "Speaking of which, the money's here—all of it. I didn't have a chance to spend any before your men snatched me."

"You'll be safer and more comfortable on the *Double Scotch*."

"I'm sick of this boat. Let's at least go back to your place on Mango Island. I can swim and play golf and go to the beach."

"My personal life is at my home. I don't do business there."

"Well, we did some *business* there last Saturday which you enjoyed. You didn't have a problem inviting me then."

"That wasn't business, my dear Gracie; that was pleasure, pure pleasure. Besides, you're much too famous. Someone would recognize you on the golf course or at the beach. You're better off here, believe me. I've got everything you need right here."

"Have you contacted Bob about the game yet?"

Vidali shook his head. "We don't want to give Bob too much time to think about this. It's better that he remains in the dark. We'll contact him with our proposal the day before the game. Twenty-four hours before kickoff is about right."

"Who is this 'we' you're talking about?"

Vidali waved a hand. "My odds makers—the guys who manage my bets."

"And what do they say?"

"Bob should have time enough to study the coach's game plan so he can figure out how to shave the right number of points. But he shouldn't have so much time that people notice a change in his behavior or so that he has time to take counter-measures."

"Counter-measures? What counter-measures could he possibly take?"

"For one thing, he has hired a private detective to find you."

Graciela raised her eyebrows. "Really? Who?"

"Carlos McCrary."

Graciela laughed. "I've met McCrary. If you ask me, he's simply a pretty face. He's probably a leg man for a bunch of ambulance-chasing attorneys. He's too young to have had much experience as a real private eye."

Vidali waved a finger at her. "You live in New York, and you don't know McCrary like we do in Port City. He's got a reputation down here from other cases he's worked. He's a former Green Beret. You gotta be smart and tough to make it in Special Forces.

He won a Bronze Star in Afghanistan, so he's not afraid of anything. He's well-connected in the police department...and he has Bob's money behind him. That's a lot of assets. We must be cautious, extremely cautious."

"Well, that doesn't change anything. Obviously, Chuck hasn't found me. Besides, I texted Bob that I was all right and I would be back before the game. He probably told McCrary to stop searching for me."

Vidali jumped to his feet, his face turning red. "You sent Bob a text?"

"I don't understand why you're upset. I didn't want Bob to worry about me."

Vidali stomped across the salon and loomed over the woman. "The whole idea for you to disappear was for Bob to worry but *not know what had happened to you.* For you to send him a text..." He faced away. "Of all the stupid..." He twisted back to face her. "Where did you find a cellphone?"

Graciela swallowed hard. "I, uh, I borrowed one from the driver."

"What driver?"

"The guy who drives the boat."

"He is called a *helmsman.* Mauricio *loaned* you his cellphone?"

"Well...not exactly." She slid the cellphone from her purse. "I saw it on the counter in the cockpit or bridge or whatever you call it, and I took it."

Vidali snatched the phone from her. "You stupid, stupid...*child.* I've been in this business for over thirty years and you think you know more than I do?" He cursed in Italian.

SIX

Carlos McCrary

S noop held up the printed report from Flamer. "Says here that Vicente Lorenzo Vidali is fifty-two years old. Third generation American, legal resident of Mango Island, Port City Beach, Florida. Married to Gina Sofia Toretto Vidali for twenty-five years. Two children: A son Vincent Lawrence, twenty-three years old, is a management trainee at an investment management firm in Chicago; a daughter June Margaret, nineteen years old, attends Bennington College."

He gazed up from the report. "Neither kid has any connection to their old man's business. The wife is a devout Catholic Italian-American, second generation. They're separated now; she won't give him a divorce. He bought her a penthouse condo in Palm Beach."

"The wife and kids could be a weak point," I observed.

"In Vidali's business, you don't mess with your competitor's family. So...not really."

"But we're not business competitors. Call PI's in Chicago, Palm Beach, and Boston. Get me candid shots of both Vidali's kids and wife, shopping maybe."

"You got a use for the photos, bud?"

"Maybe."

My cellphone whistled that I had received a text. "Message received from Bob Martinez," the computer-generated voice announced. I swiped the screen into life.

I got a text from Gracie. She's okay. Call off the hunt. Regards, Bob.

I called Bob. "That's great news, *amigo*. Where is she?"

"She didn't say, but she said she's okay and for me not to worry."

"Did she send the text from her own phone?"

"That's a funny question to ask, Eighty-Eight."

"You pay me to ask funny questions. Did she send the message from her own phone?"

Bob paused. "Well, no."

"Did you try to call her?"

"Yeah. Her phone goes straight to voicemail like it's done since Sunday."

"She may not be okay, despite what the message says. Where are you now?"

"I'm in my hotel room, resting after practice."

"Have you tried to call the phone that sent the text?"

"I didn't think of that."

"Try to call her on that phone," I said. "Wait for me. I'll be there in fifteen minutes."

I tapped the screen and a text appeared.

Querido, no tengas cuidado. Tu sabes que yo tengo que desaparecer y descansar de vez en cuando. Acuerdate de San Diego y de Key West. Me va bien. Regreso antes del Super Bowl. Con mucho carino, tu Bunny.

"What happened when you called the number this was sent from?"

"I got a standard voicemail message from the phone company."

"It didn't say whose phone it was?"

Bob shook his head. "Just that the number didn't answer and I should leave a message."

I wrote down the number. "It's area code 305. That's Miami. I'll forward the number to my researcher and get him on it." I finished my message to Flamer and asked Bob what "remember San Diego and Key West" meant.

"I think it was to prove that the message really came from Gracie, since she didn't send it from her own phone. She disappeared in San Diego and Key West last year. I'm the only one who knows that."

"When I interviewed Miyo, she told me Gracie usually crashes with her when she disappears. Let's ask Miyo if Gracie has shown up at her condo."

"What do you mean that Gracie crashes with Miyo?"

"Miyo swore me to secrecy before she would talk to me about Gracie. But she said I could tell you that her apartment is Gracie's favorite hideaway to disappear to."

"You think Gracie is there now?"

"Let's call Miyo and ask."

After two rings, Miyo's face appeared on my screen. "Hello,

Chuck. Have you called to claim that cocktail raincheck?" She winked. "I make a great Margarita."

Bob grinned at me.

I frowned. "Not yet, Miyo. I need to talk to you about Gracie."

"Have you heard from her?"

"We're not sure. I'm in Bob's hotel suite with you on speaker. Bob got a text from Gracie, but it was from a phone in area code 305. We thought she might have shown up at your place."

"Hey, Bob. Gracie texted you?"

"Hi, Miyo. Yeah, she did, but it wasn't from her phone."

"I got my 305 number when I lived in Miami. I didn't change it when I moved to Port City. What did the message say?"

"It's in Spanish," I said. "I'll translate: *Darling. Please don't worry. You know that I need to disappear and unwind sometimes. Remember San Diego and Key West. I'm fine. I'll be back before the game. All my love, your Bunny.* Does the reference to San Diego and Key West mean anything to you?"

"Last year, she called me from San Diego and sent me a first-class ticket to join her in Tijuana. A couple of months after that, she finished a photo shoot in Key West and came here to unwind for a few days. Bob, I'm sorry I never told you she was with me, but Gracie swore me to secrecy."

"Why tell me now?"

"A couple of reasons. When she disappeared from San Diego and Key West, you two were dating, but you weren't engaged. For all I knew, she wanted to escape from *you*. Remember, this was before you and I met. Now you're engaged. That's different. The other reason is Chuck says she's missing. I figure you have a right to know. Changing the subject, Chuck, what did she say at the end of the message? Something about a bunny?"

Bob smiled. "That's a pet name I use for Gracie when we're

alone. It's another signal that the text was from her. No one else would know that."

"That's precious, Bob. No wonder Gracie fell for you."

My phone chirped. "Miyo, I have a text coming in. Thanks for the help."

"You need anything else from me?"

"We're good. If you hear from Gracie, call me—anytime, day or night."

"I will and you and Bob call me if you hear from her…or when you want to collect on that raincheck."

"Deal." I disconnected.

"What did Miyo say about a raincheck for a cocktail?"

"It was nothing."

Bob grinned. "Sounded like something to me, Eighty-Eight. Come on now, don't hold out on your ol' buddy."

"When I interviewed Miyo at her place, it was almost five o'clock. She offered me a drink and I took coffee instead. I had more work to do later."

He grinned. "So, she invited you to come back another time?"

I felt uncomfortable. "Yeah."

"Why haven't you taken her up on it? She's a real nice girl. Pretty too."

"I've been kinda busy searching for Gracie. Or had you forgotten?"

"Don't change the subject, Eighty-Eight. You've been shy around girls ever since middle school. I even had to fix you up with your first date when we were at Teddy Roosevelt High. Don't tell me you're still nervous around women."

I didn't know what to say, so I said nothing.

Bob clapped me on the shoulder. "It'd be great if you and Miyo got to know each other better. Call her after all this is over."

"Yeah, yeah. I will. Now, let's get back to work. Do you know a guy named Mauricio Cuevadas?" I showed Bob the cellphone screen.

"No. Why do you ask?"

"Gracie used his phone to send the text."

"Who is he?"

I held up Bob's phone again. "Maybe I can use this to find out. Can I borrow your phone until tomorrow?"

Vicente Vidali

Vicente Vidali stood in the owner's stateroom lounge. The distant shore paraded past in stately fashion. The sun dropped behind the Port City skyline. "Mix me another drink, Dante. Fix one for yourself and Pistolet too."

Vidali brooded by the window. He stared at the darkening sky. "Dante, she's a stupid bitch."

"Women are not cut out for our business, Vic," Dante agreed.

"I think it's the hormones," added the other bodyguard.

Vidali sipped his drink. "When she first approached me with this idea, I should've run like hell. This was too good to be true."

He stood and stared out the window. "Maybe I was thinking with my dick too. She swore up and down that the dumb quarterback would fall for it. She said she had him wrapped around her finger."

"Yeah, Vic. I remember," Dante said.

"How could she be stupid enough to send a text to the stupid jock?"

"Said she didn't want him to worry too much, boss."

"I know what she said, Dante, but the whole point of her

disappearing was to get Martinez to worry, get him a little off his game after I placed the bets. She acts like she has no sense at all."

Vidali gestured with his drink and amber liquid flew across the room. "And using a freaking stolen phone. If Martinez has two brain cells to rub together, he'll know something is hinky. You don't get to be an NFL quarterback by being stupid."

He slid Graciela's cellphone from his pocket and stared at it as if it would tell him what to do now that the quarterback had been warned. "Even if Martinez doesn't tumble to something being wrong, it's for sure that McCrary will."

"You want me to get rid of the woman, boss? We're offshore. The Gulf Stream would take her body all the way to North Carolina."

"No. We need her until after the game. Martinez may want proof she's alive. We'll keep her...for now. Besides, after she calms down, maybe I'll invite her to the owner's suite one more time."

"She's too skinny, boss."

"You know what they say: The skinny ones are built for speed; the plump ones are built for comfort." Vidali finished his drink and stared at the empty glass. "Dante, I want McCrary off the case. He suspects I'm involved in the woman's disappearance. You've got to convince him Graciela has taken a brief, informal vacation."

"He's got a reputation, boss. Simpler to make him disappear."

"No. That would draw more attention to the woman's disappearance. Take Pistolet with you." He winked. "Try to reason with McCrary."

Graciela Perez

Graciela sat alone in the yacht's salon, one deck below Vidali's stateroom. The shoreline passed like a tantalizing vision, lovely and out of reach. She, too, watched the sun drop behind the skyline of Port City. She downed three more glasses of Pino Grigio and threw the empty bottle against the wall in frustration. The upholstered wall absorbed the impact and the bottle fell, unbroken, to the carpet. *I can't do anything right. I can't even break a stupid wine bottle.*

By the time the *Double Scotch* passed offshore of Miami Beach, the lights from the high-rises blazed in the dark sky. The yacht slowed to allow a container ship to exit Government Cut. It gained speed again and passed Virginia Key.

The thrum of the engines changed. The *Double Scotch* throttled down and steered west around Biscayne Key. Graciela recognized the famous lighthouse flashing its tireless rounds in the darkness. She sighed and tears rolled down her cheeks. What was going to happen to her now? Her ingenious plan to get her fiancée to throw the Super Bowl had spiraled out of her control, just like her life had spiraled out of her control.

An hour later, the mega-yacht hove to in the middle of Biscayne Bay. The hull vibrated with the short clatter of the bow anchor dropping in the shallow water.

Vicente Vidali entered the salon with a cup of coffee. "Good evening, my dear. I hope you enjoyed the sunset and the city lights on the horizon."

She glared at him through tears.

The steward followed Vidali in.

Vidali set his coffee cup down. "I'm afraid I must leave you now. I have business on shore." He pulled a cellphone from his pocket. "I'll give this back to Mauricio and tell him to be more careful with it."

From the salon, Graciela watched the crew bring the tender around from its berth at the stern. She barked at the steward, "Bring me another bottle of Pinot Grigio."

Vidali and his bodyguards descended a ladder out of sight. Twenty seconds later, the tender came into view, accelerating toward the shore.

It returned an hour later with only the crewman at the wheel.

Graciela staggered down the steps to her stateroom and cried herself to sleep.

SEVEN

Carlos McCrary

I walked into the North Shore Precinct squad room and spotted Detective Lieutenant Jorge Castellano. "I'm glad you have the seven-to-three shift this week, Jorge."

My buddy gazed up from a report he was writing. A smile broke across his face. "*¡Hola, amigo! ¿Café?*"

I responded in Spanish. "Is the coffee as bad as last week?"

"And last year. It's a tradition to have bad coffee in the squad room. Builds character."

We shook hands. "I wouldn't mess with tradition. I haven't had breakfast yet, so I'll choke down a cup." Actually, the coffee at the precinct wasn't half bad.

We walked to the coffee station.

"What gets you up at this ungodly hour, *amigo*? My shift began at 7:00 a.m., but everyone knows you like to sleep late."

"Yeah, like you."

"Seriously, Chuck. What brings you here?"

"I need a favor."

"Anything," said Jorge. He poured our coffees.

"Let's walk."

When we reached the sidewalk outside the precinct, I asked, "Can you do something off the books?"

Jorge surveyed the area to see if anyone was paying attention in the pre-dawn twilight; they weren't. "Do Cubans like coffee? For you, of course. What is it?"

I handed him Bob's cellphone. "This belongs to Bob Martinez."

Jorge stared at the phone. "*The* Bob Martinez?"

I smiled.

"How did you—?"

"Long story," I interrupted. "The short version is that Bob and I played high school football together and we've remained friends. He hired me to find his fiancée, Graciela Perez. She's a model."

"I know who she is—the Latin Angel. She's missing?"

"I'm afraid so. She disappeared late Saturday night or, more accurately, early Sunday morning, after a Super Bowl party thrown by ESPN."

"You want to file a missing person report?"

"No. Bob wants me to handle this on the down low. No cops yet."

"Why?"

"He won't tell me."

Jorge waved the phone. "What does this phone have to do with it?"

"Yesterday, Graciela sent Bob a text to this phone, but she didn't use her own phone to send it. The text was from area code 305. I need you to use your cop's super powers and tell me where Graciela's phone is. Also, where the phone that sent this message is now and its location when it sent the text."

"Can I read the text?"

"If you keep it under your hat."

He tapped the screen and a message appeared. "What does she mean by 'remember San Diego and Key West'?"

"That proved it was her who sent the text, since it didn't come from her own phone. Bob is the only one who knows she disappeared in San Diego and Key West last year." I decided not to mention Miyo, since she was not relevant to the task at hand. "Only Gracie knows that Bob calls her 'Bunny.' She definitely sent the text."

Jorge considered the screen again. "She says she's fine and she'll be back before the game. If she's okay and she'll be back, why are you still searching?"

"That's what Bob said. But I don't think she's fine. Graciela's phone goes straight to voicemail like it has since Sunday morning. The phone that sent the text goes straight to voicemail too. And that phone is registered to Mauricio Cuevadas."

"Who's that?"

"I've got a guy investigating that right now. But Bob Martinez said he never heard of him. That's why I need your cop super powers."

"Let's head back to the squad room."

Ten minutes later Jorge reared up from his computer monitor. "Graciela's phone has been switched off since Sunday at 4:04 a.m. The last time it pinged a cell tower was near the Portside development."

"Portside Marketplace is where her cellphone was turned off?"

Jorge glanced at the screen again. "Look here on the screen. It wasn't necessarily Portside Marketplace, but it was that cell tower. Portside Marina uses the same tower. The unknown phone with the 305 number that sent the message to this phone," he tapped Bob's cellphone, "used the cell tower on Mango Island."

The sun was still low in the east when I drove into the Port City Palace parking garage. Bob and I had planned to eat brunch in his suite. He had a walk-through football practice for the afternoon, followed by weight training.

A room service employee in a white coat wheeled a food cart to the door of his suite as I arrived. We came in together and the server set the table.

"Hey, Eighty-Eight." We shook hands, and he slipped the server a few bills. "That's all right, ma'am. We can serve ourselves. Thanks."

We waited for her to leave.

Bob picked up a serving dish. "You through with my cellphone yet? I'm lost without it."

"Here." I handed the phone over.

I filled both our cups, and Bob served the food.

"*Amigo*, this is worse than I thought." I played him the voicemail message sent to Gracie's flip-phone. "That's from a burner phone that belongs to a guy named Sam Torrance. His street name is Sharky. He's a drug dealer who lives in Brooklyn. I have my researcher running a report on him. I haven't heard back yet."

"If it's a burner phone, how do you know who the guy is?"

I couldn't resist. "Professional secret. I could tell you, but then…"

"…you'd have to kill me." Bob laughed. The tension in the room eased…a little.

I showed him Jerry Greenbaum's text on the flip-phone screen. I tossed the printouts of the agent's emails on the table in front of Bob. "Gracie owes money—a lot of money—to at least one really bad dude. She hasn't made a credit card payment since November.

The balances have reached their maximums. She's in debt up to her professionally-coifed hair style—again."

"Why run a credit report on Gracie? She's the victim here."

I added creamer to my coffee while I figured out how to respond.

"That's what you hired me to do—investigate. Credit card charges could tell me where she is. She hasn't charged anything since she disappeared. Her last charge was at the Port City Palace boutique Saturday afternoon. She charged that to your suite." I referred to my notes. "She bought a red bikini. The key point is that she's in over her pretty head. Desperate people do stupid things."

"What does that even mean?"

"I discovered the identity of the two men on the elevator. The main guy in the black tux is Vicente Vidali. The bald guy is an ex-con named Dante Orsinati, one of his bodyguards. Vidali is the Vic who texted her about the reservation on the Mango Island ferry. Does the name mean anything to you?"

Bob swallowed hard. "Yeah, I read about him in the newspaper. He's a mafia don in New Jersey."

"That's right. They call him Teflon Vic. The DA has never convicted him of so much as a parking ticket. He's active in the big three mafia businesses: drugs, prostitution, and gambling. He's implicated in several contract murders."

"What's he doing in Port City?"

"He owns a mansion on Mango Island. His ownership is hidden behind a Florida Land Trust. Gracie visited Teflon Vic on Mango Island Saturday afternoon, right before she disappeared. She may have been carried off in a van that belongs to a corporation that owns Vidali's casinos in New Jersey and Delaware. It's all connected."

I dropped the bomb. "Right after Gracie disappeared, somebody in Vegas bet enough money on the Cowboys to move the betting line by nine points. Vidali's casino has stopped taking bets on the Super Bowl game."

"What's that mean?"

"My professional opinion is that Teflon Vic bet a hundred million dollars or more of his own money on the Cowboys to beat the spread. He intends to fix the game."

Bob scoffed. "He's wasting his time; nobody could fix a Super Bowl Game."

"Unless they got to the quarterback."

Bob stopped chewing. "How would they do that?"

"Vidali has Graciela; you want him to return her safely. Do the math."

Bob's face turned to stone. "Is that how Gracie fits into this? She's a ransom demand? A hostage, for crissakes?"

"I don't know…yet, but I have my suspicions. Check these out." I showed him printouts of three articles on the Tawanda Grisham acid attack, along with before and after pictures of her ruined face. "Grisham's career is in the toilet, of course. We don't even want to think about what would happen to Gracie if Sharky threw acid on her."

"What's Sharky got to do with Vidali?"

I took a bite of eggs. They were perfect. "Maybe nothing. Sharky being in the mix may be a coincidence. But he is one of Gracie's many creditors. Unlike the credit card companies she owes, Sharky will maim her. Maybe with acid, or maybe by carving up her face. He's done both before. My guess is that Gracie was scared shitless; that's why she's went to Vidali. Sharky may not be connected to Vidali. But whatever Sharky is, he's bad news for Gracie that puts more pressure on her to find a way to raise money. The worse news is that Sharky might be the least of her troubles since Vidali now has her hidden away somewhere."

Bob studied the photos. "You gotta protect her, Chuck."

That was all I could take of his crap. I slammed the table with the flat of my hand. "Goddammit, I have to find her first! You've made that difficult, *amigo*. It's third and nine right now, and we're late in the fourth quarter and down by eight points. I need the resources of the cops and the FBI."

Bob stared into his cup and didn't say anything.

I dropped my fork and stalked across the room. My American grandfather Magnus McCrary taught me that trick to control my temper. Staring out the window at Seeti Bay, I counted to ten... slowly...before I did an about-face.

Bob shook his head slowly. Tears rolled down his cheeks.

He wasn't confiding in me in English. Maybe he would if I asked him in Spanish. So I did. "What won't you tell me, Roberto? What's your big, dark secret that has you so spooked you won't let me call the cops?"

I sat across from my client, my friend, and waited. And waited. And waited.

I parked my 1963 Avanti in the Mango Island ferry parking lot.

"We could at least have stopped at a drive-through on the way down, Chuck."

"You're always hungry, Snoop."

"Like you're not?"

"Ordinarily, I'd say you're right, but I had brunch with Bob so I'm not hungry. Plus, we have a lead on Graciela and I want to move on it before they move her. I'll make it up to you after we finish this part of the investigation."

"At least I get to be Good Cop this time," said Snoop.

"No can do, Snoop. You were Bad Cop last time with Alphonse. It would seem strange if I were Bad Cop this time." I rang the bell to the security office. The door buzzed and we entered.

Terrence Button was on duty. His expression hardened. "I told you not to come back here. I don't know nothing, and I didn't tell you nothing, mon."

Snoop leaned across the desk, grabbed the guard by the front of his turquoise jacket and jerked him to his feet. "Listen, dirtbag. The woman we watched on your video surveillance on Mango Island on Monday is definitely missing. You're now an accessory to kidnapping. You have two choices: Cooperate with us, or we'll let the FBI haul your sorry ass down to their office for questioning." He let Terrence's jacket loose, and the guard plopped back in his desk chair. "What's it going to be: us or the Feds?"

Terrence seemed to shrink. "What you want, mon?"

I stepped in as Good Cop. "We want to review the videos of everybody who got on or off the ferry between 4:00 p.m. and 6:00 p.m. yesterday afternoon."

He caved.

Snoop set his burger down. "Well, that was two hours of our lives we'll never get back."

We were at a table at the Fat Tummy Restaurant. I was eating a Sweep-the-Floor vegetarian pizza. It was the only thing on the menu that wouldn't congeal my arteries into cholesterol sludge. Snoop munched his usual Heart-Stopper Hamburger. He'd eaten them for years, and he was still alive. Maybe Snoop had a pact with the devil.

I sipped my iced tea. "The time wasn't wasted, Snoop. At least we know neither Gracie nor Crooked Nose nor Teflon Vic left the island during that two-hour window. That means Gracie could still be on the island."

"If the message is legit."

"It's legit."

"What do we do about that? This isn't a movie. We can't bust the door down, guns blazing."

"I've got an idea. Hank Hickham is a member of the Mango Island Club. He owns a condo there, and he owes me a favor."

The *Gator Raider Too* glided between the flashing beacons at the entrance to the Mango Island Club marina. My watch showed 11:30 p.m. Killing the running lights, I slipped the throttles back to neutral. The boat sidled to the guest dock and nudged the bumpers with a soft *squeak*.

Snoop stepped onto the dock, stern line in hand, and wrapped it several times around the nearest cleat.

I tossed him another line for the bow, and he snugged it around another cleat. I jumped off with two more lines.

"What're you doing, Chuck?"

"Attaching spring lines." I moved the line to a different cleat and ran a spring line toward the stern. I loosened the first line that Snoop had fastened.

"What? I didn't tie the boat good enough?"

"You tied it too good, Snoop. To moor a boat, you take the line once around here...across the middle here...and then flip this over. That holds the end down...like that."

"*Hmph*. Just because I'm not a sailor..."

"Don't get your panties in a wad. Any marina employee who passed would notice that the lines were snubbed wrong. He might wonder why someone who couldn't moor a boat properly was on the island. I don't want anyone to remember us." I snubbed the stern lines again too.

A powerful flashlight played across us, and an electric cart glided up the asphalt path. The driver was another security guard in a turquoise and gold jacket, a pith helmet, and white pants. "Can I help you gentlemen?"

I waved at him. "We have reservations at the Mango Island Lodge."

"May I have your name, sir?"

"Hank Hickham."

The guard got out of the cart. "You the guy who owns Hank's Bar & Grill & Bodacious Ribs? I love them ribs."

"Yeah, I love 'em too. That's my uncle. I'm named after him. He made the reservation for us. You can check if you like."

"Oh, I have to check. It's not that I don't believe you, Mr. Hickham. Rules are rules, you know." He spoke into his walkie-talkie, then nodded to us. "They've been expecting you."

"Sorry we're late. We left Key Largo this morning, and it took longer to make the run than we planned. But once you get underway…" I shrugged. "You might as well keep going, right?"

"I'll give you gentlemen and your luggage a ride to the Lodge."

"Do you meet all the arriving guests?" I asked.

"Most guests arrive by car on the ferry. I was making my regular rounds when you arrived."

"We've got things to tend to on the boat. I wouldn't want to keep you from your rounds. It's a nice night, and we only have one bag each. We'll be happy to walk."

"I don't mind waiting. It's part of our five-star service."

I glanced at Snoop. He shrugged. "Okay, thanks. We'll be a minute." I stepped aboard to fasten the hatches, flip off the lights, and kill the engines. Snoop retrieved our bags from the salon.

The guard set the bags in the back of the electric cart. He sat behind the wheel, next to me. "Is this your first time on Mango Island, Mr. Hickham?"

"Yeah. Uncle Hank talks about it all the time. He told me y'all have twenty-four-hour security." Sneaky Chuck McCrary, master interrogator.

"That's right. We have forty-seven security guards. People like me patrol the island 24/7/365."

"You mean you're not the only guard making rounds?" I mentally patted myself on the back for being so smooth.

"We have to patrol 432 acres. Superman couldn't guard 432 acres, let alone one guard. Four of us take the night shift. And we have a twenty-four-hour marine patrol. Our lodge guests can feel absolutely safe."

"That's good to know. So, you didn't come to the marina because you were expecting us?" This guy was as obvious as a newspaper headline.

The guard smiled. "Not quite. Our marine patrol observed your yacht when it was a half-mile off shore and gave us a heads-up."

"Thanks for the compliment, but the *Gator Raider Too* isn't a yacht; it's a cabin cruiser, and a small one compared to the real yachts that are moored here."

"All our guests' boats are yachts."

I had to laugh. "Very diplomatic."

The guard grinned. "When your *yacht* entered the marina, it sent a signal to the lodge and the security office. The security officer radioed me to meet you."

"That's quite a sophisticated setup. How does that work? Or is it a secret?"

"No secret. The residents know about it." The guard gestured over his shoulder. "A light beam shines across the entrance between the two beacons and above the high-water mark. Entering yachts cut the beam. That sends the signal."

"Like the photoelectric cell on a garage door opener?"

"That's right." He swerved into a circular drive and set the parking brake. "Here we are, gents."

In twenty minutes, we were in an oceanfront room on the fourth floor, overlooking the beach. I flipped off the room lights, and we sat on the balcony under the light of the half-moon. The only other light filtered up from the ornate street lamps that lined the path by the beach. I scanned the path through binoculars. "According to Google Earth, that cart path circles the entire island except for the Coast Guard station on the north. Let's time the guard on his rounds."

We observed for an hour.

"This is not good. The first round took the guard thirteen minutes, the second took twenty-two minutes, and the third took seven. It's totally unpredictable."

"It's not the same guard, Snoop. The patrol carts had three different numbers. The guards must take a semi-random route. They cover every street on the island in a reasonable frequency, but each guard takes a different route each time. Sometimes a guard circles the golf course; the next time he cruises past the condos; then he drives past the detached houses—like the one we're after."

"What're we gonna do about that?"

I stood. "We do what we came for; we rescue Graciela. It's just harder to avoid the security guards than we thought. Let's catch a nap while we can. Pick a bed."

"I'll take the one next to the balcony."

We lay down for a short nap.

At 2:30 a.m. the alarm woke us. I tossed our sports bags onto the beds. "Time to gear up."

We changed into our sneaking-around-in-the-dark outfits—black denim pants and long-sleeved, black T-shirts. We rolled our sleeves above the elbow and unzipped the pants legs to make them into black shorts. We stuffed the pant legs into the sports bags. We each slung a bag across our shoulders. "Remember, Snoop, low profile."

We remained silent on the elevator ride to the huge, open-air lobby. The three-tiered fountain in the courtyard splashed merrily as we walked across the brick patio to the entrance. We stood against one wall while a security guard cruised past the entrance in a modified golf cart. After he passed, we walked down the driveway to Mango Lodge Boulevard.

Glancing both ways, we walked across the boulevard and across a few yards of St. Augustine grass. We slipped through the bushes that edged the rough of the golf course. Fifty yards from the Lodge, I stopped to slip a watch cap from my bag. The irrigation pipes hissed and gurgled. "Oh, crap. The sprinklers are coming on. Let's move out."

We jogged across the fairway to the next hole.

I grabbed my watch cap.

"You don't need that, Chuck. Your hair is dark enough. But I gotta cover my gray."

I pulled the cap on anyway. "Cover as much skin as you can. We'll be less visible after we cross the golf course. There are street lamps on the other side, and there's a half moon tonight."

I glanced at the GPS directions on my phone, then turned off the screen. "It's about a quarter mile further. Vidali's house overlooks the third fairway." We rolled our shirtsleeves down, zipped the pants legs onto our shorts, and slipped on black gloves. That was as stealthy as we could get without camo face paint. I wasn't Special Forces anymore and had no way to remove face paint before returning to the lodge. "The security cameras are high definition. We want to blend into the foliage when we exit the golf course."

Snoop donned a similar cap and gloves. "Let's roll."

Five minutes later, I signaled a stop on the edge of the third fairway. We crouched in the blackness beneath a canopy of sea grape trees. I slid a heat-sensing, thermal-imaging camera from my bag. I waited for the viewer to warm up, then scanned the upstairs windows. "No heat source on the top floor."

I dodged through the gap in the bougainvillea privacy hedge and waited for Snoop to join me. "I'll scan the swimming pool side… No one. Wait here. I've got to get behind those bougainvillea to check the other side."

I returned a few minutes later.

Snoop whispered, "What's that on your face? Looks like blood."

"A bougainvillea attacked me while I was sneaking behind it. Don't worry; it's just a scratch."

"Those things sting like crazy. There was a bougainvillea in our yard when we bought our house. Janet made me remove it the second or third time one of our daughters got cut by the thorns."

I touched my face by habit, then remembered I wouldn't feel the blood through my gloves. "Occupational hazard."

"So, what did you find inside the house? Do we know where Graciela is being held?"

"We got nothing. No heat sources inside."

"Maybe they're all in the front of the house."

"I doubt it. The upstairs bedrooms have a golf course view. I think the house is empty."

We scurried back to the sea grapes. "Shh…" I held a finger to my lips and crouched in the shadows. Snoop followed suit.

"Down," I whispered. "Lay all the way down."

The muted whine of an electric motor grew closer. Seconds later a patrol cart halted twenty feet away on the path. The parking brake clicked as the guard set it. A two-way radio squawked. A tinny voice broke the silence. "Base to Rover Two. A condo resident reported something on the third fairway. Could be a raccoon or a loose dog, but you'd better confirm it."

"Rover Two to Base, I'm there right now." The springs squeaked as the guard exited the cart. A beam from a powerful flashlight arced its way across the bougainvillea and Royal Palms edging the fairway.

Snoop and I held our breath and lay flat on a bed of sea grape leaves, wet from the dew.

The beam flicked across the trunk of the sea grapes and passed over where we lay. In seconds, the beam passed back the other way. The radio squawked. "I don't see nothing, Base. Could have been someone's cat." The patrol cart's springs squeaked again.

"Roger that," the tinny voice replied.

The parking brake thudded off and the patrol cart moved down the path with a hum of its motor.

I waited until I no longer heard the cart or the radio, then grabbed my bag. "Is your heart beating again yet, Snoop?"

"Yeah, but I'm too old to hug wet leaves in the dark. I could do with a little less excitement."

"Let's examine the side of the house." I moved to the left and stopped again. "Is that a motion sensor?" I whispered.

A decorative seven-foot wall separated Teflon Vic's mansion from his neighbor to the north. A small box was mounted on top of the wall.

Snoop said, "Can't be. Whenever the wind blows, the swaying palms would set it off. Or a cat. It could be a security camera, though. Or maybe a laser. It's aimed along the top of the wall."

I crept close to the wall and studied the device on the thermal imager. "It's a camera." I connected the thermal imager to a remote viewer with a USB cord and held the imager above the wall, behind the camera. Studying the remote viewer, I swung the imager back and forth. "Nothing on the ground floor...Nothing on the top. Damn."

"Well, as long as we're here, we've got to check the other side and the front. Can't leave the job half done."

A cart path separated Vidali's mansion from the house to the south. "That's the path to the second hole," I whispered. I glanced both ways and lifted the imager to my eye. Walking down the cart path, I scanned both floors. When we reached the street, we curved down the sidewalk, passing in front. "Hard to tell about the ground floor when I'm looking through these bougainvillea, but the upstairs is empty. Wait here." Abandoning the path, I crawled behind the thorny plants again. A few seconds later, I rejoined Snoop. "Nobody home. And I managed not to get scratched this time."

An electric motor whirred in the distance. We moved closer to the thorny hedges that fronted Vidali's house and glanced up the street. Another patrol cart rounded the corner and headed our way.

Grabbing Snoop's sleeve, I yanked him toward the bougainvillea hedge.

Snoop jerked his arm away. "You're agile like a monkey, bud, but I'm not. Those thorns will cut me to ribbons if I hide there." He ran back the way we had come and slipped through a narrow gap between the leafy hedges into Vidali's garden. It was a big risk.

I followed right behind. "I hope there's no one home."

"No choice, kid. The roving patrols will spot us for sure unless we hide." Snoop dived to the right and dropped to the grass on the verge between hedge and patio. I dived to the left and did the same.

The patrol cart passed without slowing.

We returned to the relative safety of the third fairway and removed our caps and gloves.

Snoop said, "We know she sent the text from Mango Island. We know she didn't leave Mango Island unless she was in the trunk of a car. So where is she?"

"She could be in a condo or another house."

"That's thousands of hiding places, Chuck."

"Let's go back to the lodge."

I logged into the Mango Island Lodge Wi-Fi and read my email. "We got one from Flamer."

Snoop glanced at his watch. "Does that guy ever sleep?"

"I'm not sure Flamer is even human. He says Mauricio Cuevadas has a Coast Guard pilot license and he works for XPVV Corporation."

"What, he flies a plane for them?"

"No, Snoop, he's licensed by the Coast Guard, not the FAA. His license is to pilot a boat. Like maybe a yacht based at Portside Marina—or Mango Island. Flamer will examine the records there next." I glanced at the computer screen again. "It may take Flamer hours to hack into their systems. That means we may not hear anything else until morning. For now, let's get some sleep."

The next morning, I cranked the engines. Despite the seriousness of our mission, I took a second to appreciate the throaty rumble of the twin engines coming to life. They would need a minute to warm up, so I called Flamer. "What do you have on Cuevadas?" I was enjoying my second cup of Mango Lodge coffee in a to-go cup. Snoop and I had slept for three hours the previous night.

"Mauricio Cuevadas pilots a yacht named the *Double Scotch.* It's 164 feet long, thirty-three-foot beam, draws nine feet six inches, and cruises at eighteen knots. It docks at Portside Marina in slip E-1 and at Mango Island in slip 46. The Portside Marina issues electronic keycards to the crew and owners of yachts that dock there."

"Are they like the keycards hotels use?"

"Yeah, but these operate the gate from the parking lot to the marina. They were used to access the gate Sunday morning at four o'clock."

"The guys who snatched Graciela must have taken her to the Portside Marina and stashed her on a boat."

"Yeah. Except this boat is a ship. Mauricio Cuevadas has a permanent keycard at the marina. So does Vicente Vidali. So does a guy named Dante Orsinati. I researched him. He's the bald guy with the crooked nose whose picture you sent me. I sent you a photo from his license with the New Jersey Casino Control Commission. He's head of security for the Double Down Casino in Atlantic City and licensed to carry a concealed weapon. Three other crew members have keycards. You want their names too?"

"Not right now. Email them so I'll have them. The yacht is named *Double Scotch* and Vidali's casinos are named the Double Down. That's no coincidence. Who is the boat registered to?"

"According to the Atlantic County Tax Collector's Office, the yacht is registered to XPVV Corporation. It's on the list of slip owners at Mango Island."

"Any chance you would know where the *Double Scotch* is right now?"

"What do you think I am? The NSA?"

"For all I know, Flamer, you can access the Department of Defense surveillance satellites."

"I'm good, Chuck, but I'm not that good. Hold on a sec…Would it help to know where the boat *isn't*?"

"Sure."

"Well, it isn't at Portside Marina right now."

"You're reviewing their security video right now, aren't you?"

"Yep. It's a simple hack. And... wait a sec...it isn't at Mango Island, either."

I knocked on the doorjamb of the harbormaster's office and walked in.

A grey-haired man in a worn gold captain's hat, a turquoise denim shirt, khaki pants, and boat shoes rose from his desk. "How can I help you?"

We shook hands. "I'm Hank Hickham. I'm a guest at the Lodge—or I was until I checked out fifteen minutes ago."

"Are you the guy with the ribs?"

"No. I'm the rib guy's nephew. Uncle Hank lets me use his place here."

"I love your uncle's ribs."

I grinned, good ol' charming Chuck. "Me too. And, in response to your next question: No, I don't know the secret recipe for his barbeque sauce."

We shared a laugh. I could already feel the male bonding.

"I was supposed to meet Vic Vidali and my girlfriend here this morning. I went by slip 46 and Vic's not there. We were going to raft up near Stiltsville for a party. Have you heard from him?"

"No, sir. The *Double Scotch* was here a couple of days ago. It pulled into the slip for maybe ten minutes and then left."

"Was my girlfriend Gracie with Vic? Slender Latin brunette, five-seven, twenty-five years old? She's a real looker."

"Hang on," the Harbormaster said. He picked up a handheld radio. "Gary, Albert calling."

The radio squawked. "Gary here, Albert."

"Did the *Double Scotch* board an attractive brunette, mid-twenties, with Mr. Vidali on Tuesday when you helped them dock?"

"Nope. She was already on board. 'Attractive' ain't the half of it. I think she's some kinda super model. I recognized her from television, but she didn't get off. Only Mr. V and two other men boarded."

"Thanks, Gary. Out." Albert the Harbormaster set down the radio. "You heard. That your girlfriend?"

"Yep. Was that about 4:30?"

Albert glanced at his computer monitor. "Log shows them here from 4:17 to 4:25."

"Thanks. I must've got my signals crossed. I guess I'm supposed to meet them at Stiltsville." I headed back to my boat.

"Well?" asked Snoop.

I loosed the dock lines and tossed them to Snoop, jumped onboard, and took the wheel. "Talk to you in a minute." I waved at the dock attendant. "Fend for me?"

He waved his assent and moved to the stern.

I eased the port engine into reverse and the starboard engine into forward. It always fascinates me the way a twin-engine boat can revolve in her own length. The dock attendant placed one rubber-soled shoe against the rear rub-rail and held it away from the dock.

The *Gator Raider Too* pivoted 120 degrees. I slipped the port engine into forward and waved farewell to the dock attendant. Ten minutes later, we cleared the breakwater. I could finally talk. "Gracie was never in Vidali's house two days ago. She sent the text from the *Double Scotch*. I'll bet she's been on board since she was kidnapped. Maybe she stole the pilot's cellphone. Vidali didn't let her off when the boat stopped here. Instead, he got on and the boat left."

"That's why there was no one at Vidali's house last night. Vidali was on his boat."

"Or at the Port City Palace in his suite. I doubt he stayed on the boat for long. Too far from the action. He boarded just long enough to get Gracie far away from the shore."

"Beyond swimming distance?" Snoop asked.

"That's what I would do if I were him."

I called Flamer. "Try to get photos of Vidali's boat. I want aerial shots and front, back, and side. Can do?"

"That's a tough one, Chuck. That stuff is not a matter of public record."

"Mega-yachts are sometimes featured on the builder's website. Try to determine the builder from the registration. Or, if Vidali bought the boat from someone else, a yacht broker might have photos left over from the listing agreement."

Flamer hung up without a word. No goodbye. That's Flamer, a master of the social graces.

I pushed the throttles ahead. "Gracie's somewhere out there, Snoop."

"How do we find her?"

"We follow the plan."

"What plan is that?"

"Beats the hell outta me. You got any ideas?"

EIGHT

The intercom came to life. "Uh...Mr. McCrary, there are two...uh, two gentlemen here to see you, Mr. McCrary." Betty sounded nervous. "Wait! You can't go back there." The intercom went dead.

I had expected something like this. I switched on the secondary security cameras. I reached in the top right drawer for my Glock 17. Holding the pistol in my lap, I waited behind my desk.

My office door flew open with splinters flying from the broken latch and door jamb. Dante Orsinati and another thug stalked in. The other thug moved three steps to the side. Both men carried guns with sound suppressors. Orsinati's was a Browning .380, a nice, small gun for a concealed carry. The other guy carried a Glock like mine. As long as they pointed them at the floor, I was okay. But if either one raised the barrel...well, that's when things would get intense.

I waved with my left hand. "Is that how you exercise, Dante, kicking in unlocked doors?"

Beneath the desk, I pointed the Glock at Orsinati's private

parts. I couldn't aim any higher. Shooting through the plywood desktop would deflect the slug. If either of them pointed a gun at me, I would aim low and shoot through the thin desk panel. I might not kill Orsinati, but he would sing soprano for the rest of his life.

"Have a seat, Dante. Make yourself comfortable. My door is always open. *Mi casa es su casa*. Oh, wait, you guys may not speak Spanish. My house is your house. Anything else I can do to make you and Teflon Vic's other pet thug feel welcome?"

Orsinati pointed his gun at one of the primary security cameras and fired. The shot was actually quieter than I expected.

I glanced at the ruined camera. The Browning's barrel is less than four inches long and the suppressor doesn't help its accuracy. That was a heck of a shot. My Glock has a four-and-a-half-inch barrel and no suppressor, and I wasn't sure I could make that shot. "That wasn't very nice. My sainted grandmother gave me that camera as a confirmation present, Dante. Now I feel so much more intimidated, I might pee my pants."

Orsinati scowled at me. "You and your buddy been asking around about Graciela Perez. Gracie said to tell you she's on vacation for a couple of weeks. She don't want to be bothered right now—by neither you or the quarterback. She wants you guys to leave her alone. She asked me to tell you to back off."

"You know, Dante, I might believe that if she told me in person. Tell me where she is, and I'll drop by and have a chat. If she asks me to back off, I'll be happy to oblige."

Orsinati twirled and shot out the other camera in the opposite corner. Good thing the secondary system was recording the whole scene.

"Wow, and my sainted grandfather gave me that camera when I graduated from cosmetology school. Whatever shall I do?"

Orsinati's accomplice frowned and glanced at him for guidance.

"Next time I won't aim at your cameras, wiseass. Don't let there be a next time."

Orsinati gestured with his chin and the two men stalked from the room. They didn't bother to close the door.

I played the security footage for Jorge Castellano. He was spiffy in new lieutenant's bars. He rated a private office now like my old training officer Lieutenant Joyce Weiner.

"The shooter is Dante Orsinati, muscle for Vicente Vidali. I'd like to know who the other guy is. What do you suggest?"

"Your receptionist called 9-1-1 when she heard the shots, but you told the cops who responded that you wouldn't press charges. Why not?"

I didn't answer. Jorge knew without me telling him that I would handle this personally. *Extrajudicially*, in a manner of speaking.

"You want me to help you investigate this and I don't have a case number. That's not kosher."

"I brought donuts."

"You think you can buy me with a donut?"

"No. That's why I brought a dozen." I set the box on his desk

Jorge snatched a donut, bit off at least a third. "You get any fingerprints?"

"*Nah.* They kicked the door open like you saw. Didn't touch anything with their hands."

"Maybe that's why Orsinati kicked the door open in the first place instead of using the doorknob—he didn't want to leave any prints. I hate to admit it, but that's a moderately smart move."

"I never thought of that. Maybe you ought to be a detective." Note to self: Remember that kick-in-the-door technique for future use.

"How can I find out who the other mook is?"

Jorge took another bite of donut. "I'll run it through facial recognition. If that doesn't work, I'll print a screen shot of the guy's face and email it to the Atlantic City and Wilmington organized crime guys. They'll give me professional courtesy, but it could take a couple of days since this is low priority. Our facial recognition software will probably identify him first." He stuffed the rest of the donut in his mouth and grabbed another one.

"That's good, because a couple of days is too long, *amigo*. It's Thursday afternoon. The Super Bowl is this Sunday. If the situation is what I think it is, I gotta handle this before then."

He started on the second donut. "Refill my coffee while I run his picture."

By the time I got back, two more donuts had disappeared from the box. He took the coffee cup. "I'm printing his rap sheet. Grab it from the printer."

I did and handed it to Jorge.

"Keep it. The second gunman's name is Bradovic Pisarczik. His nickname is Pistolet Pisarczik."

"Pistolet?"

"What can I say? It's Polish for *pistol*. You wouldn't want to call him *pisser*; he'd kill you for that. Pisarczik came to the land of the free and the home the brave and sSomehow became an American citizen, so he can't be deported. He's been arrested for pistol-whipping people who annoyed Teflon Vic. No charges filed. The victims had a sudden case of amnesia." He shrugged. "No surprise."

"Thanks. It's nice to know who I'm up against." I stood.

He held out the half-empty donut box for me.

I waved it away. "Keep 'em. They're not good for my figure."

"You know you don't have to do this alone, *amigo*. Press charges and we'll rattle both these guys' cages. With your security video, we can charge both of them with aggravated assault with a firearm. We can make those charges stick real easy."

"Maybe next week. Right now, I've got too much on my plate. And I'm not alone; Snoop is in this."

Jorge shook my hand. "I'm sure he's doing his best to keep you out of trouble."

"Probably won't work, though."

"Probably not."

"Mr. Greenbaum, I'm Chuck McCrary, a friend of Graciela Perez and Bob Martinez. I am video calling from my office in Port City, Florida. This is my associate Raymond Snopolski." I pointed to Snoop standing behind me where he could view the monitor.

"What can I do for you, Mr. McCrary?" The computer monitor showed Greenbaum at a desk. An out-of-focus New York City skyline was visible through the office window behind him.

"Call me Chuck. In addition to being Gracie's friend, I am a private investigator." I held my license where the camera could focus on it. Sometimes it impresses people. Sometimes not. "Graciela is missing. Bob hired me to find her."

"Missing how long?"

"Since three o'clock Sunday morning. The last time she was seen was on a hotel security video a couple of hours after she attended an ESPN Super Bowl party. Do you know where she is?"

"Wow...this is a shock. No, I have no idea where she is." Greenbaum sipped from a blue coffee mug with *World's Greatest Agent* printed in white on the side below a smiley face. "I suppose you've tried her parents?"

"Yes."

"How about her best friend—the Asian girl—I don't recall her name offhand. It's in my file somewhere." He twirled to his left and reached for something off-camera.

"Miyoki Takashi. Yes, I've interviewed her."

Greenbaum paused. "I don't know what else to suggest, Mr. McCrary."

"Call me Chuck. What about Sharky? Would he know where Gracie is?"

His gaze darted left and right. "Who?"

"Sharky," I repeated. "Your drug connection."

Greenbaum shook a finger at the camera. "Now listen here, McCrary, I don't know any Sharky, and I don't do drugs."

"Cut the BS, Jerry. I'll refresh your memory with this text you sent to Gracie's secret cellphone, the one Bob didn't know about."

I held the phone up to the camera, showing Greenbaum the tiny flip-phone screen.

`Sharky wants his money. He is becoming insistent. You cannot ignore this any longer. He has threatened me too.`

I waited for him to react. There was a long pause.

"Jerry, I'm not a cop. I don't care what you buy from Sharky, and I don't care how much money you owe him or why. All I care about is finding your client Graciela. It's in your own best interest to help me out here."

"What do you want to know?"

"Did you know Sharky's real name is Sam Torrance?"

"No."

"You may not have known he has a police rap sheet. Arrested six times on suspicion of drug dealing, assault with a deadly weapon, and maiming."

"Maiming? What's that?"

"Sharky used a knife, maybe a carton cutter, on a poor woman's face. He cut two long slices on each cheek and one across her forehead. Never convicted. I'll play you a voicemail he sent to Gracie's secret phone."

I held the flip-phone near the computer's built-in microphone and pressed a key.

"Gracie, this is me. You better not come back to New York without my money. Have a good time at the Super Bowl. Remember that a lot of your good times come from me. Jerry's too. If you don't pay me Wednesday after the game, you'd better look over your shoulder. Remember what happened to Tawanda Grisham. But maybe I'll start with Jerry to show you I mean business. That way you might still have a career—just not an agent."

"Do you know who Tawanda Grisham is?"

Greenbaum's eyebrows raised. "Omigod. She's the actress—*was* the actress, uh, the acid attack, right? I remember the story on the news. You think Sharky would throw acid on me?"

"I've never met the man. The question is: Do *you* think he would throw acid on you?"

Greenbaum paused a few seconds, then nodded, perhaps unconsciously. "The newspapers said Tawanda Grisham's attack may have been drug-related. There were rumors she bought drugs from someone and didn't pay. The police never found out who did it. Ms. Grisham wouldn't cooperate. She feared for her life if she helped the police." He made a face. "Yeah, Sharky would throw acid." He placed both hands flat on the desk. "Okay, how can I help?"

"When was the last time you heard from Graciela?"

"Wait a sec. My calendar's right here." He moved his computer mouse. "Yeah, I remember now. She called me the day of the ESPN party."

"What did you talk about?"

"You know: who was going to be there, which people she should schmooze. Same old, same old. Routine stuff."

"Did she mention any other plans she might have?"

Greenbaum blinked. "No, she didn't."

"Did she mention Vicente Vidali?"

"Geez, don't tell me she's involved with a mobster."

"Okay, I won't tell you that. But did she ever mention him?"

"God, no. That guy kills people, for crissakes."

"How about the Double Down casinos in Atlantic City or Wilmington? She ever mention them?"

"Nope."

"Okay. I'll email you my contact information. If you think of anything that would help, or if you hear from Gracie, call me anytime, day or night."

"Wait, wait, don't go. What do you intend to do about Sharky?"

I shrugged. "Me? Nothing. Sharky's not my problem. I don't owe him any money."

———

Renate Crowell, a reporter with the *Port City Press-Journal*, took a chair in my conference room. I met her there because I didn't want her to notice the bullet holes in my office. I had repaired the office door but let the bullet holes slide for a few days. Who knew? I might need them for evidence in that assault charge Jorge wanted to file.

I sat at the coffee table. "How are things with the Princess of the *Pee-Jay*?"

"*Hmm.* 'Princess of the *Pee-Jay*'. That has a nice ring to it, handsome. But I didn't come over here to have you blow smoke up my skirt, although it could be fun for us both if you did." She laughed and picked up her coffee.

"Impossible, you always wear pants."

She glanced down at her designer jeans. "I'll wear a skirt if you want to try it sometime. I'll even lift it for you."

Renate had flirted with me every time we met for over a year. She was smart, funny, and attractive, but I never knew how to talk to women about anything personal. I retreated to the familiar. "What can I do for you?"

"You've been meeting with Bob Martinez."

"Bob and I have been friends since grade school. Everyone knows that. You want to do a human-interest story on Bob and me? Like, high school football player friends: Where are they now? One goes to hell in Iraq and Afghanistan; the other goes to the NFL?"

"Not quite. I'm chasing down a rumor, and I want your take on it."

"I don't believe much in rumors. What have you heard?"

"I recognized Bob and Graciela at the ESPN party at the Port City Palace Saturday night."

"That's not a rumor; that's an undeniable fact. I noticed their pictures in the *Pee-Jay* the next day. You must've had a staff photographer with you."

I sipped my coffee. Renate followed suit and remained silent, an old reporter's trick to get someone else to fill the silence.

I regarded her pleasantly and didn't say anything else.

"I take a photographer whenever the managing editor will let me. Since this was a Super Bowl party, it was an easy sell. The next morning, you and Bob had breakfast together in the Port City Palace coffee shop."

"Let's headline that historic meeting on the *Pee-Jay* front page tomorrow, Princess. Only a few hundred people saw us together, so you should make sure the whole world knows that we're friends. Bob even let a little boy's dad take his picture with the football hero. Human interest, maybe, but hardly newsworthy. What's your point?"

"Graciela didn't join you for breakfast."

"Neither did you."

"She's Bob's fiancée. Newspaper readers would expect them to have breakfast together."

I shrugged. "Lots of models don't eat breakfast. I'm told that it helps them keep the pounds off. Also not newsworthy."

"Graciela hasn't been seen since the ESPN party."

I seldom get in trouble for keeping quiet. I didn't know what to say, so I said nothing.

"The rumor is that she's missing."

I waited again. Waiting is one of my better skills.

"Do you know where she is?"

"No, but I don't know where the president of Lithuania is either. If you had called me on a cellphone, I wouldn't know where you were. You could call from Timbuktu. I don't know where the Port City mayor is, or the governor of Wyoming. Why should I know where Graciela is?" It didn't matter that I was laying it on too thick. Renate wouldn't believe me anyway.

"Yesterday, there were two other Super Bowl events she was expected to attend, with or without Bob. She wasn't there. Bob Martinez attended a third event where other players brought their wives or girlfriends. Bob was alone."

I raised an eyebrow. "What does this have to do with me?"

"I'd like to talk to Bob Martinez, but I don't have his cellphone number. I knew where to find you, so here I am. Besides, you're cute and have a nice ass. Care to comment?"

"You may quote me: I'm flattered that you think I'm cute. So does my mother. I'm too modest to make a comment about my nice ass, but—off the record—my ass is not my best feature, as you well know."

She laughed again. "I stepped right into that one."

"Here's another comment, which you may also quote: I am glad you are here. I am always glad to be interviewed by the Princess of the *Pee-Jay*." I leaned back in my chair. "You didn't write that down. Are you recording this on your cellphone? Would you like me to repeat it?"

"Very funny, smart guy. I want a comment on Graciela's disappearance."

"*Alleged* disappearance." I felt a guilty twinge as I stretched the truth until it almost snapped. Renate was simply earning a living. "Again, this has nothing to do with me."

"I also heard Graciela likes heroin…a lot. So much so that she went to rehab last summer."

"I never met Graciela until the three of us had dinner in New York right after the AFC Championship game. I don't know much about her—probably less than you do."

"Did you know she was in rehab last summer?"

I smiled. "Nice try. That question assumes Graciela was in rehab. I don't know whether she was, and I don't care. Her personal life and problems, if any, are none of my business…or yours. Even if the rumor were true, I wouldn't know about it. I don't travel in those circles." I lowered my voice. "A word of advice between friends?"

She raised an eyebrow.

"A professional journalist like you knows that accusations like that, if committed to print, could be considered libelous. I do remember at our dinner in New York two weeks ago, Gracie happened to mention that her agent and her attorney are both real sharks when it comes to protecting her reputation. Just saying." I smiled to soften the tone. "I know you only wanted to get a reaction out of me. I don't take it personally; you have a job to do. And I think you're cute too."

"And what about my ass?"

"No comment." But I whistled.

Renate grinned. "Can't blame a girl for trying." She flipped a page in her notepad. "I know that two suspicious guys passed her an envelope full of drugs in an elevator in the Port City Palace the night she disappeared. I've seen the pictures."

That had to be Wally, the hotel guard who showed me the security videos. There was nothing I could do about it now. I couldn't very well shoot him, and it was a juicy story. It probably made him feel important to tell a reporter. Renate might even have paid him for the pictures.

I stood to signal the meeting was over.

Renate remained seated. "I know that you and Snoop reviewed the hotel security videos of Graciela and the mysterious envelope and the two mysterious men." She paused. "And that she left the hotel at 3:30 in the morning. Alone."

I remained standing and said nothing.

Renate took the hint and stood. She paused at the door. "Read the Lifestyle section in the *Pee-Jay* tomorrow for my article on Super Bowl wives and sweethearts—including the rumor that Graciela has gone missing."

"Thanks for coming by, Renate. It's always nice to glimpse your smiling face. You can quote me on that too."

NINE

"Gracie was last seen on the *Double Scotch*," I said to Bob. "It's a mega-yacht that belongs to Vicente Vidali. You know who he is. He's bad news to anybody who comes in contact with him. Your fiancée is involved from her expertly painted toenails to her artificial eyelashes."

The Jets quarterback pushed his dinner plate away and moved to the window. "You don't know that she's there against her will."

"You're living in a dream world, *amigo*. Vidali's two thugs shot up my office to make me stop searching for her. He kidnapped her, all right."

Bob paced across the room. "Why would he do that?"

"We've been over this. The same reason most non-family kidnappers do it—for ransom."

"Ransom? Nobody's contacted me demanding money."

"Is there an echo in here? I told you: Do the math. Vidali will demand that you lose the game or he'll kill her."

"Geez. You were *serious* about that?"

"As serious as the national debt. I swear, *amigo*, sometimes your head is harder than your football helmet. You gotta let me call the cops. Now."

"But she knows Vidali, remember? They met on the hotel elevator."

"That meeting was for Vidali to pass her an envelope stuffed with cash."

"What for?"

"Well, it wasn't enough to pay her bills."

"How do you know that?"

"The envelope in the video was less than an inch thick. An inch of hundred-dollar bills is right at twenty-two thousand dollars. Vidali maybe gave her ten or fifteen thousand dollars. That would buy time on her credit cards, but it wouldn't solve her problem. No, she needs a lot more money than that."

"What if it was Euros, Eighty-Eight? They come in 500 Euro bills."

"It's a waste of time to discuss this. Where would she spend Euros? No, that envelope held something else—maybe money for her to disappear and not leave a credit card trail. Or a gesture of good faith, with more to come later."

"Okay. But what about this Sharky character? How is he involved?"

"He's one reason she's desperate for money. The credit card companies won't carve up her face or throw acid on her; Sharky will."

"What do you think she's up to?"

"Vidali passed the money to Gracie so she could disappear without using credit cards. If you don't know where she is, then Vidali can make a credible threat to harm her unless you lose the game."

"In that case, she wouldn't be on his yacht against her will."

I shrugged. "Maybe Vidali doesn't trust her to stay hidden, so he snatches her from the Palace parking garage and hides her on his yacht. Maybe Gracie had a change of heart and decided she wanted out."

"You think she's involved in this?"

"I don't know exactly what her involvement is, but it's there. That's what I've been saying. For all we know, the whole thing might have been her idea from the get-go. That's the point—we don't know. Maybe there's an innocent explanation for all this, but I doubt it. I have to find her to ask what's going on. The police could help me do that."

"No. Find her yourself, without the cops. If she's on Vidali's boat, maybe you can search the area with a helicopter."

"Tomorrow's Friday. It would take all day to search from Fort Lauderdale down to Key Largo. You're talking several thousand dollars to rent the copter, but, more than that, I don't want to waste the time when the police have their own helicopters."

"I'll write you another check." He sat at the table and slid his checkbook from a pocket.

I shook my head. "Dammit, Bob, you're wasting time. Gracie has disappeared with a mobster and murderer, and you think you can fix that by writing another check. It's gonna take more than money to solve this problem."

I set my hand on Bob's shoulder. "*Amigo*, you have a secret you're afraid will come out if we involve the police. Whatever it is, is that secret worth risking Gracie's life? C'mon, *amigo, diga me*." *Tell me*, I said in Spanish.

Bob filled in the check and handed it to me. "Here's another twenty thousand. No cops, Eighty-Eight."

I handed a set of photos of the *Double Scotch* to the helicopter pilots, Marie and Richard Leonard. I'd known Marie in Afghanistan when she'd flown supplies and airdrops for the Triple Seven, my Special Forces unit. She had met Richard over there and they married after they both rotated stateside. Marie became pregnant, and they let their enlistments expire. They organized an air charter service in Coral Gables. Good people.

Flamer had hacked the website of the company that insured the *Double Scotch* and obtained a copy of the yacht's survey. It included a complete set of photos and plans.

Marie glanced at the photos. "This is a little different from satellite photos of an LZ in Kandahar, ain't it, Sergeant?"

"Shouldn't be any enemy fire on this recon, Marie."

She handed the photos back. "You keep them. You'll be my spotter. You and Snoop."

"The *Double Scotch* is a hundred sixty-three feet long with a thirty-three-foot beam," I told the pilots. "Shouldn't be hard to recognize."

Richard took notes in a small spiral notebook. "A boat that big would stand out like a grizzly at a dog show. That means she won't be in any narrow canals like the ones dug into the mainland. What's her draft?"

I consulted my notes. "She draws nine feet six inches."

Richard eyed Marie. "She won't be near the shore, babe. She'll be in the big water or moored at a big marina. We're in luck with the tide."

"How so?" I asked.

"It's ebbing right now. She's got to stay in water that's at least ten feet deep at low tide, maybe a little deeper, because the skipper can't rely on the charts too much. The tides and currents move sand around on the bottom. Say, eleven feet to be safe. That restricts her options, especially if she's in Biscayne Bay, which is shallow. It'll make the search go faster."

Marie glanced at the sun, low on the horizon. "Dick can't use the color of the water to spot the shallow areas until the sun gets higher. All the water will appear pretty much the same for the next two hours."

"That's why I gave y'all the nautical charts. Dick, your co-pilot can help you stay over the deep areas. Begin at the Card Sound Bridge at the south end of Biscayne Bay and head north. Photos show the *Double Scotch* has a thirty-foot Zodiac tender at the stern of the bottom deck. There's a smaller Zodiac on one davit on the bow. There's a hot tub on the sun deck." I pointed them out on the photos. "That should help you identify her from the air."

"Right," Richard said. "The grizzly bear carries two Zodiacs."

"Snoop and I will fly with Marie. We'll start at Seeti Bay and work our way south in the other chopper."

Richard nodded. "What if we meet in the middle and still haven't found her?"

"She may have headed to the Bahamas or north with the Gulf Stream. We'll make that decision after we finish this first pass. Stay in touch by radio. Any questions?"

He folded his notepad and stepped up on the strut of the helicopter. "We're ready."

I gave him a thumbs-up.

Marie, Snoop, and I trotted to the other chopper. I buckled in and signaled Marie, who wound the rotors.

Marie eased the collective up. "Tallyho, Sergeant." The chopper rose like an express elevator. She tweaked the cyclic and it banked steeply over Coral Gables. Their base station shrank in the distance.

The *thump-thump-thump* of the blades carried me back to the Middle East. Old battle scars throbbed. I blinked back a tear and focused on the turquoise water of Biscayne Bay flashing by below us. It wasn't mountains and desert, and no one down there was likely to fire a Stinger missile at us. A Browning .380 maybe, but not a Stinger.

Snoop studied my face. In some ways, he knew me better than my parents. I had told him stories I could never tell them.

I glanced at him, covered my microphone with my hand, and mouthed, "I'm okay, Snoop."

I uncovered the mic and gave Marie directions. "Head up the Intracoastal to the top of Seeti Bay, then circle clockwise around the shore."

"Roger," I heard through the headset.

Ten minutes later we passed Harbor Island and my headset clicked on. "Chuck, this is Dick. You ain't gonna believe this, buddy, but we found her."

Marie was monitoring the radio and had already tilted the cyclic toward the south. "Where is she, Dick?"

"Due east of Turkey Point Nuclear halfway to Elliott Key. She's swinging at anchor. You want me to babysit her, Chuck?"

"I don't want them to know we're interested, Dick. Head back to base. We'll reconnoiter for ourselves."

It took only seventeen minutes. "Over there, Snoop, on the horizon. Geez, that sucker is gigantic."

I tapped Marie's shoulder and pointed. "Don't head straight for it. I don't want them to know we're interested. Fly down Elliott Key like any tourist. Then head toward Turkey Point. Fly slow."

"Got it." Marie banked the chopper toward the north end of Elliott Key. "I'll follow the road down to the campground." She slowed and cruised leisurely for two minutes. "I always tell customers that Elliott Key is uninhabited. The whole island is part of the Biscayne National Park. Notice those boat slips? A boat is the only way to get there."

"Or a helicopter," said Snoop.

Marie smiled. "Or a helicopter. That campground is the only place to stay overnight."

At 1,400 feet altitude, she curved for the shore.

As we came abreast of the *Double Scotch*, I studied the yacht through my binoculars. I was glad that the swim platform shown in the old photos had not been modified.

I scanned the yacht. Graciela lay on a sun lounge in a red bikini, or at least a red bikini bottom. I nudged Snoop with my elbow. "It's Graciela. She's wearing the red bikini she bought at the Palace gift shop."

"Too bad she's not topless. We could take photos for the tabloids."

I handed him the binoculars. "You need glasses, Snoop. She is topless."

Marie elbowed me in the ribs. Hard.

By noon, we had returned to the Coral Gables helicopter base. I tried to call Bob, but it went straight to voicemail. I left a message, then remembered he had a news conference scheduled for noon. I texted him:

We saw Gracie sunbathing on Vidali's boat. He has at least four crewmen aboard and maybe the gunmen that came to my office. Can I call the cops now? Or maybe the Coast Guard?

We jumped in my Avanti and headed toward Port City. Forty-five minutes later, my phone signaled a text. I was driving 65 mph on I-95, so I handed the phone to Snoop. "Read this to me."

He took the phone. "It's from Bob. It says, 'Don't do nothing yet. Meet me in my hotel room ASAP.'"

Snoop groaned. "The moron still won't let us call the cops. What the hell are we gonna do?"

"Meet the client in his hotel room ASAP, of course."

───────

Bob had given me a keycard to his suite a few days before. Snoop and I made ourselves at home until he arrived. I ordered room service hamburgers and iced tea for three. I brewed a pot of coffee in the suite's kitchen while we waited.

Bob walked in waving a section of newspaper.

I poured three coffees. "I ordered burgers and iced tea for us. We haven't had lunch and I figured you'd be hungry too."

"Thanks, Eighty-Eight. I hope the burgers are good 'cause this has been a crappy day so far."

"Want to cry on my shoulder?"

Bob tossed a section of the *Port City Press-Journal* to me. "Front page article of the Lifestyle section. The headline says *Super Bowl Wives, Sweethearts Have Tough Week.*"

I opened it and read Renate Crowell's byline. "That reporter came to my office yesterday."

"You? She came to interview *you?*"

"She's sort of a friend."

Bob jumped to his feet. "It says 'unnamed sources close to the Jets quarterback' have hinted that Gracie is missing. 'Unnamed sources'? How could you do that to me? She's 'sort of a friend'? I thought you were *my* friend, for crissakes. How could you tell a… a…*reporter* that Gracie is gone? You used a sleazy newspaper to pressure me to bring in the cops."

Snoop stepped in front of Bob. From the expression on his face, he intended to defend me from a professional athlete who was twenty-five years younger, half a head taller, and fifty pounds heavier. *You go, Snoop.*

I laid a hand on my mentor's arm. "I can handle this, Snoop. Bob and I go back all the way to grade school."

Snoop jerked his arm free. "I don't care how long he's known you. He's got no right to talk to you like that." He moved away.

I kept my voice dead calm. "It wasn't me, sport."

Bob stepped back. His temperature dropped a couple of degrees. "What do you mean?"

"I wasn't the unnamed source. I told you that your secrets were safe with me, and they are."

"Then who blabbed?"

I shrugged. "Renate and the whole world know that you and I are friends. Someone told her that you and I had breakfast Sunday morning in the coffee shop. Again, no big secret. She came to my office yesterday to confirm a rumor about Gracie not attending any Super Bowl events for the last few days. She asked me for a comment. I said I didn't know anything about Gracie being missing. She asked me about Gracie's heroin use, and about her stint in rehab. I told her I didn't know anything about Gracie's personal life and didn't care. Said Gracie's personal life wasn't my business, nor hers."

Bob took the newspaper back. "The article didn't say anything about Gracie using drugs or going to rehab."

"I don't know where Renate found out about that, but she knew, or thought she did. I couldn't ask who the source was without clueing her in that the rumors were true. And she wouldn't have identified her source even if I had asked. She also knew that Snoop and I had reviewed the hotel security videos of Vidali passing the envelope and of Gracie leaving the hotel. That means the source was Wally, the hotel security guard."

"Do we want to complain to the hotel about him?"

"Forget it," I said. "Water under the bridge."

"Okay. Why didn't the reporter say anything about the envelope?"

"I told Renate that Gracie's agent and her attorney were sharks when it came to protecting her reputation. No one knows what was in the envelope. Apparently, I worried her a little bit, but you don't know how hard she is to scare. *Amigo*, she's tough as a two-dollar steak."

"Well, the sports reporters at the press conference had read the article. They asked me where Gracie was. They blindsided me."

"What did you tell them?"

"I told them she was visiting a friend."

"And they bought that?" I would have been surprised if any reporter believed that story, but I didn't want to rain on Bob's parade.

"They asked me who the friend was." Bob smiled. "I told them I would gladly answer their questions about football, but that my personal life and Gracie's were private."

"Nice catch," said Snoop. "Hey, sorry about the attitude, Bob. I wasn't really gonna hit you."

Bob grinned. "*Whew*. I was worried." He rotated toward me. "Now tell me about finding Gracie."

I told him how we found the *Double Scotch*. "She was five miles off Turkey Point in the middle of Biscayne Bay, anchored in eleven feet of water. That whole bay is in Biscayne National Park, but this is no job for park rangers. The only way to board the boat is at sea. Actually, at over a hundred feet long, it qualifies as a ship. The ship has a regular crew of six and Vidali and his two bodyguards could be on board. Probably most of the crew will be armed. If all of them are armed, there could be nine gunmen. We need the Coast Guard for firepower. And—since we assume she's been kidnapped—we could bring in the FBI too."

Bob walked to the glass sliders. Seeti Bay spread out in the distance, but Bob's attention was elsewhere. "We can't call the cops, Eighty-Eight."

I had had enough of Bob's BS. "Listen, you jerk. The most dangerous man in New Jersey has kidnapped your fiancée. I'll bet a steak dinner against a chocolate bar that Vidali plans to text you tomorrow afternoon using Gracie's phone. He'll include a picture of Gracie holding the front page of tomorrow's newspaper to prove she's alive. The message will demand that you lose the game or at least shave the points so Vidali wins one hundred million dollars. Do you get that? One hundred million dollars. He's killed people for a lot less than that. That's how serious he is. *Now* do you think he means business?"

Bob stood like a statue. No, more like a scarecrow. Upright, rigid, but swaying like the wind was blowing him. He faced me, then cut his eyes to Snoop. He licked his lips, but didn't speak.

"Snoop," I said, "will you give us the room?"

Snoop picked up his cup. "I'll take my coffee into the bedroom. I need to catch the news anyway." He closed the bedroom door after him.

Bob sat down like a deflated balloon, his gaze aimed toward the floor.

I sat opposite. "Okay, spit it out."

Bob's eyes filled with tears. "I bet on the game."

"You bet on your own team?"

He shrugged without looking at me.

"Bob, if that gets out, your career is in the ash can. You know that, don't you? Remember Pete Rose."

A tear spilled down Bob's cheek. He studied the floor as if the solution to his problems lay at his feet.

I patted his shoulder. "Okay, buddy, we'll figure something out. Tell me about it."

Tears flowed down both cheeks. "Last September, we played the Chargers in California in a Thursday night game." He took a deep breath. "It was week three of the season. The next week was a bye week, so the team had the weekend off. I called Gracie to meet me in Las Vegas. We had a great time. Maybe we drank a little too much." He eyeballed me. "We strolled through the sports book at the casino. They had a board with the Super Bowl odds for all thirty-two teams."

"If anyone in the sports book had recognized you, you would have been in big trouble just for being there."

He shook his head. "It was late at night—or early in the morning, depending on how you look at it. The place was mostly deserted, or I would never have gone in there. That, and the fact that Gracie and I had a second bottle of wine and a couple of after-dinner liqueurs." His gaze dropped to the floor again. "To tell the God's honest truth, Eighty-Eight, I was knee-walking drunk. You know I almost never do that. We had lost our first three games. The odds against the Jets winning the Super Bowl were a hundred to one. The odds on us even making the playoffs were three to one. But I knew those three losses were a fluke. We were a better team than the score showed. Anyway…," he stared back at the floor, "I bet ten thousand dollars on the Jets to win the Super Bowl."

"I can't believe this, Bob. I hear it, but I can't believe it." I considered slapping some sense into him, then realized it was too late; that ship had sailed. And it was named *Double Scotch*.

I moved across the room. I faced him from a safe distance. Not safe for me, but safe for him; I felt like clocking the guy. He was bigger, but I was tougher. "You've risked a fifty-million-plus dollars a year career for a lousy ten-thousand-dollar bet. You stand to make half a billion dollars over your whole career. A *half billion*. And you gambled ten thousand. What in the world were you thinking? Never mind. It's clear that you weren't thinking at all."

His voice showed a little more animation. "I told you I was drunk, Eighty-Eight."

"You say that like it's an excuse."

I gazed at the heavens. "Somebody shoot me right now."

He slammed his chair arm with a fist. "All right, goddammit. Enough. I can't change the past, and I can't afford to have the bet exposed or they'll banish me from football. I'm trapped."

I recognized the look of desperation on his face.

"It's fourth and long, Eighty-Eight, and I don't know what play to call."

I held up a hand for silence. "I'll call the play this time. Where is the ticket now?"

"In the safe in my hotel closet."

"Go get it."

"Wait here." Bob knocked twice on the bedroom door and went in. A minute later, he returned. He handed me the ticket.

I studied the piece of paper. So small, so fragile, so fatal to Bob's career if it surfaced. "One thing we could do would be to throw away the ticket and kiss the ten thousand dollars goodbye. You could pretend it never happened; it's a small loss compared to your career."

"You don't know squat about sports betting, do you?"

"I lead a sheltered life. Snoop is my expert on casinos and gambling. I'd like him to join us."

Bob shrugged and walked back to the bedroom door. He opened it. "Snoop, you wanna come in?"

Snoop carried his empty cup to the kitchen and refilled it. "What's happening?"

Our lunch arrived. We sat around the dining room table and waited until the server left.

I held up the betting ticket and glanced at Bob.

He took the ticket and passed it to Snoop. "Last September,

when the odds were a hundred to one, I bet on the Jets to win the Super Bowl."

Snoop read the ticket. "Now you wish you hadn't, right? On account of you could get banned from football for life for gambling."

"Chuck said I should destroy the ticket and pretend the bet never happened." He glanced at me. "Tell Eighty-Eight why that would be a bad idea."

Snoop grinned. "Chuck, this ticket is worth maybe a half-million dollars right now, before the game is even played."

"How so?"

"The casino will buy back any bet if the odds change. You don't have to wait for the game, when the ticket will either be worth a million bucks or nothing."

"I get it," I said. "There's a market value for the ticket before the game."

"Right." Bob spread his hands. "I don't dare sell the ticket because somebody might recognize me, and I can't keep it and collect the money after we win. It doesn't seem right to let a half-million dollars go down the toilet."

"You could donate the ticket to charity. Anonymously."

"Would a charity take gambling proceeds for a donation? They might have an ethical problem with that."

"I know one that might accept the ticket and sell it before the game starts. Would you like me to arrange it?"

Bob's whole appearance changed. He seemed to get bigger even sitting at the table. "You mean that's all I have to do to get rid of this stupid ticket? Donate it?"

"Maybe even get a tax write-off. Ask your CPA."

Bob took the ticket from Snoop's hand and placed it in mine. "Who would accept a donated gambling ticket, Eighty-Eight?"

"The Port City Rescue Mission might take it. The preacher who runs it is a friend. Let me give him a call." I called the number and switched the phone to speaker.

"Rescue Mission, Brother Jim here."

"Jim, it's Chuck McCrary. I have you on speaker phone."

"Hey, Chuck, how's it going?"

"Fine, Jim. Thanks. I have a, uh, unique item to donate to the mission."

"What is it?"

"It's a sports betting ticket from a Las Vegas Casino."

"Is it a winning ticket?"

"Not yet. The ticket is for the Jets to win the Super Bowl. It's worth a million dollars if the Jets win."

"What if they lose?"

"It'll be worthless. But right now, whoever holds the ticket can sell it back to the casino for about a half-million dollars. Will the mission take money from gambling?"

"Chuck, our mission would take money from the devil himself, then put it to good use doing God's work. How did you come by this ticket? I didn't take you for a gambling man."

"It's not mine. It belongs to someone who bought it months ago. Now that person wants to donate it to a worthy cause. I told them your rescue mission was worthy."

"Thanks, Chuck. We do our best."

"Someone you trust would have to fly to Vegas tomorrow with the ticket to cash it in. The guy who owns the ticket will pay for the flight. You have anybody you'd trust with a half-million dollars?"

"I'd trust you."

"Thanks, but I'm tied up until after the Super Bowl. Anybody else?"

"Sure. I know several ministers, priests, and rabbis. I'm sure one of them will fly it out there for me. Where is the ticket now?"

In five minutes, I had used my credit card to arrange tickets to

Las Vegas at the *will call* at the Port City airport. I put my fingerprints all over the ticket as I wrapped the betting ticket in a sheet of hotel stationery. No one could hold it to the light and read it through the envelope, and anyone dusting it for prints would only find mine and Snoop's. I stuck it in a hotel envelope and wrote "Reverend Jim Holmes, Port City Rescue Mission" on it. "Snoop, take this to the concierge desk and wait for Jim. He's on the way right now."

Snoop grinned and left the room.

Bob regarded me with a contented smile. "That's a big weight off my shoulders, Eighty-Eight."

"That's why I make the big bucks."

Bob drank iced tea. "*Now* you can call the cops."

"I've been thinking about that, Bob. A Coast Guard cutter would be the normal hostage rescue craft for a target on the high seas, but Biscayne Bay, on average, is less than ten feet deep. A cutter draws nine or ten feet and they have to be able to maneuver. The bay is too shallow. The Coast Guard will need to approach the *Double Scotch* in RB-M's."

Bob set down his burger and grabbed a French fry. "What's an RB-M?"

"Response Boat-Medium. They're forty-five feet long and draw a little over three feet of water. They cruise at thirty knots and sprint up to forty. The *Double Scotch* couldn't outrun them. RB-Ms can carry up to a dozen men. They would probably send two boats for a strike force."

"How come you know so much about the Coast Guard, Eighty-Eight?"

"I'm a boat nut. Back to the subject at hand, if the crew on the *Double Scotch* notices the Coast Guard galloping to the rescue, then we could have a hostage situation. Gracie could be injured or killed. I don't want to take that chance."

"What choice do we have?" Bob washed the French fries down with iced tea.

"I'm gonna snatch Gracie off the *Double Scotch* without the crew knowing."

"How?"

"Stealth, which means I have to operate without the Coast Guard. After I have Gracie safe, I'll sic the Coast Guard on the *Double Scotch* to arrest the crew for kidnapping."

"You'll be going against a half-dozen or more guns."

"With a bit of luck, the crew won't even see me. Again—that's why I make the big bucks."

"But what if they do see you? They'll outnumber you three or four to one."

"I consider that a target-rich environment."

TEN

By 5:30 in the afternoon, the skyscrapers in downtown Port City cast long shadows across the marina. Snoop and I ran the pre-cruise checklist on the *Gator Raider Too*. Under different circumstances, it would have been a beautiful day to appreciate the sunset. I stopped stowing gear for a moment. "Did you call Janet, Snoop?"

His voice came from the cabin. "Yeah. I told her I'd be on stakeout all night."

"You didn't tell Janet this is a rescue mission? I would have bet she wouldn't be okay with that."

Snoop carried two bottles of Diet Dr. Pepper from the cabin and handed me one. "That's why I didn't tell her."

"You've been married for what, twenty-five years?"

"Twenty-seven."

"You have two daughters."

"Yeah. One in college and one in high school."

"Janet made you retire from the cops because she was worried you'd get shot and not be there for your kids."

"Among other reasons, yeah. So?"

"The odds are fairly high that you could get shot tonight if things go south."

"We won't let them go south."

"I wish I was as confident as you."

Snoop sat in the passenger chair and opened his soda. "It's a good plan. I should know; I helped you plan it."

I took the pilot's chair and opened my own soda. "If the plan's so damned good, why didn't you tell Janet what we were going to do?"

He smirked. "I don't worry her with details."

"How will she feel if she has to come identify your body at the Miami-Dade morgue?"

Snoop reached across the walkway and squeezed my shoulder. "Chuck, just because I'm not a cop anymore doesn't mean I feel any different about right and wrong. I want to make the world a better place, just like you." He took a drink and set his can in the drink holder.

"Yeah, but I don't have any dependents. There's no one who counts on me."

"How about Clint?"

Clint Watkins was my informal foster son, more like a younger brother. I'd found him on the street as a homeless teenage dropout. He had been a witness in a case I handled. I took a liking to him and, since he had no other family to speak of, I decided to send him through a private high school. "I've already spoken to my grandparents. They'll take care of him if it comes to that. You're changing the subject. Janet and the girls depend on you."

"I have a pot full of life insurance, and the girls are almost grown. Janet would be a rich widow."

"Janet and the girls will find that cold comfort if you're dead."

"Yeah, and they'll be plenty mad at you too if I get myself killed." He took another drink.

"For all we know, Snoop, Gracie could've been the one who thought this whole thing up."

"If I didn't know better, bud, I'd think you wanted to talk me out of this."

I ignored his comment. "And Bob isn't blameless in this." I chugged more Diet Dr. Pepper.

"Nope, betting on his own team proves that he ain't the sharpest knife in the drawer." He pointed a finger at me. "But his heart's in the right place. If he had bet on the other team...Well, that I would have trouble with."

"You think two flawed lovers are worth risking your life?"

Snoop paused a minute. "Why are *you* here, Chuck?"

"It's what I do. I could no more change that than I could become a unicorn. In grade school, I defended smaller kids from bullies. I've always been the knight errant."

"Well, there you go. It's what guys like us do."

"I'm happy to have you, buddy." I finished my drink, crushed the aluminum can, and dropped it in the recycle sack. "Let's stow the rest of our gear."

I fired up the twin engines and felt the power vibrate up through my feet. It was almost like I was absorbing that power to use later. Almost.

By the time the sun set at 6:05 p.m., we had cleared the breakwater at the end of the Port City ship channel. I pointed the *Raider's* bow south and shoved the throttles to the firewall. In seconds, she rose up on plane. The *Double Scotch* lay at anchor sixty-five miles away if I could fly, but there were several islands between the ship channel and there. We had to race at least eighty miles around them to reach her. I could make the first seventy-five miles in four hours. The last five miles, we would play by ear.

At nine o'clock, my radar showed Elliott Key angling back to the west. We were two miles out in the Atlantic Ocean, but the water on either side of the channel was only a foot deep. If we grounded out here, we would have to wait for high tide. The timing of the whole mission would be screwed.

I steered straight south and watched for the navigation beacons at the entrance to Caesar's Creek, the passage between Elliott Key and Old Rhodes Key. I shifted the throttles to idle. *Gator Raider Too* dropped off plane and surfed on her own wake as the wave we had created seized the boat and swept us ahead. We followed the red and green beacons through the narrow channel into the south end of Biscayne Bay, five miles south of the *Double Scotch's* last reported position.

My radar showed the target on my screen. The *Double Scotch* peeked above the horizon like a medieval castle waiting to be stormed by Vikings.

I called Marie Leonard on the satellite phone I had bought that afternoon. "Candle One, Archer here. We have reached waypoint number one. Move out."

"We're jumping off now, sergeant. Catch you on the flip side."

This wasn't Afghanistan; this was Biscayne Bay, for crissakes. What could possibly go wrong?

My radar placed the *Double Scotch* two miles ahead. It was 11:00 p.m. and the moon wouldn't rise for a couple of hours. I killed the lights. In five minutes, our eyes would fully dilate. The *Raider* cruised at just above idle speed. I glanced back at our wake. Without the moon, it would be invisible from fifty yards or more.

I made out the mega-yacht's anchor lights in the distance. The wind was four knots from the northeast. The ship must've been swinging on a single anchor. She pointed straight into the wind, as I'd hoped. So far, so good.

Snoop pointed. "One o'clock. There are the lights. Yeah, there's two of them." The two helicopters had risen over the horizon as they cruised south from Biscayne Key toward Elliott Key.

I handed the phone to Snoop. "Tell them to hang where they are for now."

"Roger." He punched the satellite phone. "Candle One, Archer says to hang there for now."

"Roger, Archer."

We angled off to the northwest to cross the *Double Scotch's* stern a half mile behind. The anchor lights on its bow and stern drew closer together. I used them like a nautical range marker. The bow light disappeared first. I continued until I had lined up the *Double Scotch's* stern light with its masthead light. Now we approached from directly astern. Right on target.

I moved the throttles back to idle. "Call Dick. Tell him to start dancing."

"Candle Two, Archer says to start dancing."

I pointed straight ahead. "We're three hundred yards off, Snoop. We'll be there in three minutes."

Ahead, the two helicopters lit their strobe lights and moved closer to the ship, approaching from the bow. From our angle, they lined up with the ship's two visible anchor lights. The strobe lights rose and fell like the opposite ends of a seesaw. It was a mesmerizing dance in the night sky—I hoped. I had instructed Marie and Dick to stay at least five hundred yards away from the ship and to remain above five hundred feet. I tried to convince myself they were in no danger. Even if someone on the *Double Scotch* tried to shoot them, they were out of handgun range. If the shooter had a rifle, which I doubted, it should be an impossible shot with the 'copters bobbing up and down. And, hopefully, the shooter wouldn't know the distance to the target. At least, that was the plan.

For two minutes, the helicopters danced in front of the ship. The *thump-thump-thump* of the choppers sent a shudder across my back. *This isn't Afghanistan and you aren't in the Triple Seven anymore*, I reminded myself. I heard the slight change in pitch when each of the pilots twisted their cyclics from falling to rising and vice versa. *You're not in Iraq either, dogface.*

Snoop scrambled onto the bow, line in hand. He glanced back at me. I could barely make him out in the darkness.

We reached fifty yards from the *Double Scotch*. I called Dick on the sat phone. "Archer to Candle Two."

"Candle Two here."

"Phase two," I said.

Thirty seconds later, I dropped the left throttle to neutral and spun the wheel to the left. I killed both engines, and the boat coasted into a curve. The bow swung across the swim platform and the *Raider* drifted sideways toward the ship.

Snoop stepped onto the swim platform and snubbed the line to a cleat. He moved to catch the stern line I tossed him and snubbed it at the other end of the platform.

I grabbed both our gear bags and stepped onto the platform.

The Vikings had crossed the drawbridge and had breached the castle gate.

I pulled my Ka-Bar knife and slashed a three-foot rip in the Zodiac's fabric. No one could chase us in that tender. The one on the bow was smaller and would take longer to launch.

I handed Snoop his bag. "Showtime."

The lounges, salon, and dining facilities were on the main deck. We climbed the steps from the swim platform. One of the helicopters' engines roared louder, then the other. I couldn't see them from the stern, but in three minutes, the two choppers would skyrocket towards the stars and head out to sea. The clock was ticking.

We crept along the walkway outside the main salon and slid open the door at the front. Snoop stood guard at the top of the stairs, and I descended to the lower deck to search the guest staterooms.

Snoop and I figured that Graciela would be in one of four staterooms on the lower deck. The first stateroom was dark. Closing the door behind me, I inhaled through my nose. Nothing. No perfume, no aftershave, no deodorant smell.

I cracked the door to number two. I recognized the same perfume I'd smelled in Bob and Gracie's hotel suite and in her rental car. I slipped into the room. Gracie must've gone to the bow to stare at the helicopters. She had to be bored out of her mind after so many days on the yacht and, like the crew, she would want to see anything out of the ordinary. I had counted on that distraction to allow us to board the mega-yacht unnoticed.

After stepping into a closet, I closed the door and peered through the louvers. Too late, I noticed the footprints of my size-twelve boat shoes imprinted on the plush carpet. Anyone coming in with Gracie would have to be blind not to notice.

I heard the rustle of clothing and soft footsteps outside. The latch on the stateroom door clicked. Shadows from the opening door moved across the carpet. The latch clicked again.

I watched Gracie's legs from the knees down as she walked to the bar. The refrigerator door opened.

I opened the closet door and stepped onto the plush carpet. "Gracie," I whispered.

She jumped back and dropped a bottle of Pinot Grigio. It rolled across the carpet. "Holy Christ!"

I picked up the wine bottle and set it on the bar. "I'm here to take you home."

Gracie wore the same outfit I had noticed on the hotel security video when she disappeared from the parking garage. "Chuck! How did you get here?"

"I've come to take you home. Do you have sneakers? Those spike heels won't do."

She studied her shoes. "How did you get here?"

"I have a boat tied to the swim platform at the stern. Do you have sneakers? If not, you'll have to go barefoot."

"I have sneakers." She moved to the closet and pointed at a pair of boat shoes on a shelf. "But I'm fine. Why do you want to take me home?"

I had been afraid of this. Gracie didn't know moonshine from moon pies.

I took her hands in mine. "Gracie, after the Super Bowl is over, Vicente Vidali won't need you anymore. You're an unnecessary complication because you could testify against him in return for a lesser sentence. He'll kill you and use your body for shark bait."

She scoffed and yanked her hands free. "This isn't a gangster movie, Chuck. This is the real world. Even a man like Vic wouldn't do that. I'm merely his guest for a couple of days."

"Gracie, look at me."

She did.

"There's a reason I'm wearing this bulletproof vest." I patted my body armor. "Vidali won't want to lose you. I'm guessing he gave orders to the crew not to let you leave. That's why he anchored the yacht five miles off the coast. He didn't want you to be tempted to swim for shore."

"Well, he's not very smart then. I don't swim that well anyway."

"Vidali will threaten to kill you unless Bob throws the Super Bowl game. Believe me when I say this: Bob will not throw the game. But whether Vidali's threats work or not, you're dead once he doesn't need you anymore."

"I don't believe you. Vic promised me."

"Promised you what?"

"That everything would be all right. That we'd make a lot of money."

"Vidali kills people who are inconvenient to him. He doesn't care what happens to you. In fact, he prefers you dead—you pose less risk that this scheme comes back to bite him in the ass." I grabbed her hands again. "He. Will. Kill. You."

Her mouth opened, closed, opened again.

Was she so far gone, or drunk, or drug-addled that she couldn't recognize her helpless position?

Tears gathered in her eyes. Her lower lip trembled. She nodded and the tears spilled over her cheeks.

She took a suitcase from the closet and set it on the bed. She grabbed a hot pink, raw silk jacket from the closet and began to fold it.

"Gracie, we can't take anything but you. Leave everything else. Wear the sneakers. We don't have much time."

She eyed the open closet, probably having a hard time coming to terms with abandoning her clothes.

"Gracie, you can replace your clothes. Bob can't replace your life. Now put on the damn sneakers."

She did.

I removed a Kevlar armored vest from the gear bag and handed it to her. "I'll help you with this."

"My God. That's a bulletproof vest."

"I hope so, and I hope you won't need it." I helped her into the vest, tugged the tabs to snug it to her slim figure. It was still too big. *Oh, well, it's the thought that counts. Better than nothing.*

Cracking the door, I heard footsteps creak above her cabin.

Someone was patrolling the main deck. The crew cabins had their own stairway down from the bow. I had counted on the crew retiring for the night after the helicopter show was over.

"Was the whole crew at the front of the boat watching the helicopters?"

"Yeah, I guess…Was that thing with the helicopters your idea?"

"*Shh*. Keep your voice down. Yes, I arranged that to distract the crew while we boarded the ship."

"We?"

"My partner Snoop Snopolski is with me. Middle-aged guy, former cop, dressed like me—also in a bulletproof vest."

I thought out loud. "Now someone on the crew is making one last walk around the deck before he turns in for the night—I hope. How many others are on board?"

"There's a steward, a pilot, a cook, and a few deckhands. Maybe half a dozen in all."

"Are you sure?"

She scowled at me. "No, I'm not sure. I don't pay attention to servants. The only people I've seen the last three days are the steward and the cook. Oh, and another guy, maybe a deckhand or something."

"There could be five or six that you saw. Is Vidali onboard?"

"He left a few days ago. Tuesday, I think it was." She finished tying her shoes and grabbed her purse. "All the days run together. I'm not even sure what today is."

"It's Friday." I glanced at my watch. "For ten more minutes. What about Dante and Pistolet, Vidali's bodyguards? They on board?"

"Dante and another creepy guy left with Vic. I haven't seen any of them since they left."

"Good. That's less people to fight."

"Fight? We have to fight?" She lifted a hand to her cheek.

"Not you, us. That's why Snoop and I are sneaking around here. That's why the bulletproof vests."

I peeked through the door again. "Let's go. Keep quiet."

We climbed the stairs to the front of the salon on the main deck. There was a ruckus from the walkway outside. I touched Gracie's arm and whispered, "Go through the main salon and out the back door to the lounge. Go down those stairs at the rear. My boat is tied to the swim platform. Get onboard. You'll find life jackets in the cabin. Put one on *over* the vest. Do not take the vest off. Stay in the cabin out of sight. Do not turn on any lights on the boat. Just wait in the dark. Snoop and I will be along soon. Now go."

I slid a Glock 17 from my shoulder holster, dropped the gear bag to the deck, and grabbed a blackjack from the bag. I glanced to make sure that Gracie was moving. She wasn't.

"Gracie, get out of here. Now."

She ran off through the salon.

I charged through the door to the walkway. Snoop was wrestling with the crewman whose footsteps I'd heard. The two men rolled on the narrow walkway, bounced between the fiberglass hull on one side and the stainless-steel braces and cables of the outside railing.

"*¡Ayuda me!*" the crewman shouted. *"Help me!"*

I clubbed him twice with the blackjack, dropped it to the deck to free my right hand, and grabbed him by the shoulders. I heaved him off Snoop. "Help me throw him over."

We heaved the groggy crewman over the railing.

"You think he'll drown, Chuck?"

"If I hit him hard enough, yeah. There's a half dozen more crew still kicking around. We'd better hurry." I abandoned the blackjack and sprinted through the salon; Snoop was close behind. We followed the route I had sent Gracie down. I snatched up the gear bag from the spot I had dropped it.

"Where's the girl?"

"Should be on the boat by now."

We pounded through the salon to the back lounge. I dodged the hot tub and hurdled over the six feet of steps that descended toward the swim platform. The fiberglass deck cracked with a bang like a gunshot under my weight. It wasn't designed for a two-hundred-pound man to jump on it. Snoop landed beside me and fiberglass splinters flew through the air. The deck split in the middle, loosening the attached swim platform.

As I clambered across the swim platform, it shuddered and shifted beneath my feet. I grabbed the rail of my boat to regain my footing.

Gracie had flicked on the cabin light. She stood in the doorway. *Did she have a death wish?*

I vaulted the rail. "Get back in the cabin and close the door," I shouted. "And turn out that damn light." I wound the engines. No time to blow the bilge.

As Snoop sprang from the broken deck to the swim platform, it broke in two pieces. He untied the bow line and threw it over the railing onto the boat. He took two quick steps toward the stern line and halted at the edge of the broken swim platform. The line's other end dangled from one stainless-steel brace.

My heart sank. The stern line was still snubbed to the cleat on the broken platform, now awash in Biscayne Bay. There was no way for Snoop to reach it.

"Forget it, Snoop. Jump on."

"We're still tied to the ship."

"You can cut the line from this end. Jump, dammit!"

A bullet shattered the side window of the *Raider*, not two feet from where I stood at the wheel.

I snapped three shots at a gunman crouched beside the hot tub. The hot tub cracked, then broke open. Water flooded the deck and sloshed down the steps. The gunman ducked for cover.

Snoop jumped onboard, and I slammed the throttles to the firewall. The *Raider* leapt six feet and jolted to a stop, knocking Snoop off his feet. I had hoped the boat's lunge would break the stern line or rip the cleat out of my hull. No such luck.

I hit the throttles again and the broken swim platform shrieked and wrenched away from the steel support, still tethered by the stern line. The *Raider* staggered away from the mega-yacht, towing the broken swim platform like a fallen water skier that wouldn't let go of the tow rope.

Snoop struggled to get up, bouncing on the deck which bucked like a trampoline.

A spotlight on the sun deck of the yacht came to life and bathed the *Raider* in its harsh glare. More shots rang out and the windshield shattered. I felt wallops on my back as two more shots punched my body armor. I pivoted toward the yacht, and another crew member joined the first gunman. I fired at the men hunkered by the ruined hot tub. One man's pistol fell to the deck and he rolled down the steps, his body tangling in the wreckage of the swim platform.

I fired again. My Glock clicked empty, forcing me to let go of the wheel to slam in a fresh magazine. I didn't care which direction the *Raider* moved, so long as it was away from that spotlight. The *Raider* gained a little speed and stabilized. Snoop managed to maneuver to his knees next to the stern line.

Two more men appeared on the sun deck. Gracie was wrong about there being a half-dozen crewmen. I had counted five so far, and none of them acted like a steward or a cook. I wondered how many more we could fight off. This had become a Whack-A-Mole game.

The *B-r-r-r-rap* of automatic weapon fire ripped from the sun deck. The muzzle flash lit the back of the yacht like a strobe light. The *Raider* shuddered as another burst raked the stern. I recognized the distinctive chatter of an M4A1 carbine. I'd heard that sound often in Iraq and Afghanistan—too often.

I snapped off several more rounds at the men on the sun deck. "Snoop, they've got serious fire power."

"Tell me something I don't know." Snoop rapid-fired at the men on the main deck.

I fired again at the shooters on the sun deck. One fell and one ran away. Another gunman changed magazines.

The *Raider* lumbered through the sea, a wounded whale straining to escape the harpoon line. I fought the wheel. The wreckage of the swim platform dragged like a sea anchor on my starboard cleat.

"Snoop, cut the stern line. Don't get your fingers caught."

More bullets smacked the boat on the starboard side. Fiberglass shards bounced off my right leg where the shots came through the hull.

As Snoop opened the clasp knife, a bullet hit him and spun him around. The knife skidded across the deck, its blade flashing in the spotlight.

I didn't spot any blood; maybe the bullet had struck his armored vest. Breathing a prayer, I yanked the throttles back to idle and released the wheel. I rapid-fired at the spotlight. One shot hit the light. It exploded like a small grenade.

Snoop lunged toward the knife and trapped it. He rolled toward the gunwale, rose to his knees, and sawed frantically on the taut stern line until it parted. "It's clear. Hit it."

I spun the wheel left and slammed the throttles full open.

The *Raider* jumped straight ahead as the swim platform fell away to our rear. I straightened the wheel, expecting her to leap up on plane.

She didn't leap; she lumbered. Something was wrong with the *Raider*.

ELEVEN

We motored into the darkness, and the gunfire stopped. The ship fell a hundred yards behind. I slipped the engines into neutral and grabbed a flashlight from a shallow locker on the cockpit wall.

I peered through the broken windshield into the pitch-black night.

The cabin door opened and the interior light played across the cockpit. Graciela climbed the steps. "Why have we stopped?"

"We're still in range of the shooters on the yacht. Go below and douse the cabin light."

"Why did you stop the boat?"

"Something's wrong with her. Go below and douse the light."

She didn't move. "What's wrong with it?"

"I don't know yet." I shined the flashlight on the bow.

A hail of automatic gunfire splashed around us. I switched off the flashlight. "For crissakes, Gracie, douse the goddam light. We're still sitting ducks."

She jumped into the cabin and slammed the door. Gracie may

have known her way around the elite salons in New York City, but she didn't have the common sense God gave a housecat.

"I've got to move farther from the yacht, Snoop. They're anchored in eleven feet of water. If we make it another half-mile west, the water is seven feet deep. We'll be safe."

Snoop sat across from me. His seat creaked as he pivoted to contemplate the distant lights of the *Double Scotch*. "We're safe until they remember they have another *Zodiac*. They'll load gunmen into the other boat and come after us."

We staggered west for ten long minutes.

I heard the cabin door open. At least Gracie had switched the light off. She climbed the steps to the cockpit and stood in the darkness between Snoop and me.

The depth gauge said six feet. I tried the flashlight again. "The bow line is supposed to be up there, Snoop. I don't see it."

"What's a bow line?" Gracie asked.

This was not a great time to interrupt me, but I felt a little guilty for shouting at her earlier. I tried to reply civilly. "The rope fastened to the front of the boat to tie us up at the dock."

Snoop had thrown the line onto the bow after he untied it. Where was it now? I peered closer. "The end loop is still fastened to the cleat. The line must be trailing in the water. My mooring lines are forty feet long. The *Raider* is thirty feet long. The bow line could have wrapped around a prop."

Snoop opened the windshield hatch and stepped onto the cabin roof. "I'll climb up front and pull the rope in."

Snoop tugged on the line. About five feet came up, then it snagged. "It won't come any farther, bud. It's caught on something." He jerked again.

"Untie the front end and bring the line to me. Gracie, if you won't stay in the cabin, at least sit over there out of the way." I pointed at the padded bench in the stern. "By the way, Gracie, this is Snoop. Snoop, Gracie."

I tugged on the line and another ten feet came up, but something under the back of the boat was holding it. "It may have wrapped around a prop. Take this line and keep tension on it. I'll reverse the props."

I eased the starboard prop into reverse and held my breath. The line rose from the water as Snoop tugged on it. I shined the light on the end. It was frayed where it had wrapped around the prop.

Graciela stepped over and grabbed the end of the line. "The propeller did *that*?"

"Yep. Now we're clear. Sit down, Gracie." I slipped the engines in gear and the *Raider* moved ahead. I pushed a little more throttle and the speed picked up, but not enough. It was still sluggish.

"It still doesn't feel right, Snoop. I'm going to hit it. Hang on." I shoved the throttles all the way. The *Raider* waddled ahead, but wouldn't get on plane.

I eased the throttles back to idle speed and handed Snoop the flashlight. "Look in the bilge."

Snoop opened the hatch and shined the light inside. "Chuck, I smell gasoline, and there's a slick on the bilge water."

I shifted the boat into neutral. "Hand me that light. Geez, that's gasoline floating on the surface. A bullet must've hit our gas tank. The bilge has too much water in it. Bullets must've hit us at the waterline."

Snoop took the light from me. "Which are we gonna do first, bud, sink or explode?"

"What!?" Gracie shrieked. "We're going to explode?"

"Sit down, Gracie. We're not going to explode. Snoop was kidding." I gave him a glare that would freeze a river.

He shrugged sheepishly. "Sorry."

I killed the engines. "Cut up an extra life vest and stick the pieces in the holes you can find. Fasten them with duct tape. Then grab the biggest pan you can find in the galley and bail."

My original plan was to rescue Gracie without being seen, then head to Convoy Point Marina, five miles west of the *Double Scotch*. We would moor in a transient slip until daylight, Snoop would drive Gracie back to the hotel in a rental car. I would refuel and take the *Raider* back home to Port City. Easy as Key Lime Pie. I didn't want Graciela out of my sight or Snoop's until I delivered her to Bob. So far, she had acted like a kid who would have wandered off chasing squirrels.

My Special Forces instructor used to quote German military strategist Helmuth von Moltke: "No battle plan survives contact with the enemy." Von Moltke was an optimist.

The GPS navigation screen showed our position. Strobe lights low in the western sky marked the Turkey Point Nuclear Generating Station. I scanned the horizon for the flashing white light that marked Pelican Bank. "Fortunately, we're now in…six feet of water. If we sink, Gracie, you can climb to the roof of the cabin and your feet won't even get wet."

I switched on the marine radio. "Coast Guard Miami, this is the *Gator Raider Too*. We have taken damage to our vessel and need assistance. Do you have a landline I can call?"

"This is Sector Miami, Skipper. I read you five by five over the radio. What is your location and situation?"

"Miami, we just rescued a kidnap victim from a mega-yacht named *Double Scotch* with half a dozen armed men on board. They could be monitoring the radio. Please give me your direct landline number."

"Roger that, Skipper." He gave me the telephone number.

I called him on the satellite phone and gave Sector Miami our GPS coordinates.

"Got it. What's this about you rescuing a kidnap victim?"

I filled him in on what we had done.

"Roger that, Skipper. We're scrambling two response teams now. Don life jackets and kill your engines. You don't want to take a chance on a spark igniting the gasoline vapors. And no smoking, of course."

"Already did that, Coast Guard."

"What's your depth, Skipper?"

I glanced at the depth gauge. We had drifted farther west. "Four feet. If we sink, we're in no immediate danger unless the bad guys come after us in their Zodiac lifeboat." I gave him a brief status report and the location of the *Double Scotch*. "They had at least six armed men on board. We may have shot two or three of them. They shot up my boat and punctured my gas tank. We made it a half-mile before we had to stop. They'll either launch the Zodiac to come after us, or they'll weigh anchor and try to escape before you get there."

"Stand by, Skipper…Skipper, it'll take us an hour-and-a-half to reach you."

"How soon could a helicopter get here?"

There was a long pause.

"Fifteen minutes if we had one available, which we don't. The helo is searching for a missing sailboat off Pompano Beach."

"That's too long anyway. If they come after us in the dingy, they're already underway. We'll defend ourselves. But you might want to dispatch some RB-Ms to round up the bad guys on the *Double Scotch*. Tell them to wear body armor. The kidnappers have automatic weapons."

"Roger that, Skipper. You want me to stay on the radio with you?"

I heard the Zodiac's engine in the distance. The dingy was a twenty-one-foot Zodiac. Its dark shape streaked through the shimmering reflection of the rising half-moon, straight toward us.

"Sorry, Miami. We're gonna be busy. The bad guys are on their way."

"Get below, Gracie."

"What's happening, Chuck?"

"Vidali's crew is coming to take you back. Or kill us all. They don't care which. You'll be safer below while Snoop and I do our thing."

I pulled a fresh magazine from my pocket to replace the used one in my Glock. "Load a fresh magazine in your pistol, Snoop."

"Already did."

"Aim for their hull. If we punch a hole in the inflatable, they'll worry more about sinking and less about shooting."

"They're three hundred yards off, Chuck. If they're smart, they'll stop a hundred yards out and spray us with automatic gunfire like a fire hose. They could make up in sheer fire power what they'd lack in accuracy."

"That's what you or I would do, but let's hope they're not that smart. Their boat is bouncing like a kid on a trampoline. That hurts their aim. And we have a relatively stable shooting platform. When they reach a hundred yards out, aim at their hull. We'll hit them before they come off plane, while the boat is bouncing in the air. Makes a bigger target."

We waited.

The Zodiac's engine noise grew louder. The hull smacked the surface with each leap across the small waves.

"Wait…wait…now." Snoop and I both rapid-fired all seventeen shells in our magazines. We replaced the spent magazines with fresh ones. Good thing we had come loaded for bear.

The Zodiac roared closer. It bounced once…again…

I rapid-fired six shots then stopped after the Zodiac's engine died. It wallowed in the moonlight, rocking back and forth thirty yards off our stern. I heard splashes as men jumped off the boat which was dimly visible in the moonlight.

"How many did you see jump, Snoop?" I whispered.

"Not sure, maybe three. What are they gonna do?"

"The water's four feet deep, so they're wading instead of swimming. They could wade to shore after they kill us. That's for sure. We're sitting ducks, silhouetted against the white hull of our boat. Put Gracie in the V-berth in the bow. Then guard her like the crown jewels."

I slammed another full magazine in my Glock, shrugged out of the life jacket, and slipped over the side into the cool water. The water was chest deep. My armored vest was the non-floating kind. Its added weight gave me traction on the sandy bottom. I was glad I'd worn my sneak-around-in-the-dark clothes, including the black watch cap I had worn to skulk around Mango Island.

Contemplating the sinking Zodiac, I waded toward the north.

Two men splashed in the moonlight about fifty feet to the southeast. The same distance as a shooting range. They were shorter than me, and only their heads and shoulders stuck above the water. That and the guns they held in the air.

I hate head shots. The targets are too small. The two men were barely lit by a half-moon, so I couldn't see well. When I fired, they would spot my muzzle flash. I couldn't ask for a do-over.

Taking a Weaver stance, I waited for the wave trough. I fired twice at the man closest to me. I think the second shell hit his head, but I had to duck beneath the waves before the second shooter fired back.

I heard a faint burst of automatic gunfire and felt shock waves from bullets striking the water above my head. The gunfire stopped.

I stood, drained the gun barrel for a couple of seconds, and fired twice at the faint outline of the second man's head. A short burst of automatic gunfire answered, but the muzzle flash aimed into the air. The machine gun fell silent.

Was there a third man? If so, where?

The fiberglass hull creaked behind me.

The third man was climbing onto my swim platform. I waited until he stood. He stepped over the gunwale, and I shot him three times in center mass. He collapsed into the cockpit of the *Raider*.

I waded to the Zodiac. Air trapped in its inflated collar kept it from sinking. The boat wallowed with its stern on the bottom, pinned by the propeller stuck in the sand.

A man slumped at the wheel in the disjointed relaxation of death. The reflective tape on the life jacket spelled *Double Scotch*. In the moonlight, the blood on his head and neck appeared black. His head rolled back and forth with the rocking of the boat, like he was saying *no…no…no…* over and over again.

The coppery fresh blood smell got to me. It didn't matter whether Snoop's bullet had hit him or mine; he was dead at my hand, along with at least three others. I faced away and vomited into the water. I ducked my head and rinsed my mouth. The clean salt water helped.

I moved to a spot fifty feet from both the Zodiac and the *Raider* and waited in the water in case any more invaders were lurking. The water temperature was above seventy degrees. I wasn't worried about hypothermia.

After a few minutes, Snoop hollered, "Chuck, I don't spot anyone moving in the moonlight. I think we're clear."

"Coast Guard Miami, this is the *Gator Raider Too*."

"This is Coast Guard Miami. Go ahead, Skipper."

"We have four casualties on the Zodiac that attacked us."

"How bad are they hurt?"

"As bad as it gets."

"Any survivors?"

"Well, all of us good guys are okay."

"Roger that. Stand by. Our response boats are about an hour out. You okay there?"

"We're good."

"Are you afloat?"

"Yeah, I got in the water and plugged the bullet holes with life jacket foam and duct tape. We bailed most of the water and spilled gasoline out of the bilge, but we still need a tow."

"Roger."

An hour later, I observed the distant lights of two Coast Guard RB-Ms arrive at the *Double Scotch*. Sound carries well over the water. I heard their loud-hailer address the ship, but couldn't make out the words from a half-mile away. The Coast Guard would notify the ship that it would be boarded. That must've been what I heard. Five minutes later, an RB-M headed our way.

The boat pulled alongside. "Permission to come aboard, Captain."

"Yes, please do. I'm Chuck McCrary."

"I'm Chief Petty Officer Mitchell."

We shook hands.

"I'd like to make sure your vessel is seaworthy before we attach a tow line."

"I doubt it's seaworthy, but I know you have to make your own inspection. Can I help, or should I get out of the way?"

Chief Mitchell smiled. "You can stand over there if you like, Captain. I'll inspect the bilge." He shined a light inside the hatch. "Seems like you have everything under control, considering what you had to work with. We'll drop a pump down there before we tow you." He pointed to a crewman on the RB-M. "Carver, get a pump down here."

"Aye, aye, Chief."

———

An hour later, I had a cell signal. Kickoff was less than forty hours away. The quarterback needed his sleep. I texted Bob instead of calling.

We have Gracie, unharmed and safe with us. We are exhausted and need to sleep now. Call me at your convenience in the morning.

I handed Gracie my phone, and she called her parents. From the side of the conversation I heard, I knew there were happy tears on both ends of the call. Gracie handed me the phone. "My parents want to speak to you and Snoop."

"Mr. and Mrs. Perez, I have you on speaker. Snoop is here with me."

"Chuck, you and Snoop saved our daughter's life. Evangelina and I wanted to thank you both for rescuing our little girl. Graciela tells us the Coast Guard is towing you to shore?"

"Yes, sir. To Convoy Point Marina, near Homestead."

"How long until you arrive?"

"About an hour."

"There shouldn't be any traffic this time of night. Evangelina and I will meet you there. Should I bring a bottle of champagne?"

"That's the best idea I've heard tonight."

I called Miyo. The phone rang four times. "Well, Chuck, I said call anytime day or night. I guess 3:30 in the morning qualifies as anytime."

"We have Gracie. She's safe with me. I knew you'd want to know."

"What happened? How did you find her?"

"That's a long story."

I heard her yawn. "Why don't you take me up on that raincheck for a cocktail sometime soon, and tell me all about it. Now that I know Gracie is safe, I'll sleep better. Right now, I can't keep my eyes open."

I made phone calls, woke a couple of guys up, and gave a few orders.

A half-hour later, we entered the navigation channel to Convoy Point. Car headlights on the shore flashed their high beams. Seconds later, my phone rang. It was Gracie's parents. Thirty minutes later, the disheveled supermodel left in her parents' car.

Then I fell into the berth in my boat, asleep before my head hit the pillow. My last thought was that Teflon Vic was still out there. He wouldn't take this lying down.

TWELVE

B ob called at seven on the dot. "Where's Gracie?"

"You're welcome, Bob, and I'm glad you're safe too." I carried my phone out to the dock so I wouldn't wake Snoop. We had moored on the end of the finger pier and the sunrise shimmered over Biscayne Bay.

He laughed. "Sorry, Eighty-Eight. Thanks for rescuing Gracie. Where is she?"

"Her parents met us at Convoy Point Marina at 4:30 this morning and took her home." I yawned and scanned like a searchlight for any place I could score a coffee.

"Are you and Snoop okay?"

"We're sleepy, but we're okay. I can't say the same for a half dozen of Vidali's crewmen."

"What happened to them?"

"They're arguing with St. Peter about whether he should let them through the Pearly Gates."

"You killed them?"

"At least four that I know of. Snoop and I wounded at least two more on the yacht, and we threw one guy overboard. You owe me big time for boat repairs. I'll tell you all about it later." I stifled a yawn.

"What about Vidali?"

"He wasn't on board, and that worries me." I spied the harbormaster's office and walked toward it. Maybe I could find coffee there.

"Tell me about the rescue."

By the time I finished sharing my harrowing tale of heroism and how Snoop and I had rescued the damsel in distress from the clutches of the evil mobster, I'd reached the harbormaster's office. The door sign said it would open at 8:00 a.m. Could I survive another hour without coffee? What if the harbormaster didn't have a coffee maker? Would Western Civilization come to an end?

I finished my story. "We got to the marina at 4:30 this morning."

"Well, we can all breathe easier now, right?"

"Nope, we can't."

"Why not?"

"*Amigo*, I'll explain everything to you after I bring Gracie there. In the meantime, don't leave your hotel room without a police escort. I've called the Port City cops to arrange it."

I glanced around the marina and spotted a cabin cruiser named *My Vacation Home* out of Norfolk, Virginia, on the next finger pier. An elderly couple sat on deck drinking coffee and enjoying the sunrise. I waved at them; they waved back. I walked in their direction. I was not above begging.

"What am I supposed to do until you and Gracie get here?"

"I called a buddy at the Port City Police Department and asked her to beef up security around your hotel and around your practice facility. I also assigned two of my operatives to guard Gracie's parents' house."

"At least Gracie's safe."

"No, she's not."

"I don't get it."

"Like I said, I'll explain after I bring Gracie to your hotel."

"How long will that take?"

"Don't you have practice today?"

"Christ, you're right. I guess you'll be here before I finish practice."

"Yeah. Yesterday, I arranged to have a rental car waiting for us here, but the car company left the keys with the harbormaster's office. The office opens at 8:00. Why don't you call Gracie and tell her I'll pick her up at nine? Call her parents' home number. She doesn't have a cellphone."

I crossed the last ten yards toward the Virginia cruiser. The smell of coffee brewing attracted me like steel to a magnet.

I reached the boat with the couple from Virginia. "Can you help a poor, sleepy pilgrim who is desperate for a cup of coffee?"

The Virginia couple summered in Norfolk and wintered on their boat. From fall to spring, they cruised the coast from Cape Hatteras to Tarpon Springs. Steve, the husband, described himself as "a recovering accountant." His wife Shirley had been an operating room nurse at Sentara Norfolk General Hospital before retiring. Nice folks who made good, strong coffee.

I had finished my second cup with them when my phone rang. It was Horatio Perez.

"Good morning, Horatio. I was about to call you. I posted two bodyguards in front of your house in case Vidali tries to kidnap Graciela again. I'll be there in another hour to take her back to the hotel."

"Something's wrong, Chuck."

"What is it?"

"Gordo is missing?"

"Gordo, Graciela's dog?"

"Yes, he's missing."

"Could he jump the fence? Dig his way out?"

"No, he's too old to jump. He's disappeared. Someone snatched him. Whoever took him left the gate open."

"Could you or Evangelina have left the gate open?"

"No. The padlock for the gate was lying on the grass. They used bolt cutters."

"When was the last time you saw Gordo?"

"Last night before we went to bed. He sleeps outside unless Graciela is here. I put him in the backyard about ten o'clock."

"When did you learn he was gone?"

"Just now. Graciela woke up and went to feed Gordo." His voice broke. "He's gone... vanished."

Snoop and I searched down the driveway to the back fence. The padlock lay in the grass next to the open gate.

"This is the way I found it," said Horatio.

Gracie's eyes were red. It could have been from a lack of sleep, but I knew she'd been crying. "Who would want to kidnap an old dog like Gordo? It's not like he's a show dog. He's not worth any money. Why would someone do that?"

Was it a coincidence that a dognapper grabbed Gordo while a kidnapper had grabbed Gordo's owner? Rule Seven: *There is no such thing as a coincidence.*

Then it hit me: Teflon Vic was a gambler who cheated to get the winning hand. He would do anything to swing the odds in his favor.

Vidali had grabbed Gordo to keep Gracie in line. But did he grab the dog while Gracie was still on the *Double Scotch*? No, Gracie's father had seen Gordo at ten last night. Vidali's crew must have called him immediately after we escaped. He had organized the dognapping in the space of a couple of hours—the work of a calculating, ruthless enemy.

I faced Gracie and Horatio. "My guess is that one of Vidali's thugs grabbed him."

Gracie teared up. "But why?"

I knew why, but I didn't have the heart to tell her. I hoped I was wrong.

After all three of us were in the rental car I had picked up at Convoy Point, I turned to Snoop. "Why don't you ask your phone for the nearest cellphone store, so Gracie can buy a new phone?"

Snoop located a store, and we stopped for Gracie to buy another phone.

I walked in with her and waited a few feet away.

Gracie opened her red Prada purse. She fished around in it, moving things from side to side, unzipping pockets, and rezipping them.

Finally, she set the bag on the counter and took the contents out, systematically lining items up on the glass. She emptied one pocket and felt around in it, held it open and peered inside. Her breath came quicker.

She carefully replaced the lipsticks, tissues, and other detritus in the pocket and zipped it closed. She unzipped the next pocket and repeated the process, her movements becoming faster and less controlled.

I stepped over. "Having trouble finding something, Gracie?"

She stopped moving. "I'm...I'm, uh, searching for my credit card." She kept emptying the purse onto the counter.

I pointed to the black Prada clutch bag she had taken from the purse and laid on the counter. "Gracie, that is a pocket book. Would your credit card be in there?"

"No, I'm looking for—" she stopped. She caught her breath and stared down at the counter. "Yes, that must be it." She opened the clutch and found a gold American Express card.

The clerk studied his cash register screen. "I'm sorry, miss. This card's been declined."

Her cheeks blazed with red. "There must be a mistake. Here, I'll use this one." She swiped another card and waited nervously for the clerk to review his screen. She breathed a sigh of relief when he opened the phone to activate it. Stiffly, she completed the transaction and we walked back to the rental car.

I closed the passenger door and walked around to the driver seat. "Next stop, the Port City Palace. I know you'll be glad to see Bob again."

"Yes, of course I will. In fact, I'll call him right now." Gracie called Bob's phone and left a message in Spanish. "It's Bunny. I'm with Chuck and Snoop and we're on our way to the hotel. I'm calling from my new phone. You can add the number from your call log. I love you, and I'll be there soon." She disconnected. "Bob didn't answer. I hope he's okay."

"I talked to him earlier. He's at practice."

"Oh, that's right. He told me when he called at Mom and Dad's earlier."

I took the entrance ramp onto I-95 northbound. "Gracie, how did Vidali manage to kidnap you right out of the hotel?"

She shook her head and didn't reply.

I drove on. "You want to tell me what happened?"

"I don't want to talk about it."

There was a break in the traffic and I took a quick peek at her. Her chin quivered.

"Gracie, did Vidali…hurt you in any way?"

She burst into tears. "Don't…" Her voice broke. "Don't say anything to Bob."

We drove in silence the rest of the way to the Palace. I knew she was a first-class fashion model; I hadn't realized she was also a first-class liar.

Snoop dropped us at the hotel entrance and went to return our rental car and bring the Avanti to the hotel.

Gracie and I stopped at the hotel reception.

The clerk smiled. "May I help you, Ms. Perez?"

"My purse was stolen and I need a new keycard."

"That's too bad," said the clerk. "I'll change the code on your door so whoever stole your purse can't get in." She punched on the keyboard. "I'll make you a new keycard."

I gave the clerk my old keycard to Bob's and Gracie's suite. "In case of emergency, I want one too."

The clerk gave Gracie a questioning look.

"Of course. Please make an extra one for Mr. McCrary," she directed the clerk.

"You'd better text Bob that his old keycard won't work anymore."

I woke from my nap on the couch when Bob opened the door to his suite. "Hey, Bob. I guess you got the message about the new keycard."

"Yeah. Where's Gracie?"

I waved over my shoulder. "Asleep in the bedroom."

He walked toward the bedroom door, and I held up a hand.

"*Amigo*, we need to talk first. Let Gracie sleep awhile. None of us got much sleep last night."

I waited for him to sit down. "This isn't over. Now that Gracie is back, you think you don't need to worry. You forget that a mobster has bet millions of dollars on the Cowboys. Vidali is not the type to leave the game to chance. He's not defeated by a long shot. Rule Fourteen: *When you think someone is out to get you, they probably are.*"

"But Gracie is free and kickoff is tomorrow. There's nothing he can do now."

I remembered Gordo, Gracie's missing dog. "You live in a world where you have to figure out what the other team is *likely* to do. You plan your response based on probabilities. You call the plays and try to predict outcomes. You have to recognize a linebacker blitz, read man-to-man or zone coverage, and sometimes dump the ball before you get sacked. That's your universe."

"Pretty much, yeah. So what?"

"In Special Forces, I trained to live in a different world. I don't worry so much about what the enemy is *likely* to do as what he is *capable* of doing. I prepare for his *capabilities*, not his *probabilities.*"

"I don't get it, Eighty-Eight."

"Let's say that you walk into a restaurant. You're thinking about what you might order."

"Okay. So?"

"Whenever I enter a restaurant, I know on a conscious level that 99 percent of the time, I'm not in danger. But I always figure out how to kill anyone or, if necessary, *everyone* in the room. After I have that kill plan firmly in mind, I think about what to order."

"My God, I never imagined such a thing."

I shrugged. "No reason you should; you're a civilian. Soldiers know different. I was Special Forces, remember?"

"I could never live like that."

"Of course not. That's why we have the military. But I had to learn to live like that to survive in Iraq and Afghanistan. Now I'm used to it. I plan in terms of Vidali's capabilities, not his probabilities. He's an organized crime boss. He organized Gordo's dognapping within two hours of us rescuing Gracie. He could order someone to break your throwing arm or even kill you. *Boom*, just like that. He wouldn't hesitate a second or have an instant's regret. You're now the best source of leverage he has."

"Oh geez. I never considered *I* could be the one in danger."

"You *weren't* in danger—until I rescued Gracie. With her free, you could be his next target. For the next..." I glanced at my watch. "For the next twenty-nine hours, I want you to think that any stranger you see could be a hit man. You have to stay out of sight."

He seemed dubious.

"One other thing, Bob. Gracie is involved in this somehow."

"Involved how?"

"She wasn't exactly kidnapped. I think she went with Vidali voluntarily, then changed her mind."

"I'll never believe Gracie would do anything to hurt me. Never."

"I'm not surprised you feel that way, *amigo*, but keep the possibility in the back of your mind. Play your cards close to your chest around her." I clapped him on the shoulder. "Now go be with Gracie. I'm gonna finish my nap."

Before going back to sleep, I patted my shoulder holster to ensure it was still within easy reach on the floor by the couch.

The click of Bob opening his bedroom door woke me. He looked like he'd witnessed a zombie apocalypse.

"What's the matter, *amigo*?" I grabbed for my Glock and sat up on the couch.

"I'm kind of freaked out, Eighty-Eight. I got a text from Gracie's phone—her old phone." He handed me his phone.

```
The woman is safe FOR NOW but don't think I
can't reach her—or you. Go look in her
rental car.
```

I handed the phone back. "Has Gracie seen this?"

"I didn't have the heart to wake her. I laid down on the bed next to her, then my phone buzzed."

"Is Gracie's rental where I left it?"

"I guess. I didn't move it." Bob walked to the kitchen counter where I had left the keys a couple of days before. "Let's check it out."

"You stay here, *amigo*. Until the Super Bowl is over, the world is a hostile place for you. Toss me the keys and I'll check it out." I strapped on my shoulder holster. "Don't open this door for anyone but Snoop or me. For Gracie's sake, don't show her that message until we know for sure what it means."

"Where's Snoop?"

"He went to return the rental car we used to bring Gracie back from Convoy Point. He'll be back soon with the Avanti. I told him to call you on the house phone before he comes up. If anybody else knocks on that door," I pointed at it, "it's dangerous. Don't even let in a housekeeper. Got it? Not even a hotel employee."

I handed him my ankle gun, a sweet little Browning .380. "You remember how to shoot?"

"Aim for center mass and squeeze the trigger."

"And remember not to *pull* the trigger, just *squeeze*."

"Right. Squeeze, don't pull. Hostile world. No one but you and Snoop, not even the housekeeper. Don't show Gracie the message."

I got off the elevator two floors above the one where I had

parked Gracie's red convertible. The guy who sent the text could have done it to lure either Bob or me into an ambush. I didn't want a shooter to surprise me as I walked through a doorway. Gracie told me that was how they got to her. The difference was they wanted Gracie alive. Bob or me, not so much.

I drew my Glock and pushed the steel door open to ninety degrees. I glanced through the crack by the hinges. No one was behind it.

As I walked down the parking ramps to my destination, I passed other hotel guests and held the pistol at my side. I reached the last ramp and edged around the support column to survey the parking deck.

I waited for two men in dark suits and a woman in a gray pantsuit to get in a sedan and drive away. No pistols bulged under their jackets, so they weren't the ones I needed to be wary of.

I walked toward Gracie's convertible. There was a slash in the top over the driver's door. That's why you never lock a convertible; any crook with a pocket knife can get in by slashing the top. And someone had.

My gut squirmed and my throat went dry. I had a sick feeling I knew what I would find in Gracie's car.

———

After the two Port City detectives left Bob and Gracie's hotel suite, I bolted the door.

Snoop appeared as sad as I had seen him in a long time. "What kind of depraved bastard slits a dog's throat?"

"Somebody inspired by *The Godfather*?"

Gracie came from the bathroom, eyes red and swollen.

"Gracie, I'm sorry for your loss. I had a dog when I was a boy. I know how much Gordo meant to you."

She nodded wordlessly and sat on the couch. Bob slipped his arm around her.

Bob's phone whistled to announce a text. "Oh, my God."

"Hand me the phone."

He did. It was another message from Graciela's old cellphone.

I can get to you anywhere. The cops cannot protect you or the girl. If the Cowboys lose by no more than four points, Graciela will live. To be clear, the Jets cannot beat the Cowboys by more than four points. If they do, she'll never live to see your wedding day.

"I need to keep this phone for a while."

"Why?"

"To find out where Gracie's phone was when he sent the text."

Gracie sat up straight. "Bob got a text from my old phone? Let me see it."

I handed the phone to her. If she had any lingering doubts that Vidali was her enemy, that ought to convince her.

As she read it, her face went white. Her left eyelid fluttered.

I took the phone back. "Now you know how serious this is. Don't leave this room, either of you. You'll be safe with Snoop here. I need my ankle gun back."

Bob handed it to me.

"Don't go out to dinner. Order room service. Let Snoop answer the door when it gets here."

Bob glanced at Gracie, then at me. "This is like a trap play in football—you let the opposing player think he's free to run right over you. He runs into the backfield, and *boom*, you blindside him. Except instead of trapping the linebacker, this Vidali guy has trapped the quarterback. I can't do what he wants, even if I wanted to."

"How you figure that, Bob?"

"No quarterback could cut the winning margin to four points or less on purpose and still win the game. The spread is too narrow." Bob slammed his fist on the arm of the couch.

"If the Jets were favored by seventeen, I could maybe shave off a touchdown or throw an interception so we'd win by ten points. But that's two scores, so we'd have a cushion and could still win the game if something went wrong. But with four points, there's no room for error. One play goes wrong and the Cowboys score seven. Even two field goals add up to six points." He hung his head. "I'm screwed. I'll have to lose the game."

"Maybe not."

"What can you do?" Bob asked.

"You don't want to know."

Jorge Castellano met me at the North Shore Precinct on his day off. That's the kind of friend he is.

He punched up his computer. "The text originated from a cell tower a hundred yards from the Port City Palace, the one on the roof of the office building across the street from the hotel."

I thought of Vidali and Orsinati and their rooms in the Palace. It took balls to send the text from the hotel, or maybe they didn't know about the technology to trace cellphones. Was Teflon Vic a tech dinosaur? Unlikely. And Dante Orsinati didn't strike me as the brightest bulb on the porch. Could they be in the hotel right now?

"Where's the phone now?"

"*Hmm.* Wait a sec…" He studied the monitor. "It's pinging off a cell tower on the south edge of downtown. Wait, it just jumped to another tower. It's on the move."

I rang the hotel manager at home. "Mr. Wallenda, this is

Chuck McCrary. Are the men in Rooms 3405 and 3406 still there, or have they checked out? Who do I need to speak with to find out?"

"First tell me about the missing guest, Ms. Perez. Did you find her?"

"Yes, sir. The men in rooms 3405 and 3406 did kidnap her. You'll hear about that on the eleven o'clock news tonight. I brought her back safe and sound to your hotel early this morning. But now her life has been threatened again. This crisis is not over. I still need your cooperation."

"If they kidnapped her, won't the police be after them? They wouldn't still be in the hotel."

"The police don't know about it yet, unless the Coast Guard told them."

"The Coast Guard? The *Coast Guard*?"

"It's complicated, Mr. Wallenda. Regardless, I believe the kidnappers could be in the hotel. Ms. Perez is still in danger, and I still need your help."

───────

The desk clerk read my business card and took me to the back office. "Mr. Wallenda called about you. How can I help, Mr. McCrary?"

"I need to know if the two men who were in rooms 3405 and 3406 are still there."

The clerk consulted the computer. "They checked out an hour ago."

I thanked her and took the elevator to Bob and Gracie's floor. I didn't use the keycard. I didn't want to surprise Snoop. He can be trigger-happy, so I knocked and stood where Snoop could see me through the peephole.

Snoop cracked the door. "Come in. Bob and Gracie are resting in the bedroom. What did you find?"

"It's definitely Vidali. He's checked out of the hotel."

"Where is he?"

"That's what I'm gonna find out, Snoop."

I called Jorge, who had hung around the precinct at my request. "Snoop is with me and I have you on speaker. Where is Graciela's phone now? Is it on?"

"Hold on a sec...well, well, well. It's pinging off a cell tower on the causeway."

"Could it be on its way to Mango Island?"

"Lemme check the cell tower map...Yeah, that tower is right near the Mango Island ferry terminal."

"You're off duty until Monday, right?" I asked. "I want to hire you to come over here and back up Snoop."

"Be there in twenty-five minutes."

"Make it twenty." I hung up.

Bob must have heard our conversation. He came out of the bedroom yawning.

"Didn't mean to wake you, Bob. Sorry."

"No problem. I heard you say something about backup. What's going on?"

"Tell you later. Right now, Snoop and I are going out on your balcony to talk."

"Stay here, guys. I want to know what's happening."

"I know you do, *amigo*, but you need to be able to tell the cops that you had no idea what we planned to do. *¿Comprende?*"

He looked thoughtful for a few seconds, then gestured toward the balcony. "Help yourselves."

Snoop waited until I slid the glass doors closed behind us. The sunset behind the hotel reflected off the high-rises across Seeti Bay and transformed their windows into sparks of flaming orange. The eastern sky over the Atlantic was already black. "How do we get to Mango Island without a boat, Chuck? The *Raider* is shot up and tied up at Convoy Point. We for sure can't take the ferry with all those security cameras."

"*We* do not need to get to Mango Island. *You* will stay here and guard Bob and Gracie, with back up from Jorge Castellano. He's on his way."

"You can't take on Vidali and his guards alone, Chuck. I'm going with you."

"Not gonna happen. You have Janet and the girls to think about. I don't have any family. Besides, if anything happens to me, you have to get Bob to the stadium in one piece." I touched his arm. "Can I count on you, Snoop?"

Snoop stared at me in the twilight. He swallowed hard. "I don't like staying here, but I'll do it."

"One more thing, Snoop. Hank Hickham invited me and a date to his stadium suite for the Super Bowl. Since I don't have a girlfriend, I promised Clint I would take him. If anything happens to me, the tickets and parking pass are in my nightstand. Promise me you'll take him for me. I don't want him to miss it."

"I promise," said Snoop, blinking like he had something in his eye.

THIRTEEN

T he only way to get to Mango Island is by boat or helicopter. Helicopter was too noisy; I couldn't attract any attention. The ferry was not an option. They keep security video of everyone who gets on and off.

Well, maybe I could parachute in, but this was real life, not a James Bond movie.

I called Mike Mahoney.

I used Mike's Marine Service facilities to rebuild the first *Gator Raider* years ago. The old boat had sunk in the New River when a hurricane slammed into Ft. Lauderdale. The insurance company paid off the owner and sold her to me for a dollar—still at the bottom of the river. I raised her from the bottom and towed her to Mike's. Mike learned that my paternal grandfather, Magnus McCrary, was a first generation American, and he pronounced me an honorary half-Irishman. Mike helped me chase down spare parts when I was young and broke. Our common love for boats, fishing, and Irish whiskey grew into a friendship.

Mike still had an Irish accent, even though he'd been a U.S.

citizen for thirty years. "Why on God's earth would you call me on a Saturday night, McCrary? You're barely half-Irish, so it's too early in the evening for you to be drunk. The sun's hardly set."

"Mahoney, I may not be straight from the *auld sod* like you or Grandpa Magnus, but it's never too early to be drunk."

"You got that right, boy-o. And what can I do for you on this beautiful evening in paradise?"

"I need to rent a boat."

"Sure you do, lad. It's gonna take four or five weeks to patch the *Raider*. I wouldn't want to go that long without a boat either. I'll send a crew down to Convoy Point on Monday to fetch her, that's for sure. And I'll rent you a nice cruiser for a good price on Tuesday, after I get back."

"Mike, I need a boat now."

"You mean like *right now*?"

"Right now. I'll be there within the hour."

"But it's Saturday night, lad. This is prime drinking time. I have to charge you a recreational penalty for disturbing my well-deserved leisure. Why would you need a boat tonight?"

I didn't dare call Hank Hickham on Saturday night before the Super Bowl. This was Port City's first time to host the Super Bowl. It would be the busiest night in the history of Hank's Bar & Grill & Bodacious Ribs. New Years' Eve, Halloween, and Arbor Day rolled into one. Hank's restaurant had been a "must see" for tourists to Port City Beach for a generation or more. With Port City full of fans for its first Super Bowl in its new billion-dollar stadium, the wait time for a table had to be hours. Even in the off season, the place made Hank a hundred grand a month. It would take a team of CPAs to figure out how much money Hank stood to make this week.

Besides, I had called Hank for a favor earlier that week when he got Snoop and me the reservation at the Mango Island Resort. But Hank had told me to call him anytime I needed a favor. He had invited me to his private box at the Port City Super Stadium to enjoy the Super Bowl the next day.

I texted him.

Call me ASAP. It's important.

A minute later he called back. "Hey, Chuck, I'm kinda busy. Whaddya need?"

"Hank, I wouldn't bother you tonight of all nights if it weren't important."

"Don't worry 'bout that none, Chuck. You never asked me for nothin' what didn't make plenty good sense. How can I help?"

"I need to get onto Mango Island again—tonight."

Even over the restaurant hubbub in the background, I heard him sigh. "Oh, Lordy. That's impossible, son. I tried a couple weeks ago to get another friend a room at the lodge. The lodge told me they been booked solid for two years. Ain't nothing I can do about that. I mean, a couple of nights ago was one thing, but tonight is impossible, even for me. The president of the United States couldn't get a room in Port City tonight, let alone on Mango Island."

"I don't want a room at the resort. I only need to get onto the island."

"I can get you a pass to take the ferry."

"I can't take the ferry."

"Why not?"

I paused a second to let him know this was serious. "I can't tell you why, but if I could, you'd agree that it's necessary. I'll go by private boat, like last time. All I need is a guest slip in the marina."

"I tried that too, son. Can't be done. Every big yacht on the East Coast is here for the game. You know that."

"What about a dinner reservation at one of the Mango Island

restaurants for, say, ten o'clock? Any excuse to get me on that
island without using the ferry will do. It's real important."

"Not gonna happen, Chuck. The restaurant's been booked for
weeks. For that matter, we closed the wait list for tables at my
restaurant after the wait time got over three hours. In case you ain't
heard, the night before the Super Bowl is like New Year's Eve, St.
Patrick's Day, and Mardi Gras, rolled into one."

"I'm desperate here, Hank. It's literally a matter of life and
death that I get onto Mango Island tonight and that I do not take the
ferry. What about a Super Bowl party? Is the Mango Island Club
having a Super Bowl party tonight?"

"Is the Pope Catholic? Of course, they're having a party. In fact,
they're having lots of parties. This is like New Year's Eve for them
too. Yeah, I can get you into that. Is there just you? You have a date
or anything?"

"Only me, Hank."

"Okay. I'll tell them you're my nephew again. I assume you
want to do this on the down low, right? You need to act the part—
monkey suit and all. It's a formal party. You know how Mango
Island is. I'll leave the invitation in my office with the night
manager, but I won't be able to meet you. You'll have to show the
invitation to dock the boat, and you can't get into the party without
it."

I buzzed down the window of my Avanti. "Thanks for meeting me,
Mike. I owe you big time."

Mike Mahoney rolled back the gate in the chain link fence and
waved me into the marina parking lot. "Come on in, lad. I wouldn't
be much of a friend if I couldn't do an occasional favor for a fellow
Irishman, even if he is merely half-Irish."

He led me into the marina office and flicked on the light. "Holy Mother of God, you're wearing a tuxedo. Why would you rent a boat on Saturday night before the Super Bowl, and wear a friggin' penguin suit?"

"I was invited to a Super Bowl party at a waterfront house on the New River," I retorted. "It's formal."

"But you can drive to them houses, boy-o. You can get there in a car; you don't need a boat."

"I'm meeting a girl there. She wants to do it on a boat. I think she likes the rocking." I winked.

Mike laughed. "Jesus H. Christ, McCrary, you're daft. What kind of boat you need, lad?"

"Practically anything with a cabin bed large enough for two. Don't care about the power or size."

"How about a cuddy?"

"Too small. I don't want to feel cramped. This is a special night with a special girl."

Mike fingered the sets of keys hanging on the wall. "Here we go. SeaRay 310 Sundancer. Very romantic. Got her on consignment. Owner said to rent her until she sells." He pocketed the keys. "I don't know how much fuel she's got. We'd better check."

I got my gear from the Avanti and followed Mike to the SeaRay.

Mike switched on the ignition. "Gauge says she's half full. Oughta be about sixty gallons. That enough for you?"

"Should be plenty to get to the New River and back. Thanks, Mike. I owe you big time."

He laughed. "No, you don't, lad. I'm charging you a bloody fortune for making me work on a Saturday night." He laughed again and stepped ashore. "I hope the girl is worth the trouble."

"Me too."

I switched on the blowers and the bilge pump. I moved to the stern and made sure the bilge ran dry in less than five seconds.

Mike stood at the bow, ready to cast off the line.

I counted to thirty, switched off the blowers, and cranked the engines. "Okay, Mike, cast off."

My stomach did somersaults as I idled out of the marina. My blood pressure had climbed and the adrenaline flowed like a river through my veins. Just like before a mission in Iraq and Afghanistan.

The SeaRay cleared the *no wake* zone, and I rammed the throttles to the firewall. The cruiser leapt in the water, bounced twice, and climbed the hill of water at the bow. The tachometer wound toward 3,000 rpm. The boat reached the top of the bow wave, nosed over, and glided up on plane. I eased the throttles back after she reached cruising speed. The engines smoothed out at a steady 2,000 rpm.

The purr of the engines had a calming effect. I took a deep breath and chilled out, at least for a while.

This time I knew what to watch for. A quarter-mile out I spotted the Mango Island marine patrol making its endless circles around the island.

I steered the SeaRay around the north end of the island, alert for the entrance to the marina. I dropped to idle speed and piloted through the breakwater. I called the harbormaster on the marine radio and got a transient slip number. The *Double Scotch* wasn't in her slip. Probably the Coast Guard had taken her to the Coast Guard base in Miami.

The Mango Island dock attendant wore the usual turquoise and gold uniform.

"I'll toss you a line."

The attendant snubbed the line at the bow, and I tossed him a stern line. "Thanks. You do this one and I'll do the spring line. I'll be here all night."

"Yes, Captain. Welcome to Mango Island. May I have the name your reservation is under?"

"I don't have a reservation. I'm here for the Super Bowl party. After the party, I'll sleep aboard the boat."

"Which party?"

I hadn't counted on that. "How many parties are there?"

"At least half a dozen, plus private parties in people's homes. Let me see your invitation."

I handed it to him.

He read the name on the invitation. "You're Hank Hickham? The guy with that rib place? I love your ribs."

"Well, I'm Hank Hickham, but my uncle is the guy with the ribs. I'm named after him. I love his ribs too."

"Tell me: How does he make that sauce?"

"Old family secret. Uncle Hank said he could tell me, but then…" I let the sentence hang in the air.

The dock attendant smiled. "I know—he'd have to kill you."

The attendant read the invitation again. "That particular party is in the Caribbean Clubhouse on the other side of the island. You'll need to take a shuttle." He called the resort on a walky-talky. "Your ride will be here in three minutes. Would you like a map of the island?"

"Yes, thanks." I took the map, slipped the attendant a tip, and walked over to the shuttle stop.

I was on the island, so I didn't need to attend the party. However, it would look out of place for me to dock and not take the shuttle, so I waited. I wanted to compare the island to the map anyway. I'd studied aerial photos of the island from Google Earth, but they might be years old. The shuttle took a cart path that Snoop and I had not used on our previous trip to the island. It skirted the edge of three more golf holes, passed the other of the island's two marinas, and angled across the other end of the street that led to Vidali's mansion.

The Caribbean Clubhouse lobby was festooned with bunting and Super Bowl banners. Huge flower arrangements in the form of team logos and colors for the Jets and the Cowboys sat on matching tables in the atrium.

I handed the invitation to a guard stationed at the entrance to the ballroom. He wore a tuxedo of Mango Island turquoise with a gold tie and cummerbund. *Nothing succeeds like excess.*

The sound of an orchestra wafted on the night breeze. The party was loud and proud.

I pushed through the crowd of beautiful people. There were two kinds of couples: beautiful women on the arms of wealthy men, and wealthy women on the arms of beautiful men. I amended that assessment to include a third type of couple when I noticed a beautiful man on the arm of a wealthy man.

I worked my way to one of the bars. I had to stay sharp tonight. "Club soda." I decided to live a little. "With a twist of lime."

I carried the drink to an out-of-the-way corner and surveyed the room. I eased back further into the corner after Dante Orsinati walked in.

Oh shit! Orsinati knew me, of course, and where Orsinati was, Teflon Vic wouldn't be far behind.

A wall of French doors opened to a garden with tables and chairs, another buffet line, and another bar. I stepped through an open door and moved into the shadows away from the bar. I sidled over to a spot where I could observe Orsinati inside, still near the entrance to the ballroom. His bald head gleamed like a cue ball on a pool table.

In seconds Pistolet Pisarczik came in. Both hoods wore tuxes.

No ill-fitting suits tonight. Nothing but the best for Vidali's thugs. I wondered how good their health plan was. Did they have dental?

I edged nearer the door to widen my viewing angle.

Vidali strode across the marble floor, as comfortable as in his own living room. A twenty-something woman with honey-colored hair clung to his arm. Look up "arm candy" in the dictionary, and you'll see her picture. Her red dress was slit to the hip on one side. Her cleavage went all the way to her waist. Every head in the vicinity, both male and female, pivoted her direction. She was that kind of woman.

I knew from Vidali's file that she wasn't his wife. She leaned on Vidali like she was half-drunk, or maybe stoned.

I felt a little sorry for her.

Vidali's mansion would probably have a handyman, a housekeeper, and maybe a cook. Ordinarily they would be at the mansion, but with this being Saturday night and Super Bowl weekend, they probably had the weekend off. The mansion should be empty. With Vidali, the mistress, and both hoods at the party, the burglar alarms at his mansion would be armed. Vidali's sophisticated alarm system would be nearly impossible to crack. Certainly, I didn't have the skill to do it.

I would wait to break in when Vidali's group left the party and returned to his place. He would disarm the alarms to go inside. That's when I would go in. I would use a door on the other side of the house—a door he didn't use often. Most people don't arm their alarms until they go to bed. If Vidali slept with a window or French door open, he might not arm them at all—or maybe he'd arm the alarms on the ground floor. Worst case, I would have a window of opportunity a few minutes long after the alarms were off.

I took a shuttle back to the SeaRay to prepare.

I closed the curtains over the windows of the SeaRay's cabin. Enough light from the marina's dock leaked through for me to dress without the interior lights. I changed into my sneaky clothes like I had before.

I studied the Mango Island map by flashlight. 176 Mango Drive lay a half-mile away as the Sandhill Crane flies, three-quarters of a mile via the shortest cart path. But someone would notice me if I took the path. I decided to follow the golf course from the seventeenth tee, which was closest to the marina, all the way around to the third hole.

The security patrol passed the marina. I had maybe five minutes before the next patrol came by.

I opened the cabin door. After grabbing the gear bag, I walked up the dock, not too fast and not too slow. I passed the harbormaster's office, crossed the cart path, and disappeared into the darkness between two mid-rise condo buildings. The golf course lay on the other side.

The hole diagram on the seventeenth tee said *484 yards, par 4*. I would wind my way 5,400 yards down the fairways to Vidali's house—walking three miles to get one-half mile. I told myself the exercise would do me good.

I hiked through the sea grapes, bottlebrush trees, and oleanders down the rough of the sixteenth and fifteenth holes to where the cart path crossed a street. The street was deserted. I sprinted across and scurried between the condos on the far side to the fourteenth green. At the street between the eleventh and tenth holes, I spotted another security patrol. I hunkered down under a copse of sea grapes for him to pass. I waited in the bushes for another patrol between the sixth and fifth holes before crossing the final street.

My objective rose in the gloom across the fairway. Two hours since I'd left the Caribbean Clubhouse. The interior lights were dark. Vidali was still at the party.

I had studied the house plans on the county property appraiser's website and the aerial photos on Google Earth. The master suite was upstairs at the back, overlooking the golf course. Of the eleven bedrooms, seven were downstairs. Downstairs rooms had one or two sets of French doors. French doors are easy to open. The downstairs had a thick bougainvillea hedge for privacy. The best downstairs views were from the four bedrooms that opened onto the pool deck. The three bedrooms on the side away from the pool had patios with wrought iron tables and chairs with deep blue cushions and matching patio umbrellas. Those patio rooms were the least desirable. They would be the last ones anybody would use. That's where I would make my entrance.

I crouched under the same sea grape that Snoop and I had hidden under a few nights before. I surveyed the scene. Home, sweet home. I squeezed my way through a gap in the bougainvillea hedge. The house and gardens had been totally dark the last time I'd been there. This time the lights over the patio doors were lit. They cast a cone of light on the French doors and the patios. The major trees had landscape lights switched on that had been dark when we'd been there before.

I hoped the lights meant that Vidali was "in residence," as the Queen calls it in Britain. That wouldn't necessarily mean he was home. If he had left the party early and beat me back to his house, then I was screwed. I fired up the thermal imaging camera and scanned the rooms I could see. They were empty.

I threaded my way behind the bougainvillea to the mansion's north side. Each of three guest rooms had a recessed light in the soffit above the French doors. I scanned the rooms through the doors. Nobody home. I breathed a sigh of relief.

I grabbed a wrought iron chair from the patio set and placed it under the light fixture. Standing on the chair, I grasped both sides of the frame and tugged it down. The corrosion on the retaining springs cut the night with a screech that would have awakened a zombie inside. I held my breath and stared through the French door, willing the room behind to remain dark.

It did.

I'd dodged a bullet on that screech. I hoped I wouldn't have to dodge a bullet for real later.

Reaching around the rim of the fixture, I unscrewed the light bulb. It was hot, even through my rubber gloves. I tossed the light bulb into the bushes.

I had to move the chair over to the eight-foot French doors to scan the top. I retrieved an electrical current sensor from my gear bag and passed it around the edge of the French doors. The burglar alarm contacts were at the top of each door. The indicator light glowed amber in the darkness as it passed across the transmitters. When Vidali disarmed his alarm, the indicator light would go dark.

It took a minute to pick the lock on the French doors. I pressed down on the pistol-grip doorknob to make sure the door was unlocked, but I wouldn't open it until the alarm was disarmed. After carrying the patio chair back to its table, I sat in the dark and watched the cart path in front of the mansion through a gap in the front hedge. Ninety minutes later, Vidali's personal electric cart passed the gap. Showtime.

I pulled my ski mask over my face.

I slipped the current sensor from my pocket. This time I knew the exact location of the alarm contacts, so I didn't need the chair. Standing on tiptoes, I held the sensor near one contact. Its amber light glowed. With my other hand, I held a stethoscope against the window. I heard a *thump*, maybe from the garage door closing.

The amber light went out, and I stowed the sensing device in the gear bag. I stashed the bag in the bushes and tugged the straps on my armored vest tighter.

Taking a deep breath, I eased the French door open and slipped inside. A sliver of light from the hall showed under the bedroom door. I locked the outside door and shined a dim flashlight around the room. Something smelled a little off.

I sniffed again. It was the same after-shave I had smelled when Orsinati and Pisarczik shot up my office. The room had a lived-in vibe. It had furniture like a guest room, but somebody lived here. The flashlight beam fell on a picture of Pistolet Pisarczik and an elderly woman on the nightstand. Mobster and mother. Even stone killers have to be born.

I glanced around the room. I had to hide. Pisarczik would visit the bathroom, maybe take a shower. The closet was out for the same reason.

My gaze fell on the ornate king-sized bed. It was a cliché, but that was my only option. I dropped to the floor and slid under the bed. I ensured my phone was off.

I lay in the silent darkness for maybe an hour. The ceiling creaked three times from someone walking across the floor above. Various doors opened and closed. Faint water sounds came through Pisarczik's open bathroom door from the pipes carrying sound from elsewhere in the mansion.

Rubber-soled shoes squeaked their way down the marble hallway. The knob clicked and the door swung open, sending a shaft of light across the Persian rug by the door. I was lying on a similar rug that the bed was centered on. It felt like silk through my rubber gloves. The door closed and a lamp on the round pedestal table came on. *A switch by the door must control it.*

One shoe squeaked on the parquet floor as Pisarczik stepped onto the rug. He walked across the carpet and sat in a leather chair next to the round table. I heard the clunk of his gun on the table.

The leather creaked as he removed his black Rockport dress shoes, then his formal black socks. He walked barefoot to the closet. The light came on when he opened the door. The clothes hamper lid slapped when he tossed in his dirty clothes.

It was chilling to be that close to a mob assassin and be unable to move if he discovered me. I scooched closer to the center of the bed.

In two minutes, he closed the bathroom door. A minute later the shower came on.

Time to boogie.

I slithered from under the bed. The gap under the hall door showed a light. I pressed my ear to the panel and listened. Nothing.

Cracking the door, I peeked down the hall. No one. I stepped into the hall and surveyed the other direction. The hall began at the marble entrance foyer and stretched maybe fifty yards to the pool deck in back. All clear. I closed the door behind me.

Since Pisarczik was in the room I had just left, Orsinati should be in another room on the same side. I tiptoed toward the back of the house. The door gap under the rear guest room was dark. That didn't mean anything. Orsinati could be in bed. I searched for a way to booby trap all three rooms.

A set of two decorative tables stood against the walls between the three guest room doors on the north. A matching set of three more tables was between the four doors on the south. Each table held a Chinese brass gong in a carved jade support. I held one gong to keep it silent and set the piece on the floor. I grabbed one end of the table and tested its weight. Solid oak, too heavy to move alone without making a noise. Instead, I grabbed the Chinese gong assembly to silence it and moved it smack in front of Pisarczik's door. I did the same with the other gongs, blocking all three doors on the north side. Vidali's thugs wouldn't rate a poolside room on the south, but I had two more gongs available. I used them to block two of the four rooms on the pool side of the hall. Couldn't hurt.

At the bottom of the stairs, I flicked off the hall lights. The same switch turned off the upstairs also.

Waiting for my eyes to adjust to the darkness, I drew my Glock and climbed the stairs.

The double doors to Vidali's master suite were locked. I held the flashlight in my mouth and pulled out my lock picks. Interior door locks are usually easier to pick than outside doors, and Vidali's door yielded quickly.

I eased the sitting room door open, praying the hinge wouldn't squeak. It didn't. I locked the doors behind me. The bedroom door stood open and a faint light came through the French doors from outside. The scent of perfume, aftershave, incense, and something else I couldn't place wafted across the room. Too late, I recognized the smell—dog.

Two dogs barked simultaneously in the bedroom. Loud enough to wake the dead—or the bodyguards in the bedrooms below.

By the time I sprinted across the sitting room and into Vidali's bedroom, he had flicked on a bedside lamp, rolled out of bed, and was stumbling naked toward the closet. I knew from the mansion's building permits that Vidali had done extensive remodeling upstairs after he bought the place. He could have fitted out the closet for a panic room to protect him from either a home invasion or a hurricane. I couldn't let him reach that refuge. In three steps, I caught him, tripped him, and kicked the pistol from his hand. The gun hit the plush carpet soundlessly and bounced a foot away.

The Pomeranians kept yapping.

I locked the door between the sitting room and bedroom.

Vidali's honey blonde, or should I say *blonde honey*, sat up in the middle of the bed, naked as a peeled mango. Her legs stretched out in front, still spread where Vidali had been a moment before. She was a natural blonde.

Blonde Honey frowned at me. Perhaps she was trying to figure out why Vidali had moved. And who the heck was this masked gunman? A satin sheet lay in a heap at the foot of the bed, spilling onto the floor. Scented candles shimmered on the chest of drawers and the two nightstands. Perfect for a romantic tryst.

I pointed at her. "You. Quiet the dogs now, or I'll slit their throats. Ask your boyfriend sometime how he feels about someone who would slit a dog's throat."

Vidali's eyes widened when I mentioned slitting a dog's throat.

Blonde Honey struggled to sit straighter. Her attention wandered the room until it focused on the dogs. She made kissing sounds. "Come here, babies. Come here." She extended her arms toward the dogs. She patted the bed beside her, but her perfect breasts barely moved. They pointed straight at me; the best that Vidali's money could buy. She'd sold her soul—and her breasts—to the devil. "It's all right, babies. Come to Mama."

The bed was high and the dogs were small. They jumped onto an upholstered set of small steps beside the bed, then up to the top. They made themselves comfortable leaning against their mistress's legs, one on each side. She stroked their heads peacefully and glanced in my direction, not quite focused. *Drunk or high?* I thought. *Maybe both.*

Vidali sat on the floor, eyes focused like lasers on the barrel of my Glock. "Who the hell are you?"

If I was right about the dogs' barking, I had maybe a minute before Vidali's reinforcements arrived. Keeping the Glock pointed at him, I moved across to the French doors and opened them both. The balcony beyond had patio furniture. The night breeze came in from the balcony and stirred the sheer drapes. Maybe the bodyguards would think I had escaped that way.

I didn't want Miss Nude Mango Island to get hurt. "Miss, you'd better take the dogs into the closet. In a couple of minutes, a bunch of armed men will break down that door and run in here with guns drawn. They'll shoot first and ask questions later. I wouldn't open the door for anyone but Vic. Or the cops—they'll be here in a couple of hours."

She pivoted toward Vidali.

He shrugged.

She scooped up a dog in each arm and scooted to the edge of the bed. Holding the dogs, she struggled to her feet and stumbled naked to the closet. She kicked the door closed behind her.

I hoped she'd be okay.

I faced Vidali. "I'm a friend of Bob Martinez and Graciela Perez."

Vidali's gaze flicked to my masked face. "Who?"

"The New York Jets quarterback and his fiancée."

"Okay, you're friends with a famous football player and a famous model. I'm happy for you. So what?"

Vidali was denying everything.

He moved to get up.

"Stay down, Vidali. I want to talk about the Super Bowl game."

"At least let me put on my robe." He pointed at a dark blue silk robe with a gold *VV* logo embroidered on the pocket. It was draped across a side chair upholstered in raw silk.

I examined the robe's pockets before I tossed it to him. I stuck his gun in my pocket. It was a Glock 17 like mine. I waited while he tied the sash. "What's behind that other door?"

"My study."

"We're going in there, but first, you're going to switch off the bedside lamp." When he stood, I grabbed the collar of his robe and pressed the barrel of the Glock into his back, three inches left of his spine, right over his heart. "You know why I have the gun on your left shoulder blade, right?"

"Yeah, yeah." He flicked off the lamp. The light from the candles and the outside landscape lighting was faint but adequate.

I gestured with the pistol. "Lead the way."

Hanging onto his collar, I walked him to the study door.

As he opened the door, the clang of a Chinese gong came faintly through the bedroom door. Those yapping dogs had woken someone downstairs.

He stiffened.

"Nothing's changed, Vidali."

The first gong falling would wake the other gunman. He would burst through the door and knock over the other gong.

Vidali punched on the light. The study was a walnut-paneled office that would have suited a Wall Street money manager. Thick green carpet, matching drapes, burgundy leather furniture, and walnut tables and bookshelves. Vidali moved toward an ornate wooden desk with a leather desk chair behind it.

"Not the desk, Vidali. You sit in the middle of the floor, legs crossed. Lean back on your hands." With weight on his hands and his legs crossed, it would take him a couple of seconds to make any kind of move. I would have ample time to act.

I stepped behind him and kicked the privacy panel on the front of his desk. *Thunk.* Bullet proof. The whole desk was armored. Maybe that building permit was to make the study into a safe room instead of the closet. Or maybe he had armored both rooms. The mobster had money enough to build any kind of fortress he wanted.

I hoped Miss Nude Mango Island would be safe if the bullets starting flying.

I searched the desk drawers and found another Glock 17 in the top left drawer. The place was lousy with them. I popped the magazine out to make sure it had the full seventeen rounds. It did. If

Vidali trusted his life to it, it was safe to use without test firing. I examined his Glock from the bedroom. It was loaded also. I ejected the magazine for a spare. With luck, the cartridges from both magazines had his fingerprints on them, or prints of one of his thugs. I shoved my own Glock into its holster. If there was a gunfight later, the bullets would come from Vidali's own guns.

I stuck the empty Glock in the top left drawer.

The top right drawer held a Smith & Wesson Model M&P R8 revolver. The Model M&P R8 holds eight .357 Magnum bullets the size of a golf ball that will stop a charging buffalo. I didn't expect to encounter any buffalo. With two Glocks, I had enough armament without the cannon. I unloaded the S&W and dropped the shells in a wastebasket under the desk. The drawer also held a wireless panic button, knife, and a Taser. I removed the batteries from the panic button and the Taser. I stuck the knife in a pocket of my vest. It never hurt to have two knives. Rule Eleven: *Always carry a knife.*

I dragged a matching burgundy leather side chair up against the paneled exterior wall ten feet away from the mob boss. Behind the paneling was a solid concrete wall with reinforced steel bars required by Port City Beach's strict building codes. No one could fire an ordinary pistol bullet through that wall.

"Let me tell you what I know. Graciela visited you here last Saturday, before she disappeared. That night, you passed her an envelope full of cash in an elevator in the Port City Palace. After you kidnapped her, you placed a large bet on the Cowboys to beat the spread."

I sat in the leather chair. "After I rescued her, you had Graciela's dog killed and dumped in her car. Bob got your message and the text you sent from Graciela's phone. I know all about you, Teflon Vic."

He stared at me with lizard eyes, but said nothing.

Why wasn't he nervous? Was his silk robe bulletproof? Maybe

he was as tough as people said, or maybe he was simply crazy. I hoped he was tough. I know how to deal with tough. Crazy is a whole 'nother thing.

Downstairs I heard the second Chinese gong fall. Not much time.

I reached into my pocket for a set of photos. "I have a message too." I walked over to Vidali and dropped the candid pictures of his wife and his children on the carpet in front of him. I sat back down and kept the Glock leveled on his forehead.

He peered at the pictures, some of which had fallen face down. His eyes widened in recognition. He leaned forward.

"Use your left hand," I said.

He scooped up the pictures, studied them, and glared at me. "You goddamn bastard. You don't have any idea what kind of trouble you've stepped in. You come into my home—my *home*— and threaten me in front of my mistress. You're a dead man if you ever get close to my family. There are rules. Family is off limits, *capisce*? We Italians *invented* the vendetta. You touch me or my family and my people will kill you, your parents, your brothers and sisters—even your grandparents. There won't be anybody named McCrary left alive after they're through with you."

I hadn't told Vidali my name, yet he knew it. He had researched me.

"Oh dear. And I hoped we could be friends."

I pulled off my ski mask and stuck it in a pocket. The thing itched like crazy. My sweaty face immediately felt better.

"Look, Vidali, I won't harm your family unless you do something really stupid and go after Graciela Perez or Bob Martinez. Then…" I let the sentence dangle. "I've got no family," which was not true, but maybe he didn't know any better. "I'm not in your so-called *business*. I'm not part of any mobster vendetta code to keep me from a hit on your family. My code is simple: I will protect my friends Bob and Graciela from your threats. I'm here to come to an understanding before your men arrive."

"What sort of understanding?"

"You take your losses, leave Bob and Graciela alone, and let the Super Bowl game play out with no interference."

"I would lose a hundred fifty million dollars, McCrary."

I shrugged. "When you gamble, sometimes you lose."

"And what do I get in return for my hundred fifty million?"

I let my expression harden to stone. "I let you, your wife, your children—and your girlfriend—live."

Vidali scoffed. "I looked you up, McCrary. You're a boy scout, a former cop, and a war hero for crissakes. You'd never kill my family—my *innocent* family who are not involved in my business. As for my girlfriend, she's a plaything—a throwaway bimbo. Her main talent is that she can suck a baseball through a garden hose. I'll give her to you after I'm through with her."

I heard the double doors to the sitting room crash in.

Teflon Vic tossed his family photos across the carpet in my direction. "You got no leverage, McCrary."

In a blinding flash of the obvious, I realized Vidali was right. I had misjudged his motivations completely. I had thought Vidali was a rational businessman, even if his business was illegal. I had figured he would cut his losses when circumstances changed against him. I would make him back off, then ride off into the sunset on my white horse. People would say "Who was that masked man?"

But Teflon Vic was not rational. He wasn't merely tough. He was also crazy. And he was certainly no businessman. The normal market has rules: You can't threaten people to make them buy your products, and you have to tell them the truth about what you're selling. These rules didn't apply to Vidali. He cheated, lied, and coerced when it suited him. He used people like his girlfriend and threw them away like used Kleenex when he finished.

And no one had ever stopped him.

He had basically said, "You can kill me, but I won't give in." That was how he rose through the mob ranks to grab the top position.

I had hurt Vidali's pride—I had invaded his home, and his honor was at stake. If it became known he had backed down to me, his reputation would be garbage. He would lose the ability to intimidate people. He simply could not afford to surrender to me; it would destroy him.

He would rather be dead.

My fallback position was to steal into his room and, if he wouldn't accept defeat, slit his throat. Vidali had ordered Gordo's throat slit. That would be poetic justice. I would disappear and no one would suspect I'd been there. The blonde bimbo was so high and so shaken that she wouldn't be able to identify me even if I hadn't worn the mask. Home free.

Except, now that I had him at gunpoint, I couldn't force myself to murder him in cold blood. He was a killer and a man who employed other killers, but he wasn't trying to kill me at that particular instant. He wasn't a Taliban sentry that I could sneak up behind and slash his throat with official U.S. Government blessing. No, right now he was a middle-aged, unarmed man dressed in a silk robe. It wouldn't be self-defense. No matter how much he deserved it, if I killed him, I could not live with it.

I had not thought this mission through all the way. I had made a rookie mistake and broken Rule Fifteen. *Never take anything for granted.* I'd projected my own values and beliefs onto Vidali. *Dumb, dumb, dumb.*

"No leverage? I've got you." I smirked. "Who knows, Vidali? You might win your bet honestly. The Cowboys could surprise you."

"I own two casinos. I take bets where the odds are with me.

You're crazy if you think I'm gonna risk a hundred fifty million bucks on a real gamble. Ain't gonna happen, McCrary. You say Graciela is your friend? That I threatened her? Bullshit. The whole scam was her idea. She wanted to disappear. You think Graciela loves that quarterback? Puh-leese. Graciela loves Graciela. Period."

He punched the air with a finger. "She put this whole deal together. She approached me in Atlantic City two days after the Jets won the AFC Championship. Told me she could fix the Super Bowl for a cut of the action. She's in for thirty points. She's as good a piece of ass as Jasmine. A little skinny for my taste, but she knows her way around a bedroom."

"Who's Jasmine?"

"The bimbo you sent to hide in the closet."

Someone knocked on the door to the bedroom. "Vic, you in there? Sorry to bother you, boss, but we heard the dogs bark. Everything okay?"

I pressed the Glock to his forehead and put a finger to my lips. The message was clear enough. I kept the pistol pointed at him and moved to close the study door.

I swung the door and noticed its weight. I examined the edge of it. The door was armored. I smacked the walnut-paneled wall with my palm. The wall was armored too. I closed the door and threw the deadbolt.

"Graciela and I planned this thing together, and I never threatened her. She was supposed to drive to Naples and hide in a hotel until after the Super Bowl game. I would text Bob using her cellphone to get him to shave a few points from the score. The Jets could still win the game. Hey, I'm a Jets fan myself. I can't let them cover the spread is all."

"How did Graciela wind up on the *Double Scotch*?"

Vidali spread his hands. "I couldn't trust the crazy bitch to stay hidden. I found out she's a junkie. You never know what a junkie will do—too unpredictable. And her face has been on too many magazine covers. Even in Naples, someone might recognize her. I was better off if she was on the *Double Scotch*, so I changed the plan." He shrugged. "Things kinda got out of hand. Now I got too much money invested in this, and I gotta ride this horse through to the end. You back off right now, and I let you walk out of here. In fact," he added, "I like to recognize a young man with talent—a guy like you. I'll cut you in for three points—that's over four million dollars, tax free. You walk away—now."

The sound of the bedroom door splintering came faintly through the study door. The gunmen were now in the bedroom trying to figure out what to do.

I pictured at least two men with guns drawn barging in to find… what? The bed was still warm from Jasmine and Vidali lying on it. The candles were lit. The balcony doors were open. The room was empty. All they knew for sure was that someone—maybe a practical joker—had placed Chinese gongs in front of their doors. And that the girlfriend's dogs had barked. I had left no sign of forced entry to the boss's sitting room.

They would have found the boss's bedroom door locked, but it was natural that the boss would lock his bedroom door when he was with his mistress. We had both heard them knock discreetly on the bedroom door and wait a respectful couple of minutes. The thugs would have discussed it among themselves before breaking the door.

Once they broke the door, then what? They had no evidence their boss was in trouble. I had frightened Vidali's Barbie doll enough to keep her quiet in the closet. No doubt Jasmine would keep the dogs quiet too. I doubted she would open the safe room door to anyone but Vidali.

They would try the bathroom and find it empty. They would walk gingerly onto the balcony to determine if their boss and his lady had stepped onto the balcony for a nightcap, or to gaze at the moon, or maybe to get it on under the stars. I had seen two chaises on the balcony when I'd opened the French doors.

The balcony had an outside stairway that went down to the pool deck. One gunman would have walked down the stairs to check around the pool. He would come back up the stairs and shrug.

I pictured the above in a couple of seconds. It would be five minutes or less before they figured out by process of elimination that Vidali was in the study.

I felt like the dog who chased a car and caught it. What could I do with Vidali now?

FOURTEEN

I leveled his own Glock at the mobster. "The second the study door fails, the first bullet goes between your eyes. You might want to call them off before that happens."

"That door ain't gonna fail. It'll withstand a two-hundred-mile-an-hour hurricane. It would take a bazooka to blow a hole in it. You're stuck in here."

"That's good to know. Your guys aren't sure where you are. We've got a few minutes until they figure it out."

"Don't be too sure of that." Vidali smirked. "What you gonna do now, hotshot? You can't kill me 'cause I'm the only leverage you got. And there are four guys with guns out there."

Vidali was right. We were at a stalemate. The sole door had at least two armed men waiting on the other side. Or four, if Vidali told the truth.

But was it the only door?

Vidali's contractors had pulled several building permits for improvements to the mansion after he bought it. Statistically, Mango Island had the highest probability of any place in the United

States of being hit by a hurricane. It was the bull's-eye in the target of Hurricane Alley. The island is seven feet above sea level in an area where a storm surge can reach fifteen feet. The town of Port City Beach, of which Mango Island is a part, has the strictest building codes in Florida. Every significant change to a building requires a permit, with blueprints. A building inspector signs off after the repairs are underway and again after they are complete before the town issues a Certificate of Occupancy.

I racked my brain to remember everything in the building permit files Flamer had sent me. Now I wished I had studied them better. Rule Six: *You never know what you'll need to know.*

If I had millions of dollars to make a house safe, I wouldn't build a safe room with just one way out. Neither would Vidali.

Moving to the wall behind the desk, I studied the paintings that hung on the walnut panels. From my peripheral vision, I observed Vidali's body language. I found the hinged painting in seconds. Swinging it open, I found a wall safe behind it. I had no interest in that; I wanted the secret escape hatch.

"How do I open the secret door?"

He stared at me like a basilisk and shook his head once.

I pointed the Glock at his legs. "The first one goes into your left knee. The second goes into your right knee. You don't want to think about where the third one goes. You have three seconds. Three…Two…"

"Twirl the knob three times to the left—"

"Not the safe. I don't want your money. I want to open the secret door. Where's the latch?"

"Next to the bottom hinge. There's a button. Push it."

The button clicked and a section of walnut paneling four feet wide and ten feet high swung out into the room.

Shoving Vidali ahead of me, I stepped onto the bare concrete floor behind the walnut paneled door. Before leaving the study, I had closed the hinged picture. Maybe the hoods didn't know about the secret exit. When they eventually got into the study, everything would appear normal.

I closed the door behind me and felt the *thunk* as it latched. Wire-caged light fixtures hung from the ten-foot ceiling and cast yellow light on the concrete steps. Now I remembered the blueprint I had studied. The stairs ended in the five-car garage.

I pushed Vidali ahead.

"Not so fast. I'm barefooted."

The industrial type stairway was built like a fire escape in a high-rise building. Aluminum scuff bars were fastened on the edge of each step to improve traction of escaping people. But they were designed for people in shoes; the edges were knife-sharp.

"Okay, you set the pace," I said. I kept him at arm's length, and he stepped gingerly down the stairway.

He stopped at the six-foot square concrete landing at the bottom. "This door leads to the garage, McCrary. You can escape that way. I'll give you five minutes before I give the alarm. This is your best chance to walk out alive. If I were you, I'd take it." He reached for the steel fire door.

I dragged him away from the door. "Quiet. Not a word. Sit on the steps...Not that one. Move two steps higher." I wanted a little more distance between him and the door. And me.

Moving to the door, I pulled the stethoscope from a pocket, placed it against the door, and listened for long seconds. Nothing.

"Stand up, Vidali." I grabbed the back of his robe again and steered him to the steel door. "Slowly, slowly. Push it open."

He set his hands shoulder width on the crash bar and pushed it down. The bar groaned then *thunked*. Everything metal corrodes sooner or later in the humid subtropics.

"Okay, now open the door—easy."

He leaned on the steel door. It swung open. The garage beyond was dark. The hinges creaked from disuse. The door swung wider.

Too late, I realized that Vidali and I were standing in the lighted stairway.

Vidali leapt into the darkness. "Shoot him! Shoot him!" He rolled to one side.

I didn't stop to think. I rapid-fired three times into the garage. At least Vidali's Glock worked.

Automatic gunfire sprayed through the open door and ricocheted off the stairs and the concrete walls. The steel-jacketed slugs scraped and pounded concrete dust and steel shavings from the wall, filling the air. I heard two distinct weapons: an AK-47 and a hand gun. Only two.

Several slugs hit my armored vest first on the front and then on the back as I jumped a 180 turn and bolted up the stairs three at a time.

The steel door *clanked* closed behind me. I prayed it didn't have a door handle on the other side.

As I reached the landing at the top of the secret stairway, the lights went out. Vidali must have flipped the breakers from inside the garage. It was as dark as the inside of a black cat's stomach.

I pushed where I thought the backside of the study door was. It opened soundlessly.

The power was off in the study, but light leaked through the window from the landscape lighting. It must have been on a separate circuit and Vidali had forgotten about that.

Moving to the window, I peeked out. The master suite balcony extended from the side of the mansion for twenty feet. A man in black stood guard with an M4A1 gun, its distinctive silhouette visible in the dim light. He divided his attention between the French doors of the master bedroom and the window where I stood in the darkness. I was above the pool deck. A large patio umbrella sheltered the poolside table right below the window.

If I opened the window, the gunman would see or hear the motion and spray me with a burst of bullets. My vest wouldn't protect me in a case like that. One lucky shot to the head or neck and I would be as dead as last year's eggnog.

Stepping back from the window, I sighted through the glass at the lone gunman. The first shot should break the glass, and the hurricane-proof glass would deflect the slug enough to miss the target. But the second shot...and the third...

I took a calming breath. *Easy squeezy, nice and easy.*

I rapid-fired four times and dove through the window. I bounced off the umbrella and landed off balance. My ankle popped and a sharp pain shot through it. I leapt into the heavy landscaping around the pool. The bougainvillea thorns gouged my face. Thorns ripped my rubber gloves and cut the backs of my hands.

I listened. Silence. There was no return fire.

I had moved too fast for the two guys from the garage to get to where I was. That meant that the man I shot on the balcony was at least a third man they had left on guard. Maybe there were just those three, plus Vidali himself, to contend with. If so, it was now "only" three against one. Maybe. Or maybe four against one.

I switched the partial magazine for the one I had taken from Vidali in the bedroom. Seventeen rounds in the spare plus ten in the first magazine. I had twenty-seven rounds of Vidali's shells, plus my own. It would have to be enough.

Standing in the shadows, I shifted my weight to my left ankle. Painful, but bearable. I had hiked and fought in Iraq and Afghanistan with worse. I swiped my cheeks and chin with the back of my hands. The shredded gloves were streaked with my blood, but only on the backs. So were the thorns that had cut me, but I doubted the CSIs would think to test the bougainvillea by the pool for DNA;

there were bougainvillea all over the grounds. If they tested, I couldn't do anything about it anyway.

I pushed behind the bushes to the bottom of the stairs from Vidali's bedroom. He hadn't had enough time to get back to his suite. He had to be in the garage still, or maybe making his way back inside the house.

Escape was not an option; I had to stop Vidali. Permanently.

I limped up the stairs. I felt for the pulse of the man I shot on the balcony. Dead. I ejected the magazine from his M4A1. The cartridges wouldn't fit a Glock, so I tossed the magazine into the pool. I hobbled into Vidali's bedroom. The power was still off. I blew out the candles.

The door between his sitting room and bedroom hung by one hinge. The landscape lighting reflected off the leaves and palm fronds and lit a wedge from the bedroom door to the sitting room doors that opened to the hall. I shined the flashlight into the sitting room. Both hall doors stood open. I limped over and shut them, but I didn't lock them. I assumed that Vidali's henchmen had flipped on the lights when they came through. I flipped the light switch next to the door. If he switched the breaker back on, the sitting room would remain dark.

Anyone entering the sitting room from either direction would walk straight across to the opposite door. Simple human nature.

There was only one suitable kill zone. A love seat on the right side backed up to the wall, ninety degrees from the direct line across the sitting room. From there, I would be invisible in the shadows until my muzzle flash revealed my position. I would have a good view of both the hall doors and the broken bedroom door. Whichever way they came, I could shoot from the dark into the dim light.

I blotted the blood from my cheeks and chin and stuffed the tissue in my pants pocket. After I stripped off the bloody rubber gloves, I zipped them into a pocket. I slipped on fresh gloves. It wouldn't do to leave any DNA at the crime scene.

The longer I waited, the more my eyes grew accustomed to the darkness.

The doorknob clicked. The pistol grip knob moved downward, and the man on the other side prepared to enter the kill zone.

I took a calming breath.

The eye responds to movement. Assuming firing position, I aimed toward the center of the room and waited for the door to open. *Easy squeezy, nice and easy.*

A hand pushed the door. It swung open all the way and banged against the door stop. Smart. The gunman made sure I was not hiding behind the door.

Silence.

A dark silhouette entered, gun held with both hands, but pointed at the floor. In the dim light, he seemed bulkier than the Pisarczik I remembered. Maybe it wasn't him. Maybe it was Orsinati. Or was it Vidali's supposed fourth man? He walked straight toward the master bedroom.

When he reached the center of the room, I double tapped him. He staggered, and I swung the Glock toward the door in case another man came in. The gunman regained his balance and reeled in my direction. I fired again, simultaneously with him. A slug pounded my vest when his muzzle flash blinded my dilated eyes.

I had hit him at least twice, yet he could still shoot. He had to be wearing a bulletproof vest. I needed to make a head shot. I hate head shots. Blinded by the muzzle flashes, I rapid-fired until I lost count. So did he until the muzzle flash of his last two shots pointed at the floor. The Glock clicked empty. I must've fired fifteen more times.

My ears rang in the sudden silence. The acrid gunpowder smell in the confined space stung my nose. I sneezed, and for an instant the smell transported me back to Afghanistan. I shook my head to clear it. The gunman didn't move. I switched the spent magazine for a full one. My own magazine was in Vidali's Glock now, but I had worn gloves when I loaded it. A future CSI would not find any fingerprints on the brass or the magazine.

Aiming the Glock at the fallen man, I limped over and kicked his gun across the room. I felt his pulse. There wasn't one. I rolled him over and felt the hard texture of the vest. His head lolled like a rag doll. I pulled out the flashlight. Orsinati's bald head gleamed in the beam.

That means that Pisarczik, the professional gunman, had the AK-47 I had heard from the garage. That was not good.

Limping into the bedroom, I rested on an upholstered chair, my back against the outside wall. In seconds, my eyesight was back to normal, but my ears still rang. A distinctive shadow crossed the light coming through the French doors. Someone was on the balcony. Someone with a bulletproof vest and a Kalashnikov. Pisarczik.

I took a breath and slowed my pulse.

A distant grandfather clock chimed four times in the silence.

The shadow on the carpet froze until the chimes stopped. It lengthened and moved to the right. The shadow stopped again.

I aimed high for the head shot. *Easy squeezy, nice and easy.*

A dark movement flashed across the threshold, flying through the air. I rapid-fired four times and tried to follow him across.

Pisarczik landed in a roll and disappeared into the darkness on the other side of the bed. I hoped he was lying flat on the floor.

"You missed me, McCrary. Now I'm gonna cut you to ribbons."

He knew from my muzzle flashes where I was. Correction: He knew where I had been when I fired. I didn't stay there.

Dropping to the floor, I belly-crawled toward the bed. I extended my Glock under the edge of the bed and aimed six inches above the floor. I fired once. The muzzle flash lit his feet and ankles. He was standing. I fired three more times and hit him at least once, maybe twice.

Pisarczik yelled and fired a burst across the bed, aiming at the chair where I had sat seconds before.

Too late, pisser. I'm not there anymore.

I crabbed sideways toward the center of the room, taking advantage of the plush carpet that absorbed sound. I didn't want him to pen me against the wall. Six rounds left. Make them count. I suppressed a sneeze when I smelled gunpowder again.

Pisarczik stumbled across the floor and dropped, groaning, into the twin of the chair I had fired from. I had hit him in the foot or ankle, but he didn't need his feet to fire a weapon.

I eased around the end of the bed toward the side where Pisarczik sat. Fishing the flashlight from a pocket with my left hand, I extended it under the bed toward where I heard Pisarczik panting. Rotating the flashlight ninety degrees to the floor, I pressed the lens against the carpet so I could flick it on without him seeing it.

I flicked the switch and tossed the flashlight out from under the bed.

He pointed the Kalashnikov at the flashlight and fired a long burst.

I frogged forward and rapid-fired at his head, well-lit by the muzzle flashes. I hate head shots. The last muzzle flash showed brains exploding against the white wall behind him. My Glock clicked empty. Again.

After stumbling to my feet, I headed toward the study. I

remembered Vidali's Smith & Wesson revolver I had found in his desk and unloaded. The cartridges were in his study.

My heart sank when I tried the door. Locked. I didn't have a bazooka; that revolver might have been on the far side of the moon.

The M4A1 was on the balcony, but I had thrown the magazine into the pool. *Note to self: Next time, keep the magazine in case you need it.*

Vidali and possibly a fourth man were lurking out there somewhere, and I was out of ammo.

I grabbed Pisarczik's AK-47 and examined the magazine. He had emptied it at the flashlight. My weapons were the knife I brought with me and the knife I stole from Vidali's desk. And two empty Glocks. Another *oh-shit* moment.

Wait a minute. Orsinati had carried a Browning .380. I struggled into the sitting room and found it. I thumbed out the magazine and examined it with the flashlight. Three rounds left. Three was better than zero.

I carried the pistol back to the bedroom and sat in the chair. Stuffing oozed from the chair from the rounds Pisarczik had fired into it. It was still the best firing position in the room.

I waited for my heart rate to slow and my eyes to dilate. Again.

A muffled bark came from the closet. Vidali's blonde Barbie doll was in there. She and her Pomeranians.

I was trespassing, so I had to disappear before the cops arrived. What was taking the cops so long? Maybe the neighbors, safe behind their double-paned windows and ensconced in their soundproof, air-conditioned palaces, hadn't heard the gunfire. Possible, but unlikely. Surely one of the security patrols would have reported the shots.

Wait, we were on an island—a private island. The cops would come by ferry. There was one ferry on duty in the wee hours of the morning. It was that time of night when response would be slow at best. Plus maybe a fifty-minute wait for the ferry. Then they would have to figure out how to get here from the ferry terminal.

And, and, and…I had maybe an hour.

"McCrary, you in there?"

It was Vidali. He sounded like he was next to the pool.

I waited.

"McCrary, you win. We need to talk."

I waited.

"McCrary, I'm unarmed. You killed my men. What more do you want? I said 'you win.' Let's talk."

I hollered out the French door, "Turn the power on and come up to your bedroom."

"Be there in three minutes, McCrary."

Five minutes later, he hollered from the hallway, "The power's on. I'm unarmed, McCrary. I'm coming in."

I held the empty Glock in my left hand and Orsinati's nearly empty Browning in my right. "Come ahead, Vidali."

He walked into view, hands up. "I'm unarmed."

"Switch on the lights."

He did.

"Take off your robe and turn around."

Vidali shrugged out of his robe and did a 360. He was unarmed.

"You can put your robe back on."

"Can I let Jasmine out of the closet now?"

I waved him permission.

He tapped on the closet door. Furious barks came from inside. Somehow the dogs knew the danger was over. Or maybe they liked to bark anytime someone knocked on the door. Whatever. "Jasmine, honey, it's Vic. Everything's okay now. You can come out."

A mumbled reply came through the door.

"I can't hear you, honey. You can come out now."

The door opened a crack. "I heard lots of guns, Vic. Is it safe?"

"Yes, it's safe. The shooting is over. You can come out."

"Great. I gotta pee something awful."

She took two steps out of the closet and swerved toward the bathroom, still naked as a nudist queen. The dogs trotted right behind. She noticed me and stopped in her tracks, swaying a little to keep her balance. She considered me through her drug-induced haze. "I remember you. You're the guy who interrupted Vic and me before we was finished."

I made a little bow where I sat. "Sorry about that. You lovebirds can finish after I leave."

She gawked at Vic, then at me. "Whatever. I gotta pee." She scurried to the bathroom and slammed the door behind her.

The dogs trotted over and sat next to the bathroom door.

I waited. Didn't know what else to do. I was in uncharted waters. I figured I'd let Vidali take the lead from here, so long as things moved in the right direction.

"She'll need clothes." Vidali stepped into the closet before I could stop him.

If the closet were a safe room, he would have more weapons inside. I set down the empty Glock and aimed the Browning with a two-hand grip.

A moment later, Vidali rolled from the closet with another Smith & Wesson in his hand. One round hit me square in the chest and another blew the corner off the upholstered chair right beside my head.

I hit him with all three Browning rounds.

Poor Jasmine. I hoped she was smart enough to stay locked in the bathroom until the cops found her. At least she would have a place to pee if they took a long time to come.

I limped to the marina—5:40 a.m. I could have made it quicker, if I hadn't had to find Graciela's cellphone. It was in a pocket in Vidali's pants in the closet. Far as I could tell, I left no evidence that either one of us had ever had anything to do with Vicente Vidali.

Poor Jasmine was so stoned she wouldn't be a credible witness, even if she was willing to talk to the cops.

Of course, there were security cameras all over Mango Island, but hundreds of tuxedoed strangers visited the island that night. I doubted they would pay attention to my little ol' boat. It was one straw in a bale of hay. All the victims were mobsters with lots of enemies. And all the bullets were from the victims' own guns. The cops would chase the wrong clues. I hoped.

As I passed the harbormaster's office, a dock attendant dozed inside, turquoise jacket tossed over the back of a chair. I let him sleep. Better he didn't notice me. My face and hands were streaked with red cuts and dried blood. I hadn't dared wash them at Vidali's for fear I'd leave my DNA in the drain.

Two minutes later I cast off and piloted the SeaRay out of the harbor. I crossed the ship channel and plucked the battery from Gracie's phone. I dropped it and the phone in forty-five feet of water. An hour after that, I cruised into Mike's Marina. I dropped the boat keys through the slot in his office door.

Halfway back to the Avanti, the adrenalin caught up with me. I leaned on the fender. The shakes overtook me. The water and the energy bars I had consumed motoring back to Mike's marina objected to the strain I'd put my body through. I pitched my cookies in the parking lot. *Macho man*, that's me.

I got in the Avanti and punched the A/C up to *frantic*. I suffered an after-action attack of the sweats.

I concentrated on breathing. I sent Bob a message:

All is well. You and Gracie are safe. No one

will bother either of you. Have a great game.
Go Jets!

I texted Snoop and Jorge:

All is well. You both are free to go home,
with my thanks.

I slipped the Avanti in gear. The adrenaline helped, but the pain in my sprained ankle made it god-awful to push in the clutch to shift gears. I managed to shift into second and drive home that way.

The sun peeked above the horizon as I arrived home and fell into bed. My last thought was what would Jorge think when he learned about the massacre on Mango Island.

FIFTEEN

I woke up at three o'clock that afternoon and turned on my cellphone. A text from Bob was waiting for me.

I can never repay you for what you've done. But at least I can pay you for your services. Bring a bill tomorrow and let's have lunch. My suite at 1:30?

I texted that I would be there and wished him and his team good luck. Then I showered and stretched my aching muscles and cleaned up the cuts on my hands and face as best I could.

"Chuck, glad you could make it. Clint, it's good to see you again. Y'all come on in." Hank Hickham grabbed my hand and shook it with the gusto only a three-hundred-pound, five-foot-nine man can muster. Then he shook Clint's hand with equal fervor. Hank was past anyone's normal retirement age, with a fringe of gray hair around his bald pate, but he had the energy of a high-school track

228

star. He had to be: It took a human dynamo to run the busiest restaurant in Florida.

Hank eyed the Band-Aids on my face, but didn't mention them. "The bar's over there and the buffet is over yonder. Make yourselves to home."

Neither Clint nor I had ever watched a live Super Bowl game. Hank had called me a month earlier to invite me to his thirty-five-yard-line stadium suite. His suite had twenty-four seats and I was surprised he'd invited me since he knew every mover and shaker in Atlantic County. I had done Hank an indirect favor the previous year, and he had become a loyal and influential friend. Apparently, he thought he still owed me, even after getting me onto Mango Island twice.

I didn't argue with him.

Clint and I had arrived a little after 6:00 p.m., a half hour before kickoff. The setting sun had dipped below the top rows of Port City Super Stadium, and the field below dazzled beneath the stadium lights. The Dallas Cowboys logo was painted in the south end zone; the New York Jets logo in the north. The NFL logo painted in the center of the field stretched between the forty-five-yard lines.

Clint grabbed two pulled-pork sandwiches and a glass of iced tea. I remembered when he was an underfed street kid bumming spare change to buy a Big Mac. I felt a swell of pride in how far Clint had come. He was now a starter on the Port City Prep varsity basketball team and an honor student.

I piled a plate with boiled shrimp, horseradish, and cocktail sauce and walked stiffly to a bar stool at a round table at the back of the spacious suite. My ankle bothered me so much when I shifted gears that I had let Clint drive the Avanti to the stadium. He had earned his learner's permit, and his eyes got big as headlights when I asked him to drive the antique car.

On the natural grass turf below, the teams finished their

introductions and lined up for the national anthem. Bob Martinez stood with the other players, staring up at the stands. There was no way he could tell which suite was which—the stadium had over a hundred of them on three different levels. Yet he pointed right at me, waved, and gave me a thumbs-up. I had to grin. I felt surprisingly good right then. I waved back.

On the field, the announcer introduced several notables to the crowd. Among them was Arnie "Bigs" Bigelow, a Hall of Fame member and retired defensive lineman for the Port City Pelicans. Back when Bigs played, he'd dominated the field so much that sports journalists had dubbed the entire Pelican defensive line *The Bigs Brigade*. After the Pelicans retired his jersey, he'd joined the Port City Police Department and worked his way up to detective. I was proud to call him a friend.

After the national anthem, I sipped my Diet Dr. Pepper, munched on shrimp, and enjoyed Clint having the time of his life.

On the field, the team captains shook hands. Honorary captains, Joe Namath of the Jets and Troy Aikman of the Cowboys, presided over the coin toss.

Hank's wife, Lorene, came over and kissed me on the cheek, carefully avoiding the Band-Aids. "Chuck, it's so nice you could come." She sat down at the table with Clint and me. She and Hank had been married over forty years and still acted like honeymooners. A few years younger than Hank, Lorene had aged well. She was proud of her silver hair and wore it long enough for its natural wave to show. A touch of lipstick and eyebrow pencil accented her slightly wrinkled face. She reminded me of one of my older aunts. She smiled at Clint and touched his forearm. Lorene is a toucher. "I don't believe I've met this young man with you. Could you introduce us?"

"Lorene, this is my friend Clint Watkins. Clint, this is Lorene Hickham."

"How do you do, ma'am?" Clint set down the remaining half of his first sandwich and stood up, wiping his hands.

She shook hands. "Any friend of Chuck's is a friend of ours. I hope you'll make yourself at home." She patted him on the shoulder and then touched my arm. "Chuck, what on earth happened to your face?"

"Cut myself shaving."

Lorene smiled knowingly. "Hank tells me not to ask you too many questions, so I'll accept that silly answer." She patted me on the shoulder and stood up. "Clint, it was a pleasure to meet you. Enjoy the game."

The Jets won the toss. Joe Namath announced that the Jets would defer. The captains returned to their sidelines.

Hank took the stool Lorene had vacated and leaned close to my ear in the deafening noise. "Everything work out okay with, uh," he glanced at Clint, "that party invitation I gave you?"

The teams lined up for the kickoff.

I gazed around the suite. Nobody other than Clint paid any attention to us. I winked at Hank.

"Where'd you get them cuts on your face?"

"Cut myself shaving." I noticed Clint's smile. While he drove us to the stadium, I had told him that I had been on a case the previous night. That was all he needed to know.

"One of them cuts is on your forehead."

I smiled. "I stood on a chair."

"I noticed you limping too."

"Then I fell off the chair and sprained my ankle." I winked. "You don't want to miss the kickoff, Hank." The kicker was running toward the ball. Hank gave Clint and me each a fatherly pat on the shoulder and left to rejoin his other guests.

Down below, the Cowboys kick returner took a knee in the end zone.

Clint was working on his second sandwich. I refilled my plate.

Bob Martinez and the Jets offense took the field for the first snap of the Super Bowl.

I switched on my phone and it whistled. My sprained ankle had bothered me all during the Super Bowl and Hank's post-game party. At home after the game, I turned off my phone, crashed, and slept ten hours. Bob's text read:

    I'm up early and I'm starving to death. Let's
    make lunch at 1:00. Don't forget to bring your
    bill.

I texted back,

    Great. See you then.

Bob limped badly as he led me out to the balcony. I was limping just as much.

I sat at the table across from him. "What happened to you, *amigo*? I thought you won the game. You look like you've been rode hard and put up wet."

"It's part of the game. I'm always beat up and sore the day after. Those two-ton linemen chow down on me something fierce." He motioned to the server, who poured our coffee. "I see that you're walking wounded too. What's your excuse, Eighty-Eight? You get sacked by a charging defensive lineman? How did you get those cuts on your face?"

"It's part of the game, except my game is different from yours. It's merely a sprained ankle." I clapped him on the shoulder and we sat down at the table. "Will Gracie be joining us?"

"Uh, Gracie doesn't feel well." He forced a smile. "Let's eat. You can give me your bill after lunch."

He waved at the server who was standing by. She removed the covers from our plates, and the aroma of mushrooms, salsa, bacon and God-knows-what-else filled my nose. "What are these?"

"My own special omelet: jalapeños, cheddar, bacon, mushrooms, chopped onions, and chopped ham. All topped with salsa."

"Reminds me of the sweep-the-floor pizza I sometimes order." I cut off a piece of omelet. "It's delicious."

We ate in silence for a moment.

"How does it feel to be Super Bowl MVP?"

Bob grinned like he'd won the lottery. In a way, he had. "Almost better than sex, Eighty-Eight. Almost. The icing on the cake is the two-million-dollar contract bonus for the MVP designation. My agent threw that one in when the Jets traded the Browns for me." He lifted his juice glass, and we toasted the Jets victory. "Thirty-five to twenty, we even beat the spread." He set his juice down. "How'd it go with Vidali?"

I glanced at the server. "Let's finish our championship breakfast. We'll talk later."

He took the hint.

An hour later, the server wheeled our dirty dishes away and we were alone. Seeti Bay sparkled below in the afternoon sun.

"Have you read the paper today?" I asked.

"Yeah. I clipped out the articles about the game for *Mamacita's* scrapbook."

"I meant the front page."

"They were on the front page. This is the Super Bowl, Eighty-Eight. What page did you expect them to be on?"

"I meant the front page of the first section, not the sports section. The story with the headline, '*Mango Island Mobsters Shoot*

It Out.'" I picked up the first section of the *Port City Press-Journal* that the server had brought with our breakfast and handed it to Bob.

I finished my coffee while he read the article.

He shook his head unconsciously. At the bottom of the third column, he flipped to the continuation on page three. He pursed his lips like he was about to whistle, but he didn't.

"Wow," he said softly as he leaned back in his chair. "Four mobsters all dead. Says here that Vidali killed three of his own men outright with a Glock. The third man killed Vidali with his Browning .380 after Vidali shot him. All the bullets came from the mobsters' own guns." He set the paper down. "How'd you manage that?"

"Me? As that fight went down at 4:00 a.m. the day of the Super Bowl, I was nowhere near 176 Mango Drive. I went to a party in Fort Lauderdale." I raised my hand like I was taking an oath, but I crossed my fingers. Bob and I did that as kids in Bowie Elementary School back in Adams Creek.

Bob smiled a half-smile. "So, it's a coincidence that the guy who threatened me and Gracie got into a gunfight and got himself killed right before the Super Bowl game?"

"Rule Seven, Bob: *There is no such thing as a coincidence.*"

"Huh? What's rule seven?"

"My personal rules about how to be a good private eye. Rule Seven is there is no such thing as a coincidence."

"So, it's *not* a coincidence that Vidali got into a gunfight with his own men."

"My daddy used to say, 'All I know is what I read in the paper.' If the *Press-Journal* says it was a shootout amongst the bad guys themselves, then that's what it was. Let's leave it at that."

"I don't know what to say, Eighty-Eight. You risked your life for me and Gracie, and you did it more than once. How can I put a value on that?"

"You can't, but the good news is that you don't have to. It's what I do for a living. Like your bruises, sometimes that's part of the game." I reached inside my jacket. "Here's the bill you asked for."

To his credit, Bob didn't flinch when he spotted the total. It was less than he made in a week, especially Super Bowl week, but not much less. He handed me a check. "It's totally inadequate to say thank you, but I'm no good with words."

"No need, Bob." I stuck the check in my jacket. "Now let's talk about Gracie. I had a conversation with someone who tried to fix the Super Bowl game. I got answers that explained things."

"You had a conversation with a certain someone. But he's dead and you were in Fort Lauderdale."

"For the sake of conversation, let's assume I had a séance with his spirit during his crossing to meet the devil. The spirit said that Graciela approached him at his New Jersey casino two days after the AFC Championship game. He said the whole idea to fix the Super Bowl was hers. She claimed she had you wrapped around her finger, and she could make you throw the game."

"I don't believe you."

I shrugged. "Not my problem if you don't believe the spirit. I'm telling you what the spirit said." I reached in my pocket and tossed him an envelope. "You recognize that?"

Bob opened it. "It's full of cash. Is that the envelope Vidali passed to Gracie in the elevator?"

"It is. I snagged it from her purse right after we rescued her from Vidali's yacht. It's evidence in case anything ever goes to trial. It's the money Vidali gave her to go hide at a hotel in Naples." I took the envelope back and stuck it in my pocket.

"That's the Naples you mentioned the other day?"

"Yeah, Naples, Florida. A nice resort town on the Gulf Coast. That was the address she punched into the GPS but didn't drive to."

"Then why would Vidali kidnap her?"

"He had second thoughts about her ability to stay hidden until after the game. He was afraid someone in Naples would recognize her, so he kidnapped her and held her on his yacht."

Bob didn't say anything. He stared into the middle distance at nothing.

I guess it was a lot for him to take in. I sipped coffee and waited.

He stood up and paced a couple of steps. "Gracie was behind the whole thing?"

I nodded. "She didn't have the resources to pull it off—that's where Vidali's cash and contacts in Las Vegas came in—but the whole scheme was her idea."

"God knows, she has expensive tastes."

"And an expensive drug habit," I amended.

He spread his feet and set his fists on his hips. "Gracie kicked that habit last summer."

I shook my head. "She began using again in September about the time you played San Diego in week three. When you were in Vegas after that game, whose idea was it to go into the sports book? Was it Gracie?"

"Omigod." He seemed like he'd been smacked with a two-by-four. "Gracie said she'd never been in a sports book and wanted to see what it looked like. Said she wanted to check the Super Bowl odds—just for fun." His face reddened beneath his tan. "She said it would be fun to place a hundred-to-one bet on the Jets."

"Gracie owes a lot of money to a drug dealer named Sam Torrance a/k/a Sharky. He threatened to throw acid on her face. He's done it to other women."

Bob hung his head. "She must have been so desperate…"

He raised his gaze. "Why didn't she come to me? I have more money than I could ever spend. I helped her before. I've always helped her." He slammed the table with his non-throwing hand.

"Why not come to me? By God, I'm her freaking fiancé. I could've helped her." He regarded me through tears as the truth sank in. "I could've helped her."

I reached the hotel lobby, and my phone whistled that I'd missed a call from Jorge Castellano. He didn't leave a voicemail.

"Hey, Jorge, it's Chuck. I was in an elevator and had no signal. You tried to call?"

"My squad has been handed the Vidali case. We need to talk."

"Sure, what's on your mind?"

"Not over the phone. Can you come to the precinct?"

"Always glad to help our men and women in blue. I'm in the lobby of the Port City Palace. I'll be there in…forty-five minutes."

"Thanks for coming, Chuck. Coffee?"

"Sure."

Detective Lieutenant Jorge Castellano and I walked to the coffee station and Jorge grabbed the carafe. "A little cream, no sugar, right?"

"You remembered."

"I'm a lieutenant of detectives now. I remember everything."

"Does it get old, being perfect?"

He shrugged, then poured our coffees. "I'll get used to it."

When we were in his office, he closed the glass door. "I assigned the case to Kelly and Bigs." Kelly Contreras was the senior detective of the two. She had spotted Bigs Bigelow after he'd trained at the police academy and become a ride-along, unpaid volunteer in the NFL off-season. After retiring from the NFL, Bigs began a second career as a patrolman. After he earned his detective rank, Kelly grabbed him as a partner. I'd worked with them before. Good cops.

"Kelly wants to talk to you, but I told her I wanted you first."

I stirred my coffee and waited for the other shoe to drop. This was tricky. When we were both patrolmen, Jorge saved my life by taking a bullet meant for me. Then I saved his life when he was framed for murder. Call it even. He was one of my best friends. I would lie to him if I had to, but I wouldn't like it.

"Vicente Vidali was shot dead in his mansion early yesterday morning. Neighbors reported they heard something, maybe gunshots, around 3:30 to 4:00 in the morning. Hard to say because they were asleep behind double-paned windows."

He paused, so I said *hmm* to let him know I'd heard him.

"Dante Orsinati and Pistolet Pisarczik were among the guys found dead."

"Aren't those the two guys who shot up my office?"

"Yeah. Small world."

I didn't want to risk another *hmm*, so I said, "How about that?"

"You texted me that all was well and I could end the protection detail. You know anything about what happened on Mango Island, Chuck?" He regarded me closely.

"Why would I know anything about that?" I didn't lie exactly. I didn't answer the question, but I didn't lie.

"Orsinati and Pisarczik shot up your office. They worked for Vicente Vidali. They were all killed at Vidali's house on Mango Island. Graciela Perez's text was sent from Mango Island, using the phone of a guy who worked on Vidali's yacht. You rescued Graciela from Vidali's yacht. Saturday afternoon, I told you that Graciela's phone was near the Mango Island ferry terminal. Everything connects to everything else." He set his coffee cup down and nailed me with a dead-eye cop stare. "And it all connects to you."

Jorge waited for me to respond.

I seldom get in trouble with my mouth closed. I decided to go with a winner and shut up.

"Well?" he said.

I said *hmm* again. I was getting into a rhythm.

"And you're limping and you have cuts all over your face, like you've been in a fight."

"Tripped on my balcony and cut myself shaving."

"A lot of coincidences there, *amigo*."

I sipped my coffee.

"You always say 'There is no such thing as a coincidence.' Your rule six."

"Rule seven."

"Okay, seven. There is no such thing as a coincidence."

"The complete rule seven says *There is no such thing as a coincidence—except when there is.*" I set down my cup. "Sometimes coincidences do happen."

"Tell me what went down at Vidali's place. Just between the two of us."

I spread my hands, palms up. "I couldn't possibly tell you what went down at Vidali's place. Why are you asking me? Am I a suspect?"

Jorge contemplated me for a long time. "Okay. Kelly and Bigs want to talk to you."

As I walked out of Jorge's office, trying not to limp, he stopped me. "For what it's worth, *amigo*, I deleted that 'all is well' text you sent me from my phone. I told Snoop to delete it too."

He shook my hand. "It never happened."

I grinned at my friend. "*What* never happened?"

I sat on one side of the table. Kelly and Bigs sat on the other between me and the door. They didn't mean anything by it; that's the way cops do it. I did it that way when I was a police detective.

After *hello-how-are-you* all around, Kelly plopped a three-ring binder and a manila folder on the table. "This interview is being videoed and recorded. Please acknowledge that you are aware of that."

I did, and she read me my Miranda rights. "Chuck, do you want an attorney?"

"Remember the last time you read me my Miranda rights?" I grinned. "It was when you and Bigs arrested me for murder. No hard feelings."

She forced a smile. Maybe she was still embarrassed about that arrest. "This is simply routine. You willing to talk without an attorney?"

"Sure. How can I help you?"

"We've got questions."

"What kind of questions?" When I was new to interrogation, Snoop had taught me, "The guy that asks the questions controls the interview." Maybe I could ask a few of my own to steer her in another direction.

"About the Mango Island Massacre," she said.

The *Port City Press-Journal* had called the gunfight the Mango Island Massacre. I thought it was kinda catchy.

Kelly set an eight by ten crime-scene picture in front of me. "This is Vicente Vidali, the way we found him in his bedroom yesterday." His blue silk robe had fallen open in front and his chest and the robe were both covered in blood. He had the Smith & Wesson revolver clutched in his right hand. He had rolled onto his back before he died.

I picked up the photo and studied it. "Lotta blood on his chest. How many times was he hit?"

She ignored me. "Do you know Vidali?"

"I know him by reputation. I had a researcher do a complete background check, and I recognize his face from the security videos I reviewed at the Port City Palace. Have you watched those yet?"

"This is the first we've heard about security videos. Tell me about them." She flipped open a note pad.

I filled her in on my activities, beginning with my Sunday breakfast with Bob. I included nearly everything that had transpired until I delivered Gracie safely to the hotel. I was specific and thorough. Rule Four: *Always be specific when you lie. Include as much truth as possible.* I wanted to give Kelly and Bigs lots to do that involved things they would find out anyway. It would keep them busy to verify everything Snoop and I had done. They would be able to fill lots of pages of their crime notebook. A thicker notebook would give their conclusions more weight, pun intended. "How many times was Vidali shot?"

This time Kelly responded, probably because I was so cooperative. "Three."

"Whose shells hit him?"

"Browning .380's. Don't know whose they were. We found a Browning near Dante Orsinati."

"He shot up my security camera with a .380. You could compare those slugs with ballistics from the Mango Island Massacre. That could tie them to Orsinati."

"Where are the slugs from your office?"

"Still in the ceiling. I left them there in case I wanted to file assault charges against the shooters."

"We'll send a CSI guy to your office to collect them."

I studied another photo. "What room is this?"

"The sitting room."

"Where in the house is that?"

"At the entrance to Vidali's bedroom. It's like his own private living room."

"*Hmm.* Must be nice to have that kind of money. Is that a Browning in the photo? Is that Orsinati's?"

"Yeah, he must've dropped it when Vidali shot him."

"Is that a vest he's wearing?"

"Yeah, we found three nine-millimeter slugs in the vest. And two hits to his head were consistent with a nine."

"The picture of Vidali shows him holding a revolver."

"Yeah, but we found an empty Glock near him. He must've emptied the Glock at Orsinati. Then he went to his closet for the S&W. We found a niche in the closet the right size for the S&W. The closet had been modified as a safe room."

"Must have been a long shoot-out, huh?"

"The girl claims she heard about a hundred gunshots. Of course, she's a stoner, so who knows?"

"This girl?" I picked up another photo. "Who is she?"

"Jasmine Burke. Vidali's girlfriend."

"Pretty girl. A shame she was tied up with a guy like Vidali. Is she a witness?"

Bigs scoffed. "Define *witness*. She was half-stoned when this went down. She hid in Vidali's bathroom for hours until we got to the scene. She was incoherent about armed gunmen busting into Vidali's bedroom while she and Vidali were getting it on hot and heavy."

I laughed. "Gives a whole new meaning to *coitus interruptus*. She said Vidali's own men broke in? Why would they break in while he was banging his girlfriend? Was it a palace coup? Maybe a rival mob bribed Vidali's bodyguards. If they did, that would be a good time to catch Vidali with his pants down. Pun intended."

Kelly smiled. "Who knows? The girl babbled all kinds of

nonsense. She was stark naked when the responding officers broke down the bathroom door. She wouldn't open it."

"Did she actually witness anything?"

Kelly shrugged and eyed Bigs. He shrugged too. "I don't think she knows *what* she saw."

"If this were my case, I'd ask Atlantic City Organized Crime cops about a rival gang trying to muscle in on Vidali in New Jersey and Wilmington, Delaware. That would explain a lot. Might provide the motive for the shootout."

She made a note. "I'll call Atlantic City and Wilmington."

SIXTEEN

I opened the front door. "Come in. You look like you didn't get much sleep last night."

Bob had called earlier to say he wanted to talk to me before he flew back home.

We sat on my condo's balcony overlooking Seeti Bay. This time of the morning it was in the shade.

Bob stared toward the bay, but I don't think he saw it. I don't think he perceived anything but what was in his own mind. Maybe he had something too important to discuss over the telephone. Or he needed a shoulder to cry on. I waited.

"I talked to Gracie about the Super Bowl bet and about this Vidali guy."

"Talk is always good for a relationship." There I was, mouthing platitudes. Me, who got so tongue-tied around women that I couldn't even ask Miyoki Takashi for a date. Carlos McCrary, relationship counselor. Talk about irony.

Grandpa Magnus McCrary often told me, "Everyone has a story

to tell. Sometimes the best thing you can do for them is to listen to it." I listened.

"We had a big fight after you left yesterday, Eighty-Eight. Gracie finally admitted everything. Said she was desperate for money. Said she didn't want to ask me again. She felt guilty that I bailed her out twice before. She wanted to stand on her own feet. That's rich, 'stand on her own feet' by blackmailing me into losing a game. I guess she didn't think it all the way through. That's why she approached Vidali. She swears she'll never use drugs again."

"Do you think she means it?"

"She always means it." Bob studied the fingernails of his left hand. "That's the trouble; Gracie is sincere as a saint when she says it. But *doing* it…" He shrugged. "That's a whole 'nother thing."

"*Hmm.*" I wanted Bob to know I heard him, but I didn't signal my opinion about Gracie. She was his problem and his business, not mine. A philosopher could make an equally good argument either way about her sincerity. Or lack of it.

"Gracie said Sharky sent her another message yesterday morning. Says he has to have his money by tomorrow or else he's coming after her."

He sighed. "She's scared shitless."

"With good reason. Sharky has a well-earned reputation as an acid-throwing face-cutter."

Bob lapsed into silence again.

"You want coffee, Bob? I made a pot."

"That'd be good, Eighty-Eight."

I poured our coffees, and he talked again. "I called Papa about this."

It was my turn to say something. "What did Papa Martinez say?"

Bob sighed. "He said I shouldn't throw good money after bad."

"That sounds like Papa."

"*Mamacita* said Gracie should learn that actions have consequences."

"You made any decisions yet?"

"I made one." His gaze shifted to back to the horizon. "Getting married right now is not a good idea. I think maybe I didn't know Gracie as well as I thought I did. I decided to postpone the wedding, Eighty-Eight."

"You told Gracie yet?"

He nodded. "She left yesterday after our fight. She's gonna visit her folks."

"*Hmm.*" Good old wishy-washy McCrary. "You make any other decisions—like about paying Sharky to go away?"

"*Nah*, but I haven't said 'no' yet either." He clasped his hands together. "The thing is: Despite everything she's done, I still love her. Or at least I love the *memory* of her—the memory of who I thought she was." He rubbed his hands together like he was rubbing an invisible football. "Hell, I don't know how I feel. All I know is I don't want anything bad to happen to her, even if we never get back together."

There it was—the conflict between head and heart. The head says "do this," and the heart says "no way."

"Love is a powerful force." McCrary, the wise philosopher. I was chock full of wisdom today.

"It's not like I can't afford to pay this dirt bag. With the Super Bowl win, my agent tells me I'll make over a hundred million this year." Now he rubbed his hands against each other, like he was fighting himself. "But then I'm the one who solves Gracie's problem—not her. Like I did with the credit cards and the drug rehab last summer. Apparently, she's learned nothing about what *Mamacita* said—actions have consequences. She's done this before; she could do it again. I wonder if I'm not paying her way for her to kill herself."

He frowned. "Maybe I'm loving her to death."

"I hope not," I said, merely to say something.

"Yeah. Me too." He stared at the horizon again.

We sat and drank coffee. The clouds drifted across the sky.

Finally, Bob checked his Rolex. "Well, I have to go to the airport or I'll miss my flight home."

"What time do you land in New York?"

"New York? New York ain't *home*, Eighty-Eight. New York is where I *live*. Home is Adams Creek. I'm flying to Houston and renting a car. I'm gonna visit Papa and *Mamacita*. Try to get my head around this situation with Gracie."

"Please give them my love."

"I will, Eighty-Eight. I seem to give everybody love, even people who don't deserve it."

A couple of days later, Miyo called. "Chuck, two detectives visited me—a woman named Kelly Contreras and the largest man I have ever personally met. His name was Arnold Bigelow. They said they're friends of yours."

"They are. Are you a football fan?"

"No, why do you ask?"

"The reason Arnie Bigelow is so big is that he's a former defensive lineman for the Port City Pelicans."

"That's our local football team, isn't it?"

"Yes. Arnie's nickname is 'Bigs' Bigelow."

"Well, he's certainly big enough for the nickname. Do you know why they interviewed me?"

"They're investigating Vicente Vidali's death. Maybe they think that Gracie's kidnapping is connected somehow."

"I told them what I told you. I don't think it helped much. The good news is that their visit reminded me I'd given you a raincheck for a cocktail. Yesterday, I shipped off the last of my paintings to New York for that gallery show."

"Congratulations. I know that's a load off your mind."

"Do you like Margaritas?"

"One of my favorite things to drink."

"Why don't you come to my place for a Margarita or three?"

"You know the wedding has been postponed, right?"

"What's that got to do with anything? You promised to tell me the story about how you rescued Gracie. Come on over. We'll watch the sunset."

I didn't remember a promise, but I wanted to see Miyo. "Thanks, I'll be there."

"Good. See you at five."

Miyo opened the door like she was raising a curtain. The first thing I noticed was her perfume. This time there was no paint odor. Her art paraphernalia had been removed from the room behind her and it had been transformed into a normal apartment. She wore a hot pink halter top and matching walking shorts above hemp sandals with gold buckles. She had three-inch gold hoops in her ears and a heavy woven gold chain necklace. Her fingernails and toenails were painted hot pink. So were her lips. Just the thing to wear for sunset watching.

I caught myself staring.

"Come in, Chuck." She positioned a hand on the back of my neck, drew my head down, and kissed me on the cheek. She took my hand and led me through the studio and onto the balcony.

Her penthouse had a full-length balcony on the west that overlooked Seetiweekifenokee Bay. The bay sparkled from the sun

248

dropping toward the downtown skyscrapers. An icy pitcher of Margaritas had spread a condensation ring on the glass-topped table. A nearby tray held a saucer of salt, a small plate of cut limes, and two stemmed glasses.

"Are you salty or non-salty?" she asked.

"Salty."

She wiped the rims of both glasses with a damp cloth and twirled the rims in the salt. She poured our drinks and stuck a wedge of lime on each glass. She handed me mine. "What shall we drink to?"

I took the glass, but I couldn't think of a toast. I stared at her like a deer in the headlights.

She laughed. "It's not that hard a question."

I flushed. I seemed to do that a lot around her. "I'm not very good at this."

"At what?"

"At...at..." I made a vague gesture. "At social stuff...small talk...with women."

Smiling, she raised an eyebrow. "If I were a man, what would you toast?"

"I'd say 'to the Jets for winning the Super Bowl.'"

She clinked her glass against mine. "To the Jets for winning the Super Bowl."

We drank.

"*Ta-da*," she said, "that wasn't so hard, was it?"

I grinned. I often do that with women when I can't think of anything to say. They seem to like it.

"Look, Chuck. I don't know what your experience is with women, and I don't care. All I knew about you at first is that Bob Martinez chose you to be his best man. Bob is one of the most honest, nicest men I know. Being Bob's best man is worth two points. I observed the way you handled yourself professionally when you interviewed me. I admire your skill. That's worth a couple of more points. After that, you all but got killed rescuing my best friend. I gave you five points for that."

"Points?"

She grinned. "That's my way of saying you did something good, something I like. Like giving a school kid a gold star." She stroked my arm with a finger. "I Googled you after those detectives left and before I called you. Now I'd like to know you better. I didn't ask you here to entertain me, or charm me, or impress me. I'm already impressed. Simply talk to me."

"How am I doing so far?"

She laughed. "You haven't won any more points, but the night is young."

"So, I've got plenty of time to put my foot in my mouth."

She gripped my forearm lightly. "Can I give you a little advice about women?"

"My mother says everyone knows more than I do about *something*. Therefore, there is always something I can learn from anyone. You gotta know more about women than I do. Ergo..." I shrugged.

"My advice is to treat a woman like you would a man." She squeezed my arm.

I stared at her hand. It felt really warm on my arm. And smooth.

"Tell me what you're thinking right now," Miyo said.

"I'm thinking that I wouldn't tell a man that his hand feels good on my arm."

She cracked up. "Okay. Let's amend the rule. Treat a woman like a man in everything except when it comes to gender differences."

"That sounds profound. Wait a minute so I can write that down."

"Oh, clever man, that's worth one more point." She laughed again. I liked the sound.

She squeezed my arm before moving her hand. "Have you heard from Bob lately?"

"He stopped by my place on the way to the airport Tuesday. Said he and Gracie had postponed the wedding. What have you heard from Gracie?"

"She's at her parents' place, crying her eyes out."

"Has she visited you?"

"No. She knows I'll kick her butt." She sipped her Margarita.

"Why would you do that?"

"Where do I start? She gets through rehab, then screws it up and goes back to using. *Boom*." She made a kicking motion. "She has a first-class modeling career going, and she's in danger of sniffing that up her nose. *Boom* again." She made another kick. "She hooks the most eligible bachelor in New York City, and she pisses that away. Strike three with a double *boom*." She leaned back against the flowered cushion of the wrought-iron chair. "Take your pick."

"Sounds like she's really good at making bad decisions."

"You can say that again."

"Sounds like she's really good at making bad decisions."

Miyo grinned over her Margarita glass. "That's worth one more point."

After that the conversation flowed freely. We grilled hamburgers on the balcony and mixed more Margaritas. I felt more comfortable with her than I had with a woman in a long time.

My landline rang. In my half-awake stupor, I knew it was my landline because I had turned my cellphone off. I had stayed at Miyo's until late and taken a cab home. The combination of two pitchers of Margaritas and Miyo's perfume had left me half-drunk. I planned to go back for the Avanti in the morning. "Yeah."

"Eighty-Eight, it's me."

I glanced at the clock. 12:10 a.m. "Yeah, Bob. You in Adams Creek?"

"Yeah. Why?"

"You do know that it's an hour later here, right?"

"Sorry to wake you, buddy, but Gracie called me."

"Congratulations. Did she wake you up in the middle of the night too?"

"She spotted Sharky. He's stalking her."

"Has she gone back to New York?"

"No. She's still in Miami with her folks."

"Sharky is in Miami?"

"Yeah. She says Sharky came for his money."

I tossed the sheet back and stood up. "Does she have it?"

"No. That's why she called me."

"Do her parents have the money?"

"*Nah.* They're good folks, but they live from paycheck to paycheck like most people."

"What do you want me to do?"

There was a long pause. I realized Bob hadn't thought this out. His thought process had gone no further than *Gracie is in trouble and good ol' Eighty-Eight is nearby. I think I'll call good ol' Eighty-Eight. He'll know what to do.*

"I don't know, Eighty-Eight. Can you help her?"

I started to walk into the kitchen in case I needed coffee. Fortunately, my landline has a cordless phone. "What kind of help did you have in mind?"

"Protect her, maybe?"

"Sure, I can protect her. I'll use two guys to cover her sixteen hours a day. It'll be expensive and I'll do it, but that's solely a short-term solution."

"How so?"

"It doesn't solve the underlying problem of her debt to Sharky. Sharky will still be there. Or he'll be in New York if she goes back there. I can't protect her in New York City; I don't know the territory."

"I'm not worried about the long term. I simply want to make sure she's okay while she stays with her folks."

"How long are you willing to pay me to protect her? A week? A month? What happens when she goes back to New York? Sharky won't go away on his own. She'll still owe him money. Protection for Gracie is not a long-term solution."

"Then I don't know what else to do, Eighty-Eight. What play would you call?"

There it was. Bob's problem was about to become my problem.

Whatever I said could be the wrong thing. If I were in Bob's position, the right solution for me might be the wrong solution for him. On the other hand, I would never be in Bob's position. If I had a girlfriend involved with drugs, I'd run for the exit like a scalded dog.

If I had a girlfriend. Someone I loved. Which I didn't. Hell, I didn't know what I would do in Bob's shoes.

"I'm stumped, Bob. You're damned if you do, and damned if you don't."

"How so?"

"If you hire me to protect her, that doesn't solve the Sharky problem. If you pay off Sharky, that doesn't solve the Graciela-standing-on-her-own-two-feet problem. Bad outcome either way."

"So, what play should I call?"

"What's best for Gracie?"

"*Amigo*, I ain't no deep thinker. Finding my third outlet receiver is about as far ahead as I plan. Everything else I leave to my agent and my CPA."

"What does your agent recommend?"

"He thinks I should tell Gracie to take a hike. He thinks she's a distraction to my career. He also says that Gracie's own agent, who is a friend of his, tells him that Gracie is coming unglued and her career is headed for the crapper."

"And your CPA. What does he think?"

"I haven't asked him. It's really not his area of responsibility."

"Okay, here's what I think: Let's go for the short-term solution. Protect Gracie for a few days while you think about the long-term. Maybe something will come to me, or maybe you'll have an idea. Okay?"

I glanced at the clock. 12:15 a.m. "Gracie at her parents' house now?"

"Yeah."

"I'll call her and work out a bodyguard schedule. Send me fifteen thousand as a retainer. That'll cover about a week."

"Fifteen thousand a *week*?" His voice climbed an octave as he said the last word. Even a guy making two million a week can get sticker-shock.

"Two guys eight hours a day each, plus my time to search for Sharky. I told you it would be expensive."

After Bob hung up, I called Gracie and told her not to leave home until I got there at ten o'clock the next morning.

I arranged for Snoop and Frank Bennett, a young Port City cop on vacation for a couple of weeks, to alternate watches outside the house.

Gracie ought to be safe until morning...unless Sharky had brought reinforcements. That was unlikely, I hoped.

"Chuck, so nice of you to come." Gracie air-kissed the neighborhood of my cheek. She looked like the supermodel she was: perfect makeup, perfect hair, perfectly accessorized, wearing an oh-so-casual but outrageously expensive shorts-and-top set.

"Come in. Would you care for coffee?

Her parents both rose to their feet as I stepped into their modest living room. Both had apparently taken the day off from work. They seemed shaken. No surprise there.

"You remember my parents, Horatio and Evangelina." Gracie gestured toward them like she was showing a luxury car in a television commercial.

I said hello to her parents and asked them to excuse us so Gracie and I could talk privately.

Gracie's façade of denial was so thick, I would need a meat cleaver to cut it. "Let's get one thing straight: This is not a social call. You're in danger. Bob hired me to protect you, at least temporarily. I can't protect you forever. Let's not pretend things are normal. You understand that?"

Her face got serious. "I understand."

"Have the Port City Police contacted you yet?"

"Why would they contact me again? I already told them and the FBI all about the kidnapping."

"Lots of things have happened since then. Vicente Vidali and a bunch of his hoods were killed under mysterious circumstances."

Gracie pursed her lips. "The Mango Island Massacre the newspaper called it."

"Right. The cops are investigating those deaths. They may want to interview you again. They interviewed Miyo. We both know that your role in this thing is…let's say 'murky.' If the cops contact you, you'll need a criminal attorney. Call Vicky Ramirez and ask her to recommend one. If the Port City detectives want to interview you, I advise you to insist your attorney be present."

"If I could afford an attorney, I could afford to pay off Sharky.

I'm broke." She lowered her head. "I can't do anything right—not anything *important*. I sniffed all my money up my nose."

"Take a public defender then, but don't say a word to the police without your attorney present. Not one word. Don't wait for them to read you your rights before you ask for an attorney. If they show up at all, tell them you want your attorney present. Got it?"

Her bottom lip trembled. "Is there any chance Bob will pay off Sharky?"

"Ask Bob. All I know is he doesn't want you killed or maimed. How much do you owe Sharky?"

"Forty-five thousand dollars."

"Geez. That's enough money for Sharky to invest in a trip down here to collect. Plus, it doesn't hurt that it's seventeen degrees in New York. Another excuse for him to come to Miami."

She cupped her face in both hands for a moment.

"Tell me about Sharky contacting you."

"Yesterday, he texted my other phone. You know, the flip-phone I left in my rental."

I had returned her flip-phone when I brought her back to the Port City Palace the previous Saturday. "Let me read the message."

Her hand shook as she gave me the phone. All it said was:

Tawanda Grisham.

Her chin quivered as she took the phone back. "I thought Sharky was in New York. Then, last night, Mom and Dad and I got back from the restaurant and there he was."

Her voice broke. "He…he was…on the sidewalk in front of this house, leaning on the lamp post. He wore a baseball cap and a hoodie, so I didn't recognize him at first. I got out of the car, and he flipped the hoodie back and took off his baseball cap so I could see his face under the street light. The bastard didn't say anything; he simply stared at me. Then, as I walked to the front door, he pointed that finger at me."

Her voice became ragged. "He…he followed me…tracked me with that *finger* all the way to the front porch. He said I'd better have his money tomorrow night when he comes back. That's when I called Bob." Tears spilled down her cheeks, trailing black mascara tracks. "Oh, Chuck, I'm so scared," she sobbed, hands in front of her face again.

I waited while she gathered herself.

"What's going to happen to me?"

"In the short run, nothing. I'll protect you. I'll post Snoop or another of my men outside the house or with you when you leave, all day, sixteen hours a day. My man will go with you wherever you go, and he'll escort you safely home at night. He or another man will be on duty outside the next morning. When you want to go out, he'll go with you. Snoop is on the way here right now."

"Sharky said he'd come back tonight."

"I'll be here if he does."

"Thank you."

I waved it off. "Did Sharky have a car?"

"I…I guess. I didn't notice."

"When he left, how did he leave? Did he walk? Drive? Someone pick him up?"

"I was so shaken up that I didn't think to look out the window."

"You said he was in a hoodie. What color was it? What else was he wearing?"

"It was a light-gray hoodie. And blue jeans."

"Shoes?"

"Didn't notice. Sandals, I think. I'm not sure. Maybe motorcycle boots."

A lot of help she was. Not. "What about the baseball hat? Describe it."

Gracie gazed upward, trying to picture it in her mind. "Black with the New York Yankees NY logo in white on the front."

"That's great. If you spot him again anywhere else, I want to know everything you observe. Which direction he came from, which direction he leaves in, what he's wearing, what kind of vehicle. If you can, get a license plate. Snap a picture with your phone, if nothing else."

"I guess I could do that."

I patted her shoulder. "Yes, you can. I know that you can be as strong as you need to be. "While I said it, the words tasted bad in my mouth. I knew no such thing. From what Miyo had told me, she would take any excuse as a reason to fail. "I will review your home's physical security now. I'll be back in fifteen minutes."

I studied the perimeter of the house. Horatio had replaced the broken padlock on the backyard fence. Several years before, Gracie's parents had planted Crown of Thorns under each window. The plants were mature and heavy with flowers that hid the wicked spines. They were a good defense if anyone tried to break in through a window. The bad news was that the locks on the front and back doors were cheap and easily broken. I sent Horatio to the hardware store to get better deadbolts. He was handy with tools and promised he'd have the new ones installed before sunset.

Snoop showed up at ten o'clock. I gave him a mug shot of Sharky and an extra to give to Frank Bennett when he showed up at four.

Then I went in to talk to her parents.

Since midnight, this day had shaped up like the old Chinese curse: May you live in interesting times. I was definitely living in "interesting times."

So was Graciela, but hers were of her own making.

"Evangelina, a woman in the house across the street kept an eye on Horatio and me through the window when we were in front of your house. How well do you know her?"

"That's Señora Guzman. She's lived in the neighborhood forever. I've known her since Graciela was a baby and we first moved here. Why do you ask?"

"Sharky is out there somewhere. I'd feel better if I laid eyes on him, instead of waiting for him to come back. I'd rather play offense than defense. Maybe Señora Guzman noticed something last night. Would you introduce me to her?"

Señora Guzman opened her front door while Evangelina and I were walking up the sidewalk. She gave Evangelina a big hug and welcomed me in heavily-accented English.

I returned her welcome in Spanish, and she grinned like I was a long-lost relative. She was barely five feet tall, with salt-and-pepper gray hair she wore in a bun. She weighed maybe ninety-five pounds if she carried a brick in the front pocket of her calf-length blue dress. It was eighty degrees, but she wore a white knit shawl over her long sleeves. She reminded me of Estrella, the cook at my Mexican grandmother's hacienda. Estrella always had an empanada for me when I visited as a small boy. I liked Señora Guzman immediately.

Evangelina told Señora Guzman I had rescued Graciela from Vidali's yacht, and she hugged me like I had saved her own life. She insisted on serving freshly baked *pastelitos*, a Cuban pastry filled with guava and cream cheese. She made us each a *cortadito*, a sweet Cuban coffee. I had the feeling Señora Guzman didn't have company often and wanted to take advantage of our visit. I enjoyed the Old Home Week feeling.

Evangelina and Señora Guzman caught up on all the neighborhood gossip while I enjoyed my *pastelito* and *cortadito*. We had a sizeable Little Havana in Port City, but nothing like the original neighborhood in Miami. Señora Guzman was quick to tell me she had come with her parents from Havana in 1960 when she was a teenager. She cursed Fidel and Raul Castro and made a sign, maybe to ward off evil.

Señora Guzman was the neighborhood busybody. She watched a lot of cop shows on *Telemundo* and was a one-woman Neighborhood Watch program. She had surveilled Sharky on the sidewalk the night before, and had written down the license number of the car he was driving. She gave me a detailed description, including the make, model, and color.

I said goodbye with another big hug. This time she drew my head down with both hands and kissed me firmly on the cheek. "You protect my Gracielita, Carlitos. God be with you."

Returning to the van, I booted my tablet and researched Sharky's license number. A stolen car or at least a stolen plate would give me grounds to sic the Miami cops on him. No such luck: It was a rental car plate that matched the description Señora Guzman had given me.

My nondescript white Caravan was like a million others, so it was effectively invisible. I cruised the neighborhood in widening circles. At sunset, I found Sharky's rental in the parking lot of a diner a half mile away.

I parked in a lot across the street where I could observe the door to the diner. I slipped on a reversible windbreaker and sunglasses and walked across. Opening the door, the place smelled so good that my stomach reminded me I hadn't eaten since the coffee and pastry Señora Guzman had fed me. My mouth watered, but I wasn't there to eat.

Sharky was alone at the long counter. I read in a magazine

somewhere that invading someone's space makes them feel intimidated. If it was printed in a magazine, it had to be true, right? I took an empty seat beside him. He had a plate of *picadillo*, sweet plantains, and yuca.

He frowned in my direction. "Who the hell are you?" He didn't seem intimidated yet, so I gave him a business card. He glanced at it, but didn't seem impressed by that either. Maybe I should add a logo of crossed daggers.

I spoke softly. "Leave Graciela Perez alone, Samuel."

That got his attention, so I pressed my small advantage. "You are Samuel Torrance, but you prefer that people call you Sharky because you think it's cool. You live in Brooklyn." I rattled off his street address and phone number. "You were arrested and released for maiming Tawanda Grisham." I recited his rap sheet from memory. It was obvious I'd done my homework. I even impressed myself.

So far, he didn't seem intimidated. More like irritated.

I went on. "I know all about you, Samuel, but you don't know anything about me. I suggest when you get back to whatever spider hole you're staying in tonight, you Google me." I grabbed a plantain chunk off his plate and ate it, invading his space more. "I'm about to become your worst nightmare. If you're smart, you'll write off the debt, turn in that rented Impala out front, and fly back to New York. If you're smart, you'll forget you ever knew Graciela Perez. If you're smart, you'll stay alive a little longer."

I stood and made sure Sharky spotted the gun under my windbreaker. I walked out without looking back. Maybe that would impress him. I had my doubts.

Turning left outside the diner door, I walked a half-block down the street. Once out of sight, I lost the sunglasses, turned my windbreaker inside out from the black to the red side, and donned my Port City Pilots baseball cap. I walked back to the Caravan on the other side of the street.

Sharky's back was to the window. Even through binoculars, it was hard to discern what he was doing. I hoped he would Google me. As far as I knew, he'd never committed a capital crime, so I hoped I wouldn't have to kill him. Surely, after he found out what a super-sleuth tough guy and major righter-of-wrongs I was, he'd turn tail and slink back to Brooklyn—or not. .

Dad always said, "Wish in one hand and spit in the other and see which gets full first." I was wishing.

Sharky left an hour later, and I followed him to a cheap motel on US 1 with a sign that said *Yes, we have waterbeds and DVD players*. I wondered if they rented rooms by the hour.

Sharky walked out of the motel office, climbed the metal stairs, and entered a room on the second floor. Thirty minutes after he'd gone into his room, I stuck a GPS tracker under the back bumper of his rental car. Two quick Cuban sandwiches from a nearby fast-food place calmed my growling stomach while I eyed the GPS monitor. Sharky's car never moved.

Waiting outside the motel, I planned to follow him if he returned to Gracie's parents' house. The sole thing I learned was that the motel did rent rooms by the hour. Sharky must have decided that tonight wasn't his night. Perhaps I had shaken his confidence. Wishing again.

At 2:00 a.m., I gave up and went home.

The next day was Saturday. At 11:00 a.m., Sharky's car had not moved from where he'd left it the night before. At noon, I followed him to an Italian restaurant. At 1:30, I followed him to an adult video store.

I called Snoop while I waited outside the XXX Adult Emporium *Couples welcome!!!* Snoop was bored. On a protection detail, boring is good.

Sharky emerged carrying a plain white plastic bag. Maybe he had bought a DVD of *Gone with the Wind*. I followed him back to the no-tell motel.

At 4:30, a silver Cadillac double-parked in the motel lot. A teenage girl in four-inch gold heels, a white halter top that hardly met the legal minimum, and a red skirt that barely covered her assets, got out. As the girl walked around the car, the driver rolled down his window and said something. She walked back and leaned into the window for a short consultation. The skirt hiked up to reveal a transparent black thong something-or-other. She was probably here for a financial analysts' conference. She didn't carry a briefcase, though, simply a silver-sequined clutch purse.

She climbed the stairs carefully, glanced at a piece of paper in her hand, and took out a container of breath spray from the clutch. She squirted the spray into her mouth, returned it to the purse, and tugged the skirt down. It covered her behind, but barely. She knocked on Sharky's door. Maybe she wasn't there for a financial analysts' conference after all. Maybe Sharky didn't want to watch *Gone with the Wind* alone.

Sharky would be occupied with the rent-a-bimbo for an hour or so, so I drove down *Calle Ocho* to a little Cuban restaurant I knew. We didn't have them like that in Port City. I parked on a side street and ordered three *Media Noches* and a to-go thermos of Cuban coffee from the walk-up window.

I took up post again outside Sharky's motel and called Frank Bennett. Frank was bored too. Hooray.

About 6:30, the silver Cadillac returned and double-parked. The teenager left Sharky's room and got back in the Cadillac. She handed her purse to the driver, who removed some bills and tossed it back to the girl. Life in the big city.

I munched on the *Media Noches*, drank the Cuban coffee, and hung around 'til midnight.

Sunday morning at 9:00, I returned to Sharky's motel. His car was gone. I punched up the GPS monitor. The signal said the car was at Miami International Airport.

I called Snoop.

"Yeah, bud. I'm on post out front. Been here since 8:00."

"I can't find Sharky. The GPS I stuck on his car says the car is at MIA. He must've returned it to the rental company sometime in the night."

"Maybe he gave up and went back to Brooklyn."

"Or maybe he made my tail and got another car."

"Now who's the pessimist?"

I called Jorge. "Need another favor of your cop super-powers, *amigo*. A New York drug dealer is in Miami. He threatened my client, a woman. I want to know where his cellphone is right now." I gave him the number.

"This have anything to do with the Vidali case?"

"That case is closed. This is a different case, a protection gig. I had an eye on the guy, name of Samuel Torrance from Brooklyn, New York. He gave me the slip. I need to find him again."

"Hang on." He was gone for a couple of minutes. "The phone is in Miami. I'll forward you the address."

My heart dropped into my stomach. The address was the home of Gracie's parents. I bounced out of the parking lot and said a little prayer as I drove at warp speed.

SEVENTEEN

I jerked to a stop at the curb, right behind Snoop's car. Evangelina's Honda SUV was in the driveway behind Horatio's Ford Focus.

Snoop got out and walked back to my van. "Nothing's happened since we talked."

I called Graciela's new cellphone. It rang a few times and went to voicemail. I called her flip-phone. Same thing. I called Horatio and Evangelina's home number. Four rings and it went to voicemail.

This couldn't be good. Sharky was inside listening to the phones ring. A ringing phone always puts me on edge. Sharky didn't need to be any more on edge than he was.

How had he gotten inside? I called his cellphone.

"You finished leaving your voicemail messages? Whaddya want, McCrary?"

"Can I come in?"

"You got my money, hot shot?"

"Yeah."

"Step outside your van and show it to me."

I walked around the van and stood on the sidewalk. A finger bent a blind in the living room window. I pulled out the envelope Vidali had given Gracie. I fanned the sheaf of bills where Sharky would spot them. At that distance, fifteen grand might look like forty-five.

I stuck the envelope in my pants pocket. "Can I come in now?"

"Take off your coat."

I took off my windbreaker.

"And your shoulder holster."

I shrugged out of my holster.

"Throw them in the back of your van."

I did.

"Turn around where I can see your back."

I did that too.

"Tell your pal to get in his car and drive away."

I faced Snoop. "He wants you to get in your car and drive away."

Snoop went to his car, opened the door, and stood there. He shot me a questioning glance over the roof.

"It'll be okay, Snoop. You go home." I winked at him.

He sighed and drove away.

"He's gone."

"Okay, hot shot, you can come in. The door's unlocked."

I walked up the sidewalk and climbed the steps. The front door had the old locks on it, broken. Horatio hadn't installed the deadbolts like he had promised. I hoped he wouldn't have cause to regret his procrastination. I stepped through the door and closed it behind me.

Graciela sat on the upholstered couch where her parents had served Snoop and me Cuban coffee a few days earlier. So much had happened since then that it felt like much longer. Her parents sat on either side of her. All three had their wrists duct taped in front. All three wore pajamas and robes. Physically, they seemed okay.

Sharky had broken into their house sometime after Frank Bennett went off duty and before Snoop got there. Maybe he caught them at breakfast, then forced Gracie to duct tape them while he held the knife to her throat. A roll of duct tape lay on the floor beside the couch.

The drug dealer stood behind Gracie. His left hand clutched her shoulder. His right hand held a wicked-looking carpet knife at her throat. He wasn't going to use acid this time. Dried tears tracked Gracie's cheeks.

The curved blade in Sharky's hand was like an obscene boomerang on the end of the wooden handle. I didn't spot any blood on it. I wondered if he used that carpet knife on the other girl he maimed, the one with cuts on her cheeks and forehead.

Horatio sat like a statue, not leaning on the arm of the couch. Evangelina's lips moved in silent prayer. Despite the tape, her fingers thumbed an imaginary rosary, counting Hail Marys. I hoped to God they worked.

"Gimme the money, hot shot."

"Move the knife away from her throat."

"Gimme the freakin' money, or I'll slit her beautiful little supermodel throat."

"Sharky, you've done a lot of bad stuff, but you never killed anyone. Florida has capital punishment so you don't want to murder anyone here; you'll get the needle. What you want is to get your money and escape in one piece. I want that too. We all want that. Now, let's make that happen. Move the knife away from her throat."

He shifted his weight from one foot to the other. He squeezed her shoulder tighter. I saw the carpet knife press a crease in Gracie's throat. A drop of blood oozed around the point and ran an inch down her neck.

I slipped the fat envelope from my pants pocket and held it in my left hand. "Move the knife and I'll give you this money."

He eased up on the knife. The crease disappeared and I felt a little hope.

"Gimme the money."

"Move the knife."

He did. Maybe an inch. "Stop playing games and gimme my money."

"Sharky, you're gonna walk out of here regardless." I gestured at the front door with my chin. "Why don't you come over here and I'll hand it to you on your way out. I presume you parked around the next corner? Shouldn't be a long walk."

I could hear the gears click in his twisted mind as he considered that. "Show me the money again."

I opened the envelope flap to show him the bills inside. I tugged a few bills an inch out of the envelope. "They're all hundreds. Here. It's yours." I left the flap open and extended the envelope in my right hand, willing him to come take it.

Her grabbed Gracie's hair and jerked her head around as he leaned close to her face. "Don't move one muscle until I'm out the door. You hear me, bitch?"

She managed to nod her head. Her lips trembled. Her cheeks were wet.

He wrenched Gracie's head back, leaned over, and licked the drop of blood off her neck.

Gracie cringed as his tongue slid across her skin leaving a glistening pink trail.

Sharky released her hair. He punched the carpet knife in the back of the couch. As he walked around the end, he cut a long slash in the fabric. Foam rubber oozed from the cut. "That could be you, *Latin Angel*. You wouldn't look like no angel no more."

He waved the carpet knife at me as he crossed the living room. "Give me my money and get out of my way, hot shot."

I stepped to the left and held the envelope out to the right, in front of the door. He would count the money as soon as he left and discover it was thirty thousand short. He'd be back, if not immediately, then later in New York.

And I wouldn't be there to protect Gracie.

That was unacceptable; I had to do something now or Gracie would pay with her life or her career.

Sharky held the knife inches from my face as he reached for the envelope with his left hand.

As his hand touched the envelope, I dropped it.

Instinctively, he grabbed for the envelope with his left hand.

I seized his right wrist like a vise and twisted the curved blade up and away from my face.

Sharky grabbed my wrist with his other hand, struggling to regain control of the knife. He was stronger than I had expected. It felt like he was chinning himself on my left arm and the arm began to droop.

I couldn't let that wicked curved blade near me. I slammed my other fist into his solar plexus as hard as I could.

Breath exploded from his mouth, spraying me with droplets of spit. He dropped his left arm to protect his stomach.

I kneed him in the balls hard enough to lift him off the floor. The carpet knife dropped to the floor. Gravity is my friend.

I clung to his right wrist like it was the last lifeboat on the *Titanic*. I hammered his throat with my other fist. Another right to the heart and he collapsed on the floor.

He rolled over and reached for the carpet knife. I kicked him in the head. He was still moving, so I kicked him again. I picked up the wicked knife and threw it through the doorway into the kitchen.

It was over.

Grabbing the roll of duct tape, I secured his wrists and ankles, then called 9-1-1.

Kelly put her notebook away. "Bigs, you got anything else?"

"I'm good."

She smiled at me. "I guess that wraps it up."

Two uniforms in a black-and-white had taken Sharky away. The CSIs had finished their duties and detectives Kelly Contreras and Bigs Bigelow had another collar on their record. I have no idea how they got a case in Miami-Dade County transferred to the Port City Police Department in Atlantic County, but there you are. Sometimes the law works in strange ways.

The three of us shook hands and the two detectives left.

Gracie came in from the kitchen where she had been waiting. "What happens now, Chuck?"

"Well, I'm going to call Miyo and ask her for a real date for tomorrow night. Then I'm going home and sleep for about fourteen hours."

"No. I mean what's going to happen to me?"

I spread my hands, palms up. "I don't have a crystal ball, Gracie. Your future is mostly what you make of it."

"Do you think Bob will take me back?"

"You'll have to ask him."

"He's mad at me. Will you ask him for me?"

"No."

She sat on the couch in the same spot she'd been that morning. "You're no help."

"I'm no help? Rescuing you from a kidnapping gangster who intended to murder you, that was no help? Rescuing you from your drug dealer who threatened to maim you, that was no help? Getting him on attempted murder for his attack on me, that was no help? What do you want from me, lady?"

Her face got cloudy. "I don't know. I just…" She cried…again. "I feel so helpless."

There it was again—the helpless facade. It was hard for me to believe that Gracie could be so devious, but she was performing her act right in front of me. I wasn't buying the crying or the helplessness. I hoped Bob wouldn't buy it either when she tried it on him. Again.

"To paraphrase Forrest Gump: Helpless is as helpless does." I sat down across from her. "I don't know what you'll do with your life, Gracie. It's your life. It's not mine, and it's not Bob's. You will write your own life story. You can't hire a ghost writer."

I touched her hand. "You've had several wake-up calls, Gracie. I suggest you look at yourself in the mirror and see yourself as you really are. In the real world, there is such a thing as cause and effect. You need to reflect on the bad effects from the numerous bad decisions you've made. Maybe you need therapy; that's not my area of expertise. I hope you grow up and take responsibility for your actions. I really do. But it's up to you and no one else."

I stood. "Now, if you'll give my regards to your parents when they return, I'll be on my way."

As I started my Dodge Caravan, I felt like I was mounting my white horse and riding into the sunset. *Hi-yo, Silver.*

The End

DANGEROUS FRIENDS

CARLOS MCCRARY PI, BOOK 4

I stood on the bottom step and knocked. The drape above the window a/c unit moved and an eye peeked out. Nothing happened. I knocked again. "Steve, it's Chuck McCrary. I'm here to treat you to lunch."

I called his phone. I heard it ringing behind the door, but he didn't answer.

The front door opened a crack, held by the safety chain. "What do you want?" The room behind him was dark as a cave.

"I told you; I'm here to buy you lunch."

"I don't know you. I don't know you at all actually."

"I'm Chuck McCrary, a friend of Michelle Babcock."

Wallace's eyes darted back and forth for a second. He nodded, perhaps to himself. "Wait… wait here." He closed the door. I couldn't hear if he was sliding the safety chain off. I heard his voice from inside. "Come in."

I opened the door and stepped into the apartment. After the bright sunshine, I could barely see. Dim light squeezed around the heavy drapes in the front windows.

It was so dark I could scarcely make out Wallace standing on the far side the bed, a revolver in his hand. Pointed at me.

"Raise your hands, McCrary." He held the revolver in two shaky hands. He shifted his weight, dancing from one foot to the other.

"That's not necessary, Steve. I'm here to help you."

"Never call me Steve. Never call me Steve. You don't have the right to call me Steve. You don't have that right, McCrary. I've earned the right to be called *Dr. Wallace*." He waved the gun up and down to emphasize his point. "I sometimes let dear friends call me Steven. Yes I do, I do actually. But you are not a dear friend; I don't know you."

I make it a policy never to argue with people who are pointing a gun at me. Especially nervous, twitchy, crazy people. "Sorry, Dr. Wallace. It's okay for you to call me Chuck though. Everyone does." I smiled. "I'm here to help."

Wallace relaxed a smidgeon. On a ten-point scale, the tension in the room declined from 9.9 to maybe 9.5, or maybe that was just me. I didn't raise my hands, but I kept them where he could see them.

Wallace waved the revolver. "How can you help me? I don't need any help. I'm fine actually. I especially don't need *your* help, McCrary. How can you help me?"

"Redwood..." I watched to notice if his eyes widened. They did and I continued. "Redwood sent eleven people to kill you..." His eyes widened more. "Four of them are waiting near your apartment as we speak. They came from Chicago to kill you. They already killed James Ponder. I came here to save you from them."

"I don't need saving. I'm fine actually. I'm just fine. Redwood would never kill me; I'm central to the operation. Central." He smiled as if he loved hearing his own words. "Central to the

274

operation. James was merely a pawn. A pawn and a dupe, McCrary. He's no great loss. No loss at all actually."

"Please call me Chuck, Dr. Wallace. Everyone calls me Chuck. May I sit down? We need to talk."

"Sit down? Sit down?"

I pointed at the ancient Formica and chrome dinette suite. "I can make coffee or tea and we can talk."

Wallace wobbled two jerky steps toward me, waving the gun. "I have tea, McCrary. Do you know how to make tea?"

"Sure, Dr. Wallace." I moved toward the kitchen; Wallace moved toward the front door like we were twirling in a slow dance.

"Why don't you relax in that chair by the front door while I make the tea?" The farther away from me he was, the more likely he would miss if he did shoot.

I filled the teapot, positioned it on the burner, and switched it on. "Thank you, Dr. Wallace." I opened the cabinet and found a box of teabags. "And the cups?"

"Second cabinet."

Wallace shuffled one more step sideways. His leg bumped the chair.

"Dr. Wallace, since you're standing beside the chair, why don't you sit down and I'll fix the tea?" The teapot whistled.

The revolver wavered. "Maybe I will sit down. I've not been sleeping well actually. Not well at all."

As Wallace twisted to move the chair, I made my own move.

Two steps, a side kick at his hand, and the gun flew across the room.

I breathed again and retrieved the revolver. "Sit down, Dr. Wallace. We need to talk."

Available in Paperback and eBook from Your Favorite Bookstore or Online Retailer

ABOUT THE AUTHOR

Dallas Gorham's books combine murder, mystery, and general mayhem with a touch of humor—all done with a PG-13 rating. His Carlos McCrary, Private Investigator, Mystery Thriller Series can be read and enjoyed in any order.

Dallas writes in the mystery, thriller, and suspense genres. (Take your pick: His novels have all three elements) His stories will get your heart pounding and leave you wanting more. He writes to hit hard, have a good time, and leave as few grammar errors as possible (or is it "grammatical errors"? Hmm.)

In his previous life, Dallas worked as a shoe salesman, grocery store sacker, florist deliverer, auditor, management consultant, association executive, accountant, radio announcer, and a paid assassin for the Florida Board of Cosmetology. (He is lying about one of those jobs.) If you ask him about it, he will deny ever having worked as an auditor.

Dallas is a sixth-generation Texan and a proud Texas Longhorn, having earned a Bachelor of Business Administration at the University of Texas at Austin. He graduated in the top three-quarters of his class, maybe. He has also been known to lie about his class ranking.

Dallas, the writer, and his wife moved to Florida years ago to escape Dallas, the city, winters (Brrrr. Way too cold) and summers (Whew. Way too hot). Like his fictional hero, Chuck McCrary, he lives in Florida in a waterfront home where he and his wife watch the sunset over the lake most days. He is a member of Mystery Writers of America and the Florida Writers Association.

Dallas is married to his one-and-only wife who treats him far better than he deserves. They have two grown sons, of whom they are inordinately proud. They also have seven grandchildren who are the smartest, most handsome, and most beautiful grandchildren in the known universe. He and his wife spend waaaay too much money on their love of travel. They have visited all 50 states and over 90 foreign countries, the most recent of which was Indonesia, where their cruise ship stopped at Kuala Lumpur.

Dallas writes an occasional blog post at http://dallasgorham. com/blog that is sometimes funny, but not nearly as funny as he thinks. The website also has more information about his books. To get an email whenever the author releases a new title (and sometimes a free book), sign up for the VIP newsletter at http://dallasgorham.com/

If you have too much time on your hands, you can follow him at the following social media links:

www.DallasGorham.com

facebook.com/DallasGorham
twitter.com/DallasGorham
amazon.com/author/B00J4LISCS

www.ingramcontent.com/pod-product-compliance
Lightning Source LLC
Chambersburg PA
CBHW051336020726
47501CB00007B/2114